If I Was To Tell You Something

PETER FARRELL

Copyright © 2023 Peter Farrell
All rights reserved.

Chapter One

Brian lifts his blood-stained hands up before his eyes. The stink overwhelms him. He goes over to the old Belfast sink in the dark, dirty locker room and uses a scrubber to eliminate the now hard-dried evidence of slaughter. He then removes his sweaty, stained overalls from yet another twelve-hour shift. This is a ritual he's done Monday to Friday since leaving school seventeen years ago, working in this filthy, loud, and smelly leather factory.

He looks up into the broken, speckled mirror; bloodshot, blue eyes stare back. The frown-wrinkles across his forehead remind him of how old he feels. His hair is still thick and rugged; thankfully, it was what caught Linda's eye when she first saw him. But the grey of his sideboards is overtaking his chestnut mop and creeping upwards across his scalp. He shrugs involuntarily; at least his shoulders still stand broad, belying his years. He stretches to his full six foot two and flicks his forelock backwards.

"Thank god it's Friday. I feel wiped out," he says, turning to his mates, Dave and Deano. Deano pushes past him.

"Sorry, Brian! I'm in a real hurry." Deano smiles. "I've got to meet someone, and I'm already late." He squeezes past Dave and rushes out of the suffocating small space all the factory workers share to change their clothes before and after shifts. His jeans are clean, and his leather jacket hangs casually over a white pressed shirt.

"That's the fastest I've seen you move all week!"

Deano disappears into the corridor. They hear the front door to the building slam shut behind him. The draft brings some welcome fresh air into the staleness of the changing room.

"God! The things we do to keep the wolves from the door. Put the light on, will you, Dave? There must be an easier way of making a living." Brian lowers himself down heavily onto the bench with a sigh and pulls his brown-stained trainers off. He throws them into his open locker and pulls out his boots.

"You could always earn some extra money like Deano," Dave replies.

"Yeah but spending the next ten years in jail kind of puts me off. Then again, is working in this shithole any worse than prison?"

"Yeah, you're not far wrong there. Anyway, you up to much this weekend?"

"Kid's football tomorrow morning. Apart from that, nothing much. What about you?"

"I'm gonna get absolutely intoxicated all weekend."

With his boots back on, Brian stands to pat his friend on the shoulder. Dave is a head shorter than he is and a few years younger, so Brian always feels protective of him. He's glad that Dave doesn't follow in Deano's footsteps.

"Ha! Well, don't get too drunk, Dave. See you Monday, mate!" They part outside the factory.

With his tall height and being slightly overweight, Brian struggles to get into his small Corsa. He's done this journey twice a day since leaving school and could find his way home blindfolded if need be.

Driving home through Liverpool, the weather forecast is announced, but he switches it off, laughing to himself. "Yeah, we know! It's raining," he says out loud.

At home, he strolls through the front door of their three-bedroomed terraced house, throwing the Corsa keys onto the hall table as he passes. He ignores the two letters on the table. Linda will deal with them later, no doubt. Probably bills.

"Hello, love! Had a nice day?" Linda calls from the kitchen.

"No, not really. Why, did you?" he replies, joining her in the kitchen and reaching to put the kettle on. He turns to listen to her story, always pleasantly surprised by how beautiful she is, with her long, wavy black hair and dark brown eyes. Although they are both in their thirties now, she has struggled to keep her svelte figure but never seems to age in his eyes.

"Well, it was a kind of a strange day," she drawls in her American accent. "A bloke came into the shop earlier. He didn't have enough money to pay for his food. Barbara, on the next till, was dead snotty with him and buzzed for the manager. When John came down, he was even worse. He was quite aggressive and threatened to call the police. I didn't expect him to have such a heart of stone with an embarrassed customer, though!"

"Wish I'd have been there. I'd have given him a proper reason to get aggressive. And that horrible cow is just as bad. So, what happened to this man?"

"Well, John and Barbara literally marched him out of the store and told him not to enter the supermarket again."

"Wow!" Brian pictured the man being thrown out of the supermarket. "Poor bloke didn't have enough money for his food… I thought I had a bad day at the stink factory, but there's always someone worse off than you are. Where are the kids, Linda?"

"Oh, Ruby's having dinner at her friend Mary's, her official new 'bestie,' and Liam is at Nanny Sandra's. He wanted to stay at your mom's tonight, but I told Sandra he's got soccer in the morning."

"Dinner? Soccer? You're not in the States now, Linda. You mean tea and football. Oh, and she ain't my 'mom'. She's my 'mum'."

"Oh, I'm terribly sorry, you English snob."

"Not a problem, you crazy Yank."

"Funnily enough, I was talking to my mom earlier. Sorry, I mean, mummy."

"I don't say 'mummy', Linda. In fact, I've never used the word 'mummy' in my life."

"Yes, well, anyway, Mom asked me when we are going over to visit her and Dad next."

"No pressure there, then, Linda! We couldn't even afford to go to Alton Towers a few weeks ago, and now you're talking about visiting your mum and dad in New York again?"

"Again Brian? Again? I haven't been home for almost four years now. Our kids were tots the last time they saw Mom and Dad. Ruby is nearly eight, and Liam is ten now. You see your mom almost every day! Our Sandra makes damn sure she sees her little boy, Brian!" Linda stops abruptly.

Brian is shocked by her response. She must be missing her parents, but they really don't have the money for a trip right now.

"I'd ask Mom and Dad to help with the travel costs, but they haven't got much money themselves. Couldn't we get a loan or re-mortgage the house, Brian?" Linda's voice is pleading.

Brian feels his exhaustion again and lowers his head dejectedly. "Like I said, Linda, no pressure there, then!"

Chapter Two

It's Saturday morning in an overcast spring Merseyside. Linda and Brian are up early for Liam's school football match.

"Come on, Ruby! Hurry up! Liam is going to be late for his football," Linda shouts from the kitchen.

Brian drops three slices of bread into the toaster and reaches above Linda's head to retrieve the Frosties from the cupboard. He sets them on the table in their cosy kitchen diner.

"Think I'll need to get a new set of hinges for this door. When did this happen?"

"You might have to buy the complete door. It's been wonky for a while," Linda replies, sipping her tea. She sets her tea on the table and spreads margarine on a slice of toast.

Brian tries to fit the cupboard door back on its dodgy hinge while Ruby plonks herself at the table and Linda pours her a bowl of Frosties.

"Why do I have to go, Mum? I hate football. It's such a boy's game!"

"Girls play football too, you know. When you're Liam's age, you might have to play football in school. Coach Walker told me last week that the girls are already playing in Year 7. He might start them younger next year. Anyway, we go to support your brother, Ruby… and afterwards, as a treat, we can get something to eat and make a day of it."

After throwing their dirty dishes in the sink, they pull on their waterproofs and scramble into the car to pick up Liam from Sandra's. Brian's mum doesn't live that far away. Thankfully, Sandra and Liam are waiting at the front door of her semi when they arrive so they can get off quickly.

"Hi, Sandra. How was Liam last night?" asks Linda, stepping out of the car.

"He was lovely as always. We had a great night, didn't we, Liam? Chocolate, sweets, and Coke. Oh, and he told me about his speller of the week sticker award in school."

"Well, he is half-American, Sandra. He's bound to be half clever," says Linda with a smile. "What do you say to your nan, Liam?"

"Thanks, Nan. See you! Bye." Liam rushes into the car.

Sandra holds the door for him and leans in to say hello to Ruby and Brian.

"Hi, Mum. Sorry we can't stop. Liam will be late for his football. Are you still coming tomorrow for dinner?"

"Yes, that's if you're not doing anything."

"No, it'll be lovely to see you, Sandra," says Linda. "I've got your favourite sticky toffee pudding. And if you come early, you can watch your son peel the potatoes."

"She's quite funny for an American, Mum, isn't she?" says Brian sarcastically.

"Thanks for minding Liam. See you tomorrow, Sandra. Come for six," says Linda.

Sandra is laughing as she waves them all goodbye.

"Who are you playing today, Liam?" Brian asks as they pull up to a set of traffic lights.

"Tinsley Road Primary School."

"I'm supporting Tinsley," says Ruby, "as that's where I live."

"Traitor!" Liam retorts. "You're my sister. You should support me. And anyway, it's your school too, so you should support St. David's."

"I don't care. I hate football. And even if Coach Walker does classes for my year, I'm never going to play."

"Girls suck at football anyway," Liam countered, grimacing at his sister.

"Calm down, you two! You've only been together for a couple of minutes!" Linda says, exasperated.

A silver Range Rover Evoque pulls up alongside as Brian stops at a set of red lights. Deafening music blares and the horn is beeping. The driver is shouting at Brian.

"Oh look, it's your mate, Deano," says Liam, excitedly waving his arms to Deano.

"Ha, look at the posing bastard in his new car!" Brian scoffs but lowers his window to greet him.

"Hiya, Brian. Hello, Linda. Where are you going with your lovely family?" asks Deano.

"The big football match today, Deano. St. David's Primary playing Tinsley Primary. Where you off to?" asks Brian.

"Wow. Exciting game for you lot!" He winks at Liam. "Me? Oh, you know. Got a few blokes to see here and there and then off for a drink at The Feathers this afternoon."

"The Feathers? I thought the police closed that pub down," laughs Brian.

"Ha, no, they'd never do that. Villains would be scattered across all of Liverpool, making their job impossible. This way, they know where all the rogues are." Deano smiles. "Anyway, it's under new management now."

"Ha, same horse, different jockey then," laughs Brian.

"Could be a late one on the beer today," Deano continues.

"Still, Sunday tomorrow and enough time to recover for the shithole on Monday." The lights change colour. "Bye Linda, bye Ruby. You knock 'em dead in that match, Liam! See you Monday, Brian," Deano puts his foot down on the accelerator.

"See you, mate," says Brian, but Deano's already gone.

"Wow, what a lovely car Deano has. How can he afford a cracking car working in the factory?" asks Linda.

"You don't wanna know, Linda. You don't wanna know, love."

"What, you mean drugs?" asks Linda.

"I think it's just part of the young trend today. They eventually grow out of it," says Brian.

"I wouldn't want to be looking over my shoulder all the time and worrying that the drug squad might kick in our door."

"I know, but as I say, I think it's just a silly young phase he's going through."

"I don't understand, though. Why would you want to work in a dirty factory if you can afford a car like that?"

"I don't know — maybe to portray the image of a hardworking, honest guy? Or maybe he just enjoys working in shite." Brian laughs.

"He wants to be careful. He's got such a lovely girl, that Debbie."

"I know. I often think that. I wouldn't like to see anything happen to him. Deep down, he's a good lad, is Deano. Honestly, he'd do anything for you."

Linda grips Brian's hand. "You're a good man, Brian Jackson, my Jacko."

Chapter Three

They arrive at the football club, and Brian notices that most of Liam's team is already there. A light drizzle casts a grey veil over the pitch, and Brian zips up his waterproof against the wind. The children bundle out of the car.

"It looks like the game must be still on, then?" Linda sounds disappointed and wraps her scarf around her head to keep her hair dry.

"I'll walk over to the shop and get Liam a drink and some crisps for after the game. Do you want to come with me, Ruby?" asks Brian.

"No, I can't be bothered, Dad."

Brian glances down at his daughter; she looks like she would have preferred to stay in bed rather than join the family outing, but Brian had felt Liam needed all the support he could get. He watched Liam run off to join his mates.

"Would you like anything, Ruby?" he asks.

"I'll have a blackcurrant juice and salt and vinegar crisps, please, Dad."

Brian heads to the corner supermarket across the street from the pitch. As he opens the shop door, he hears a woman's terrifying screams and a loud crash. Inside the shop, an elderly Asian shopkeeper is being attacked by a young man. A wooden flap in the counter, which usually separates the shopkeeper from the customers, has been raised so the attacker can access the till. A tray of Terry's Chocolate Oranges gets knocked to the floor as the two men struggle with each other. The shopkeeper's slight frame seems miniscule in contrast with the six-foot skinhead, who has his hands around the man's throat. A young woman with a long dark plait is screaming hysterically in a doorway behind the two men. She starts tugging at the youth, but with one arm, he easily shoves her back through the doorway while still choking the old man with his other hand.

Without any plan, Brian begins punching the young thug. The attacker knocks the old man to the floor with a punch to the face but swiftly transfers his attention to Brian. The young girl runs to her father, and the two watch the youth throw his punches towards Brian. Fortunately for Brian, he can handle himself.

After receiving a combination of blows that any boxer would be proud of, the young man is now beginning to understand what it is like to be on the receiving end of a beating. The thug realises that he's up against a stronger opponent. Trying to get his cash here today doesn't seem like such a good idea anymore. He picks himself up from the floor and spits some blood out of his mouth before pushing his face up close to Brian's.

Brian notices an ugly violet tattoo on the youth's right cheek.

"You haven't fucking heard the last of this," violet tattoo spits at him. "You're fucking dead!" He then leaves the shop.

Brian leans down to help the shopkeeper to his feet. He and the daughter between them help the old man stand.

"Are you okay?" Brian asks. "Don't worry about him. He's gone," Brian reassures.

The shopkeeper looks rather dishevelled and is slightly out of breath. His right eye has started to swell, and blood trickles from his lip. He rubs his neck where the youth had clinched him.

"Thank you for your help. They think they can come in here and take whatever they like without paying. It's all for drugs, you know. That's all—just for drugs. They're not even worried about the cameras that I've had fitted." His voice shakes as he speaks.

The young girl, who looks about twenty, is crying her eyes out. She puts an arm around her father.

"I wish you would just leave them, Dad," she whimpers. "They could be carrying knives or something." Then she turns to pick up biscuit packets, which had been knocked to the floor in the fray.

"No respect, not one of them," says the shopkeeper. "No point calling the police, either, Gemma. You know what I've told you before."

"But Dad…"

"No! Absolutely not! Then we'll have more trouble on our doorstep. You listen to me, girl!"

Brian could see fear in the man's eyes as he spoke to his daughter. The old man turned his attention to Brian.

"Now, what can I get you? I'm very grateful to you for intervening, and I hope it won't cause you any trouble. Are you hurt?"

The rapid transition to normality somewhat took Brian aback, but recognising how upset the girl was and how the old man's hands were now shaking from the shock, he decided he'd better leave them in peace as quickly as possible. But still, he was worried for their safety.

"No, no, I'm fine. I'll just have these bottles of blackcurrant juice and crisps, please? And I hope you'll let me give you some advice?"

"Yeah, sure," replies the shopkeeper. "I'm always open to advice from someone who has my back," the man replied. He shook his hand, pointing to the back room, indicating to his daughter to go there.

"I'd think seriously about employing some extra staff, preferably somebody big, who can deal with these thugs."

"What about you?" the shopkeeper asks with a little smile, his eyes looking hopeful.

"I'm afraid not. I'm an overworked husband, father, and underpaid leather worker," laughs Brian as he walks out of the shop, letting the door close behind him.

When he arrives back at the pitch, the team are already playing. Brian tells Linda about the thug.

"Sometimes, I wish we didn't live around here. This place has gone down the pan," he says.

"Well, that's good old England for you, Brian."

"That's rich coming from someone from Brooklyn."

"Hey, Brooklyn is a great community. So don't you diss my hometown, you English snob! Go for it, Liam!" She punches the air as Liam tries for a goal.

The motley crew of parents, now completely dampened by the constant drizzle, try to feign excitement that the home team might finally get a goal.

Brian starts laughing.

"Good try, Liam," he shouts towards his son. "Only kidding, Linda. Calm down, you crazy Yank."

Unfortunately, Liam's team are defeated 3-0. Brian watches his dejected son walk off the pitch.

"Never mind, son! It's only a game," says Brian. "Here's your drink and crisps. Let's go to McDonald's for a Happy Meal. And if your mum apologises for calling me an English snob, we'll get her one as well."

Linda throws Brian a sarcastic smile.

"Can I have a Happy Meal too, Dad?" asks Ruby.

"What, for my little girl? Too right."

Chapter Four

It's Saturday night, and the kids are safely tucked up in bed. Brian and Linda are treating themselves to a quiet drink after gorging themselves on an Indian meal delivered from The Raj restaurant. The aroma of spices still lingers from their eating on their laps in front of the false electric fire. With the lights low, Brian can't see the worn carpet or tired dark blue cord sofa cushions, and he feels cosy and relaxed. Linda picks up their discarded plates from the small tables on either side of the sofa and drops them in the kitchen sink, returning with a bottle in hand.

As Brian flicks through the TV channels, she winds the corkscrew into the bottle.

"Isn't it amazing?" she says.

"Isn't what amazing?"

"How all the troubles of the world can quickly disappear when you open a bottle of Côtes du Rhône."

"I'd rather have a few Stella. Red wine always gives me a blinding headache the next day."

"Oh, I'd rather have my Côtes du Rhône than a beer any day!" she says, heading to the kitchen to fetch him a Stella. "Anything good on TV?" she asks, sitting back down on the sofa.

"Nothing, absolute rubbish. Just another load of repeats." Brian sits checking his lottery tickets on his phone.

"What time is your mom coming for dinner tomorrow?"

"I'm not sure, didn't you say about 6 p.m.? And yes, you're allowed to call it dinner on a Sunday, Linda."

"Hooray for good old little England and its Sunday roast dinners," says a slightly tipsy Linda sarcastically as she raises her glass of wine. "Have we got any good movies recorded, Brian?"

"You mean films, Linda."

"Movies, films, who cares, Brian. Do we have anything good recorded, or don't we?"

But Brian is in a world of his own, checking his lottery tickets.

"Are you listening to me? Have we got anything recorded worth watching?"

"Hold your horses! I've got some winning numbers on this ticket here." Next to him on the sofa sits a ripped pile of discarded losing tickets.

"Pass me the remote, Brian. I'll have a look myself."

"That can't be right."

"What can't?"

"Hey, hold on. There's a shit load of winning numbers on this ticket," he says. "I think I've got five numbers. No, that can't be right."

"So, I take it that there's nothing recorded. Pass me the goddamn remote, Brian!"

Brian sits up. "I need to check these numbers properly. Fuck me, Linda. I've got five numbers here."

"Mind your language, Brian. The kids aren't asleep, you know. You've had too much to drink! Besides, if you've five numbers, what's all this 'I've got five numbers' business? You mean, we've got five numbers."

"Linda, I ain't kidding. Take a look for yourself. I've got five fucking numbers, I'm telling you."

"Keep your voice down, Brian. Do you want our children to grow up uncouth like their father? Not only did you just repeat the F-word, but you also just said that I-word again. You mean we've got five numbers, not I."

"Yours, mine, ours, who gives a shit? Here, have a look for yourself. Unless I'm going round the bend, this ticket is showing…" Brian lowers his voice to whisper sarcastically. "…five fucking winning numbers! That's worth about a hundred grand!" He hands Linda the ticket.

Linda checks through the numbers on her phone, with the lottery ticket shaking in her hand.

"Oh my god, Brian! Oh my god!"

"Told you!"

"You've made a mistake here."

"That's why I asked you to check it."

"It's not five numbers, my love."

"Give it here. Let me have another look!"

"It's not five numbers. It's six fucking numbers!" Linda shrieks.

"No way!"

"I've just checked it again. Yes, it's definitely six numbers."

"No way."

"Brian, I've just rechecked it twice. It's six winning numbers, I'm telling you. Oh my god, Brian. We've got six fucking numbers. That's the jackpot."

"Give me that ticket!" Brian painstakingly goes through each number once again very slowly. "Oh my god, it's six numbers. I'm fucking shaking like a leaf here. I'm taking a picture of this ticket in case we lose it."

Brian takes a photograph of the ticket and tells Linda to take one with her phone, too.

"So, what do we do now? I can't think straight."

Linda looks at the back of the ticket.

"It says here that we can phone them in the morning. We can ask them then how much we've won."

"Yeah, but first of all, we need to ask them if we've definitely won," says Brian in a worried voice.

"Brian, we've definitely won. We have six winning numbers on this ticket. We just need to find out how much we've won."

"Oh my god. Don't lose that ticket. I'll put it on top of the kitchen cupboard so it's out of reach of the kids," says Brian. He takes the ticket. He reaches up and places it above the now doorless kitchen cupboard by the sink. He registers the fact the door has come off completely but can't focus on that right now. He takes a breath and runs the cold water tap to splash his face. He stands for a moment, looking out onto their small patch of turf in the back garden, where Liam has a small goalpost for football practice. He turns to head back into the living room and kicks something with his foot. There's a large bang as the cupboard door, propped up against the base unit, falls flat to the kitchen floor, knocking one of the chairs. Brian picks it up, rests it back where it had been left and returns to the living room, grabbing his beer and knocking it back. He stands in front of the muted TV.

"I wonder how much it's worth?" he asks.

"It depends on how many other people also have winning numbers. So I wouldn't go building your hopes up just yet. It may not be a big pay-out."

"How do you mean?"

"Well, if a few other people get six numbers, then the prize money gets shared and divided between them, obviously."

"Pass me that bottle of wine."

"I thought you didn't like wine?"

"I'm shaking here. I've never seen that many numbers before."

"You're saying the I-word again, honey."

"How much do you think we're talking?" asks Brian.

"I've told you. I don't know. As I said, if there are other people with winning numbers, then it gets shared. And the more people who have won, the more it gets shared. Do you need me to write that down, Brian?"

"Which means less of a pay-out," says Brian, disappointed.

"Well, yes, exactly, so let's not build our hopes up."

"Well, even if a good few people have won, it's still got to be worth at least a couple of hundred thousand. Oh my god. I can't believe this. I feel dizzy."

"Come and sit down, Brian. There's nothing you can do right now."

"They shouldn't make people wait until the next day like that. They should have a twenty-four-hour hotline you can call." Brian paces up and down the living room floor.

"Brian, it says here that if you believe you have won over £50,000, then telephone the National Lottery Line. We're going to have to wait until tomorrow to phone up. So please sit down. There's nothing we can do right now."

Brian eventually sits down.

"What time do they open in the morning?"

"I'm just checking that on my phone now. Here we go. It says their office opens at 9 a.m. We only have to wait until in the morning." Linda picks up the remote again and starts flicking through the channels.

Brian empties the last dregs of Linda's Côtes du Rhône. "I've no more beer. Do you have any more wine in the cupboard?"

"God, for somebody who doesn't like wine, you sure know how to knock it back. There're those bottles of Prosecco under the stairs, but I was keeping them for presents."

"That'll do. I need a drink."

"So do I! Fetch me a glass, too."

When the Prosecco is nearly finished, Brian notices that Linda has lost the calmness she showed earlier. She suddenly bursts into tears.

"Are you okay, love?" he asks.

"I'm sorry, I can't help it."

"What's the matter? You should be happy. Once we get this confirmed, I'm packing in that filthy job, and you don't have to spend all week in that supermarket. We should be happy, love," says Brian.

Linda is now sobbing her heart out.

"You're such a hard-working husband and great dad. I know that's a horrible factory where you work, but you do it all to look after us."

"It's okay, love," Brian puts his arms around her and pulls her close. He switches off the episode of Casualty that neither of them can concentrate on.

"Let me say this please, Brian," Linda continues sobbing, her cheeks now flushed from all the wine and her words a little slurred. "We've struggled over the years. We've all gone without, including the kids, because we've had no fucking money." Linda's shoulders start shaking involuntarily. "Our children are in for a future that we never had, Brian."

"I know. I was thinking the same."

"Can we visit Mom and Dad, Brian? And Karen and Dan? I haven't seen them all in four years. Wait until they see Liam and Ruby." She pulls a tissue out of her cardigan pocket and blows her nose noisily into it.

"Not only are we going to the Big Apple to see your folks, Linda, but we're also flying first class, babe."

Brian tells Alexa to play Frank Sinatra's New York, New York.

Linda's up on her unsteady feet, singing about her hometown.

"I love you so much, you English snob," she giggles, putting her arms around his neck and swaying against him.

"And I love you too, you crazy Yank," says Brian, now beginning to feel the effects of mixing beer, red and sparkling wine.

Chapter Five

On Sunday morning, Liam and Ruby come running in to shake them awake. Brian hadn't remembered to close the curtains, so the sun was already warming the room. The reflection from Linda's dressing table mirror, which she'd carefully transported back with her on the flight last time they'd visited her family home, is painful to his sore eyes.

"Are you getting up, Mum?" asks Ruby.

"Come on, Dad! You and Mum are really lazy. Me and Ruby are hungry," moans Liam.

"Okay, we're getting up now. Let me get dressed," says Linda.

"What was all that singing and loud music last night?" asks Ruby as the two of them leave the room.

"Oh my god. My head is killing me," Linda throws back their floral duvet. "I haven't drunk that much in years."

"Was that a dream last night? Because the last I remember, I won the lottery," Brian squints against the sunlight and drops his legs down so he can sit on the edge of the bed. He can't think straight.

"You mean we won? We, we, we, Brian. And don't forget what I said last night. If loads of other people have won too, it gets shared." Linda opens the louvre-doored wardrobe and tilts her head on one side for a moment before retrieving a pair of jeans and a t-shirt from a hanger.

"Yeah, but it's still got to be a good few quid, Linda. What did we do with the ticket?" Brian retrieves the clothes he had worn on Saturday and starts pulling them on.

"Don't worry, it's safe. It's on top of the kitchen cupboards, well away from the kids. Are you going to phone?" she asks. "You can't wear that top again, Brian. You got curry down it last night, and your mum's coming tonight. I'll find you a new one." She rummages on the shelves on Brian's side of the wardrobe that stretches across her side of the bedroom.

"Well, yeah, we definitely need to contact them to confirm we've won, and I'll ask how much it is. Thanks!" He catches the clean black t-shirt.

"I like this one. It's nice and loose," Brian says as he pulls the garment over his head.

"I feel a bit nervous, Brian."

The whining of Liam and Ruby arguing down in the living room reaches them in the bedroom.

"Me too. Let's first get the kids something to eat and keep calm. Then I'll phone, and we'll know one way or the other." Brian rushes downstairs to arbitrate. His heart sinks when he sees the dirty dishes in the sink, the foil trays abandoned on the kitchen table from the takeaway curry, and the empty beer and wine bottles littered around the kitchen, some also visible through the arch to the living room.

"Oh my god, look at the state of this place. I can't remember going to bed," says Linda from behind him.

"Nor me," replies Brian.

Liam and Ruby are sat in the living room, bickering over what to watch on TV.

"Stop it, you two! Bring those glasses into the kitchen for us, Liam! If you help us tidy up, I'll cook us a full English. This place is a mess."

The children jump up enthusiastically and gather the wine glasses and beer bottles. Brian picks up the loose cupboard door and moves it out into the hallway so he can get to the fridge. He pulls the bacon and four eggs out and puts the frying pan on the hob.

"Help me tidy the kitchen before you cook, love," Linda asks.

"Are you kidding me, Linda? I can't do anything else until I get this win confirmed. The kids will help. I just hope there's not been some kind of mistake. I'll help when I come off the phone, but I definitely need this confirmed first."

Liam holds his nose as he drops the empty curry foils into the bin. With a mutual goal now, the children have switched from a full-blown argument to joint mirth over the remains of their parents' evening. They start to wash the dishes, giggling relentlessly.

"I'll go into the front room to phone them," Brian suggests, reaching for the ticket. There's no peace to be found in the kitchen. Liam and Ruby are now flicking bubbles at each other, having poured far too much Fairy liquid into the kitchen sink.

"Go easy on the soap, guys! We're not made of money, you know!" he teases, catching Linda's eye and whispering, "Just yet."

Brian leaves the kitchen and front room doors open, and he occasionally turns to watch Linda from where he is standing in the front room across the hall. Linda tells the children to quiet down, puts some bread in the toaster, and starts to fry the bacon. She shifts the bacon around with a wooden spatula anxiously, and eventually serves it out on four plates and starts to break the eggs into the pan. Brian seems to be moving from one voice to another as questions are asked and he's transferred again and again. Eventually he's heard what he needs to know and thanks the voice at the other end.

"Right, kids, you can eat in front of the telly if you like. You've been so good clearing up for us," says Linda.

"Wow, thanks, Mum," says Ruby. They grab their plates and toast and plonk themselves down on the rug in front of the TV.

"You can choose what we watch, Liam. My turn next time," Ruby says happily.

Brian walks slowly into the kitchen, looking like he's just seen a ghost and stares at Linda without saying a word.

"Well, what happened? You managed to get through to someone, yeah?" Linda keeps her voice low so as not to attract the children's attention.

"Yeah, I spoke to them," Brian almost whispers. "And? So, what happened? Have we won or not?"

Brian is still staring at Linda as if in a trance.

"Oh yeah, we've won, alright."

"Phew, thank god for that," she says. "So, everything's okay then?"

"Everything is fine, love. Everything is fine, my love."

"What do you mean, 'Everything is fine, my love'? Well, come on! What the bloody hell did they say?"

"They're calling here on Tuesday to collect the ticket and check our identification, but we've definitely won."

"Thank god! Did they say how much?"

"Yes, they did."

"Well, how bloody much? God, you're doing my head in, Brian. Spit it out!"

"We're millionaires, Linda."

"No way! No way!" she calls out. The children glance briefly at their parents and then return to their feast.

"Is there any more toast, Mum?" Ruby calls.

Linda starts quickly pacing uncontrollably around the kitchen in a state of euphoria. She picks up the remaining toast, butters it, and takes it to the children. She returns to stand in front of Brian.

"Oh my god," she whispers again. "We've won a million pounds, Brian? I can't believe it. Oh my god. I've dreamt of something like this happening all my life. We've won a million pounds. Jesus Christ, sorry, Lord! I didn't mean that. Oh my god! I can't believe it."

Brian has to physically grab Linda by the shoulders to stop her from running crazily around the kitchen.

"Linda, we've won more than a million, love."

"What?"

"We've won seventeen million."

"What?"

Linda sits down at the kitchen table.

"Seventeen million smackaroonies, Linda."

"Oh my god," she says. "I feel dizzy."

Brian fetches the Scotch from the front living room and pours them each a large shot. They knock them back.

"They've just said to me on the phone that after they've seen our ticket on Tuesday and checked our identification, we'll have the money in our bank by Thursday."

"Oh my god!" Linda pours another shot of whisky.

"Let's just try and calm down, Linda. Brian looks down at the egg and bacon on the plates. "Perhaps we'd better eat now. We had enough alcohol in us last night, and now we're downing the Scotch!" He puts some more bread in the toaster.

"Oh my god, Brian! What are we going to tell the kids?"

"We won't say anything just yet. Come on, for Christ's sake, Linda, let's get ourselves together."

"Yeah, you're right. Yeah, let's get ourselves together. You're right. Let's eat. Let's think," says Linda.

"Wow, I just can't believe it. Where do we begin to start with all of this, Brian?" Linda scrapes butter across her toast.

"Well, I know the very first thing I'm going to do."

"And what's that?"

"I can't wait to phone work in the morning and tell them something I've been dying to tell them for years: to shove that job right up their arses."

"Aren't you better off waiting until we get the money, Brian?"

"Why? You don't think I'm going into that factory tomorrow, do you? I'll never be in that horrible dirty shithole ever again. We've definitely won. They just told me that. They only want to check our identities and see the winning ticket on Tuesday. So, unless we've suddenly changed our names or we lose that ticket, we're millionaires, Linda."

"Have you put the ticket back on top of the kitchen cupboard?"

Brian reaches up to the cupboard to check.

"Yeah, it's safe. You'll still have to work in the supermarket, though," Brian says, laughing.

"Yeah, of course!" she says, laughing. "I might even buy it and sack my dickhead manager," she laughs.

"And that nasty cow, Barbara," Brian laughs back.

"I don't know about you, Brian, but I don't want to leave the house today. I need to try to take all of this in."

"Yeah, me too. We'll get some food delivered Later. I need to take it in as well."

"Oh, I've just thought! We invited your mom for Sunday dinner this evening."

"Okay, I'll phone her and tell her we're not feeling too well. I definitely need time alone today," says Brian, dipping a piece of toast into his cold fried egg.

Chapter Six

Monday morning arrives, and Brian and Linda are still in a complete state of shock, having checked and rechecked the ticket a thousand more times. Each time, Brian carefully reaches up to replace the ticket in its secret hiding place.

"Did you have any homework, Liam? And where's your school bag? I hope you didn't leave it at Nanny Sandra's!"

"Nah, it's upstairs," Liam calls to her from where he's lying on the rug in front of the TV, watching an old Danger Mouse cartoon.

"Well, go and fetch it then, Liam! Hurry up! You're going to be late!"

Liam gets to his feet and tucks his white shirt into his black school trousers.

"And while you're up there, tell Ruby that she's left it too late for any breakfast now." Linda squeezes the dishcloth out and starts wiping the kitchen table, skirting around Ruby's empty bowl, which she leaves where it is in case Ruby still wants to grab some cereal quickly.

"You definitely not going to work then, love?" Linda slips her arm around Brian from behind as he pours them each a cuppa.

"Are you kidding me? I've told you. I'm finished with that place. But if it makes you happy, I won't tell them I've left until the money is in our account. I'll phone them and say I'm taking a few sick days as I'm not too well. How does that sound?"

"Yeah. I think I'd prefer to see the money in the bank first, love."

Brian takes his mobile out of his jeans pocket and phones his company, Langhams Tannery.

"Oh, hello, Christine. Can you put me through to personnel? Oh, Mrs Pendlebury? Yes, it's Brian Jackson here. I'm sorry, but I won't be able to make it to work for the next few days. I've been coughing my guts up all night. I'm hoping to see a doctor but will phone you when I'm feeling better." Brian is silent for a moment. "Thank you, Mrs Pendlebury. I sure will rest up, thank you! Bye."

"Were they okay about it, Brian?"

"I couldn't care less. I only did it to keep you happy." Brian grins. "She's got a soft spot for me, that Mrs Pendlebury, ever since we looked after her cat that time she went to visit her cousin. She'd do anything for me now. Right, I'll drop the kids off at school, and when I get back, we'll have a morning shop and stop off at a TGI Friday's on the way back. How does that sound?"

"Sounds great. I'll phone John as well and tell them I've caught something from you. Then I'm going to relax in a nice hot bubble bath. I feel so bloody nervous. I keep thinking it's all a dream, or we've made some kind of mistake."

"Stop worrying! We're millionaires, love," Brian whispers so the kids won't hear and kisses her on her cheek.

Brian bundles Liam and Ruby into the car. Ruby takes her bowl of Frosties with her and continues munching in the backseat. Liam jumps in front and buckles up.

Linda rings John and tries to cough between words. She's always been a hopeless liar. She then goes upstairs to run a bath. Sandra gave her some Champney bubble bath the previous Christmas, which she opens and sniffs.

She can't smell anything, so she pours a generous dollop into the bath. While it's running, she picks up Ruby's pyjamas and flings them into the laundry basket with her own.

She steps into the now frothy rose-scented water, checking it's not too hot. She sinks down with a gentle sigh. As she lies there, she tries her best to relax, but she's so excited about returning home to New York and the possibility of seeing her parents, Nancy and Bob, her little sister, Karen, and Karen's husband, Tom. She also can't wait to see her younger brother, Dan. Liam and Ruby affectionately call Dan 'Uncle Buck'. Linda laughs, remembering. She can't wait to see her home on the edge of Brooklyn. How strange it would be to return to East New York, a real working-class neighbourhood, as a millionaire! What would her parents say? As she lies in the water, her phone starts buzzing on the shelf over the sink. She'll leave it. It can't be important. But it continues, so she heaves herself up to full height and leans across the edge of the bath to see who it is. If it's work or Sandra, she'll leave it ring. But it's Brian. She quickly jumps out of the bath, dries her hands on a towel and grabs the mobile.

"Oh, hello. The Jackson residence. How can I help you?" she asks in her best English accent.

"Oh, I can tell you've just come into money, Linda Jackson. You've turned English posh!" Brian laughs. "Just to bring you back down to earth, we've only got a bloody puncture. And just in case you don't know, the days of me bending down to change a tyre are well and truly over."

"And you're calling me posh, Brian Jackson? You're too good to change a tyre on a car now, are you? Anyway, I'm not bothered who changes the tyre, but what about the kids getting to school?"

"Don't worry about them. They're sorted. Your friend, Jenny, is it? The one who looks like she's had ten too many face lifts? She was driving past and is dropping them off with her little ones, which was very kind of her. Listen, I'm walking up to Archie's garage. I'm going to ask him to get one of his lads to come out and fix the tyre. I'll be back when I've got this sorted, love, okay?"

"No worries. Hey, tell you what! If everything's okay with the money tomorrow, we'll be buying a new car anyway."

"You mean when everything is sorted tomorrow, Linda? Yeah, too right, we will. That Corsa was on its way out anyway. In fact, I'll ask Archie to tow it back to his garage, scrap it, and send me the bill. See you soon. One of Archie's lads can drop me back home."

Linda steps back into the bath, daydreaming of walking through Central Park with the kids. The water has gone cold, so she turns the hot tap on to try to warm it up. She wonders if they might buy a jacuzzi for the summer. The children would love it.

Chapter Seven

For Brian, Tuesday morning couldn't come soon enough; his heart beats fast when he hears the doorbell. He opens their half-glazed front door, expecting a man in a suit with a briefcase, but a short, dumpy woman stands on the doorstep, grinning at him. She thrusts her hand towards him while at the same time tilting her head to one side.

"You must be Mr Jackson. I'm Christine. Christine Edgerton. I'm from the National Lottery. I believe you're expecting me?" Her voice is shockingly high-pitched, and Brian has to try hard not to look surprised.

"Yes, and please call me Brian." Brian shakes her hand vigorously and ushers her straight into the living room.

"Please come in. This is my wife, Linda. Linda, this is Christine Edgerton from the Lottery."

"Hello," Linda says, wiping her hands on a kitchen towel.

"Very pleased to meet you both," Christine says, offering Linda her hand to shake.

The living room suddenly seems tiny to Brian with the three of them standing there. He feels nervous and isn't sure whether to treat the meeting like an interview or to start asking questions about the money.

"Would you like a cup of tea or coffee?" Linda asks.

"Yes, of course—what would you like to drink?" Brian echoes, relieved that at least Linda is in control of the situation.

"Well, now, Linda! I'd love a cup of tea, please. White, two sugars," screeches their guest. Brian feels distracted by the unpleasantness of her voice.

"Do you want one, love?" Linda asks Brian.

"Yes, thanks." He smiles at Linda.

"Please sit down," Linda calls as she heads to the kitchen sink.

"Well now both! How are you?" Christine asks.

"We still can't believe this is happening to us," says Brian.

Linda returns to join them while the kettle boils.

"That's normal." A high-pitched giggle erupts after every sentence. "Everyone feels like that at first. I've been in this job for three years now, and I'm yet to meet someone who could take it all with a pinch of salt."

Christine's words and voice are grating on Brian's nerves. Her Cheshire cat grin switches between himself and Linda in a rather unnerving way. Perhaps he's just tired from lack of sleep with all the excitement.

Linda returns to the kitchen when she hears the kettle switch off.

"Well, now! Before we do anything else, shall we get the formalities out of the way? This shouldn't take too long."

Brian sits, nodding his head while Linda busies herself with the tea. Eventually she returns carrying a tray with three mugs of tea and a sugar bowl.

"Brian, love, just bring that side table out, will you, and set it between us?" she asks.

He jumps up, glad to have something to do, and places the largest of their nest of tables between himself on the armchair and Christine, who is sitting on the sofa. Linda sits next to Christine and passes a mug of tea to her.

"Please help yourself to sugar."

Christine shovels three spoons into her mug.

"Well, now, thank you! Love my sugar, I do. I expect you can tell from my shape?" She giggles again. The sound has a squeaky scream-like quality. He smiles at her but notices a frown pass Linda's face. She looks like she's struggling too.

"Mmm, lovely. Nothing like a nice cup of tea, is there! Well, now! Have you filled out the back of the ticket?" Christine asks.

Relieved that, at last, they can get on with the business, Brian jumps up again.

"Yes, here it is." He leans over to hand it to Christine Edgerton.

"Well, now! Thank you. Firstly, just to check those six magic numbers." Christine pulls a black Moleskine notebook out of an oversized shoulder bag lying by her feet. She opens the book with one hand and holds the by-now somewhat worn ticket in the other. She transfers her glance between the ticket and the notebook. Brian and Linda's gazes are glued to her. Brian involuntarily holds his breath until the Cheshire cat smile returns.

"Yes, they're correct." She laughs again, and Brian cringes inwardly.

"And now just to check all the other reference numbers on the ticket..." Again, a pause while she flicks her head back and forth between her book and the ticket. "Well, now! Yes, they're all correct as well. So, all I need now is two forms of identification, please?"

"I've got our passports and driving licenses, if that's okay?" asks Brian.

Christine Edgerton takes each document in turn and seems to note everything from each in her black book. Brian and Linda gulp their tea loudly and wait.

"That's marvellous, and yes, everything is in place here. I can now officially validate your good fortune. Congratulations!"

"Is that it?" asks Linda.

"Yes," Christine responds, again switching her grin between the two of them.

"So, the seventeen million pounds is now officially ours?" asks Brian.

"Yes, that's everything confirmed. The total sum is seventeen million, three hundred and forty-seven thousand pounds. And depending on where you want the money deposited, you should receive it by Thursday. It could even go in earlier than that."

"Wow, I still can't believe it," says Linda, as she accidentally bumps into Christine.

"Oh, sorry, this room is very cramped," says Linda.

"You're gonna need a bigger house," says Christine, which unfortunately triggers a raucous bout of laughter from Christine. Brian tries to ignore it and smiles.

"We also provide further information and help with insurance, investments, even health and wellbeing."

"I can't believe this is happening to us," repeats Brian.

"Yes, it must seem very strange indeed. It will eventually sink in, but it can be quite a shock. Some people struggle with that. That's why we offer support for health and wellbeing. We can put you in touch with other winners if you think that will help, you know, talking to someone who's already experienced all this. Can I ask you both, are you going public? Or do you wish to remain anonymous? We normally recommend that you don't do anything immediately, well, until you've had time for all of this to sink in."

"Oh, we haven't even thought about any of that," Linda replies. "What would you do?"

"Well now, Linda, we always advise winners to think carefully about it. If you're an outgoing type of person, you might enjoy the publicity. If, on the other hand, you're pretty private people, then it might not suit you. So, you need to think it through carefully."

"No, I mean, what would you do personally yourself? Would you go public if it was you?" Linda asks Christine.

Christine seems surprised by the question. Brian watches her, interested to hear how she will answer.

"Oh, I see. You mean, if it was me?" she stutters. "Okay, off the record, I would not go public, as I'm what you would call a private kind of person. So, no, to answer your question and, as I say, off the record, I would keep it quiet, but that's just me." She takes a deep breath and seems to recover her usual banter. "Well, now! You'd be surprised by the people I've met who do go public and those who choose not to! It's never the ones you expect who keep it private!" she giggles. "Again, off the record. This is just me speaking. If you really intend to keep this private, I would not tell one single person, including family. But as I say, that's just me."

Brian stares at Christine, happy to ignore her high-pitched laughter and "Well, nows," so long as she can transfer the money and they can keep everything private.

"You see loads of people announcing winnings in the papers and on TV, but I don't think I'd want to do that," he says. "You must get hassled by loads of people with begging letters and stuff like that."

"It would be nice, though, Brian, to help people, like certain charities," Linda interrupts. "I've always wanted to donate to the NSPCC. It seems such a good cause, helping prevent cruelty to children."

"Well, now! I think it's best not to rush into anything at this stage. Take your time for this to sink in," advises Christine again, temporarily lowering her voice to a more serious tone.

"Yeah, you're right," replies Brian.

"Good. Well, now! I must be off!" Christine sets her mug back on the table and rummages in her bag. "I won't keep you any longer. Here are some leaflets on the different banks I mentioned. Once you've decided on which bank, you need to let us know the details. The sooner, the better, of course. Here's a card with my number. We can point you in the right direction for any health or investment support. We always give our big winners financial advice from Coutts & Co. — the same bank used by The Royal Family. Here's their leaflet." She rings the name of a contact on the leaflet before putting her pen and Moleskine book back in her bag. "Providing you let us know today about the account, you could receive the money by Thursday. Don't forget, if you need to speak to me or my office, we're always available."

Brian and Linda wave Christine goodbye from the front door, calling out their thanks. As they re-enter the front room, Linda begins to cry.

"Are you okay, love? asks Brian.

"I still can't believe it. We've literally struggled and struggled for years. We've worked so hard to make ends meet… and now this has happened. I want to see my mom and dad. I want to see my baby sister and brother."

"Well, there's not a thing in the world stopping us now, Linda. America, here we come!"

"I love you so much, Brian Jackson," Linda says, hugging him. "Jesus, what an awful laugh, though. I couldn't wait for her to leave!"

"Yes." Brian starts laughing. "It was hard to take her seriously, wasn't it? Still, worth it for the money!"

"Yes. Absolutely. Well, now, Brian…" Linda imitates Christine's high-pitched giggle, and they both fall back onto the sofa with tears of laughter this time.

Chapter Eight

The next couple of days are all a bit of a blur. The money has landed safely into their new bank account, and Brian and Linda are trying to come to terms with being millionaires.

With the kids in school, they are about to go into Liverpool city centre to buy some new clothes for them all for their trip to America.

"Afterwards, we can stop off at that new posh restaurant we saw advertised in The Echo," says Brian.

"Sounds a brilliant idea," Linda replies, although she's wondering whether splashing their money around so soon is a good idea.

"Tell you what, I'll ask my mum to collect the kids from school, and we won't have to rush back," Brian adds.

"Talking about your mom, Brian, I couldn't sleep a wink last night."

"Why, what do you mean?"

"Well, firstly, have you told your mom that we're going to see my folks in America? And more importantly, when the hell are we going to tell our families about our win?"

"Well, actually, I was going to tell my mum and Billy we're going to America later. With regard to the money, I don't really know when the best time is to tell her that. I'd certainly like you to be with me."

"I know exactly what you mean. I was speaking to Karen the other night, and I could hardly say over the phone, 'Oh, by the way, sis, I've won seventeen million pounds.' I'm going to have to tell them all face to face. If Sandra collects the kids from school and drops them off later, we could tell her then?"

"Let me think about that one, Linda. I'm not sure about telling her with the kids here. I mean, don't get me wrong, I can't wait to tell them all, and I certainly can't wait to help them all out."

"Well, I'm not going to let my dad struggle anymore in that old decrepit townhouse in Brooklyn, with him struggling to climb the stairs. I want to buy them a beautiful bungalow."

"Yeah, and we will."

"And your mom, too. We'll be buying her and Billy something here as well."

"Yeah, too right. We'll definitely be looking after our families. But I honestly don't know where to start, though, and it's making me feel so anxious."

Linda puts her arms around Brian.

"I feel the same, love. We have to remember this is still a huge shock to us. I just think it's best if we don't do anything rash until we've let it all sink in."

"So does that mean I can't visit a couple of car showrooms and pick up my Porsche whilst we're out today?"

Linda starts laughing.

"I think we'll leave the car for now. Anyway, if we're going to visit my folks, the car will only be stuck outside the house."

"Yeah, that's true."

Brian hears a car beeping its horn.

"The taxi's here. Make sure you've got your new bank cards. I've got mine."

Brian pulls their parkas off the coat stand in the hall and passes Linda hers. Together, they leave the house without tidying the mugs from the living room or clearing the children's breakfast things. Laughing, they jump in the taxi and head for town.

"Where do you want dropping off, mate?" the taxi driver asks them as they reach the centre.

"Drop us off at The Albert Dock, please," Brian says.

"I need to go to Primark first for the kids' stuff," Linda says.

"Forget Primark, Linda! We're only buying the best from now on."

Linda looks nervously at the taxi driver and frowns at Brian. She wonders whether the driver has guessed anything.

"What?" Brian asks, pulling a face back at Linda. He rummages in his pocket and pulls out his shiny new credit card.

"Can I pay on a card, mate?" he asks.

"Sure." The driver starts tapping numbers into a machine and hands it to Brian. Linda climbs out.

"Brian, perhaps we should hire a car for a while. It's going to cost a fortune to keep using taxis, and people will notice."

"So what if they do notice? I don't care. They can think what they like," Brian says as they walk towards the Albert Dock.

"Mmmm. You say that now. But you might not like it if The Echo gets wind of it, or the national press for that matter."

"Come on, you! We're supposed to be enjoying ourselves!" Brian admonishes. "I'm just going to ring mum about picking the kids up; you go ahead."

After a couple of hours at The Albert Dock, they walk down to the Metquarter, where Linda can't resist shopping in the Cricket boutique, with its vast designer range.

"I've always dreamt of shopping here, Brian. I've often thought how wonderful it must be not having to look at the price tags, and now that's us! The only labels I'm looking at are the sizes," says Linda.

"I didn't realise that we had so many fantastic shops in Liverpool."

"Brian, do you men not know anything? It is a well-known fact that Liverpool has the best shopping experience in the world, after New York, of course."

Linda is now looking forward to browsing the malls in the States, where the lights are always on full, and the atmosphere just smells of wealth, doughnuts and Asian noodles from the food halls. Brain tries a suit on, but he just doesn't look right in it. His shoulders are too broad, and the trousers are a tad too short.

"We'll have to go to Primark for t-shirts, Brian. They've got nothing here in Liam's or Ruby's size."

"I've told you we can't go to Primark anymore, Linda. We've got far too much money now," says Brian, laughing. "Can we head for The Shabu now? My feet are killing me."

"Oh my god, you really are now an English snob."

"Look what I bought from Boots while you were in Jaeger."

Brian passes Linda a small Boots carrier bag.

"Ominous. What is it?"

"Take a look."

She looks into the bag and pulls out a white box.

"Wow, Brian! Diorissimo, my favourite… and it's the perfume, not the eau de toilette! You remembered after all these years." Tears well up in Linda's eyes. She feels overwhelmed by his generosity and thoughtfulness.

"But I haven't got you anything. I feel awful."

"There's plenty of time for that. And anyway, that's not the point. I want to get my lady Linda what she deserves. Now let's get a move on. I'm starving."

"You certainly know how to woo a woman, Brian. Perfume and then a Michelin star-rated Japanese restaurant. Did you book?"

"Trust me. They'll give us a table."

Reassured by Brian's extravagant gift, Linda starts to feel more relaxed about spending money. Just as they are about to leave the shopping centre, a Harvey Nichols coat in a shop window catches her eye.

"Brian, that is so you!" she says. "Come on. You have to try it on."

Within six minutes, they are leaving the shop with a hip-length tan leather coat on Brian's shoulders. Linda has used her shiny new credit card for the sum of £1685. Brian's old black parka is stuffed in the H&M bag with the children's jean shorts. As they exit the shopping centre, Brian pulls it out and drops it in a bin. He then retrieves it quickly and extracts his wallet from the right pocket before returning it to the bin.

"Whoops! That was close. Nearly lost my new credit cards!" he laughs.

Linda frowns. That dark little cloud keeps hovering in the back of her mind.

"Be careful, Brian. We mustn't get complacent."

"Stop worrying, you! You need a drink."

They find their way to the restaurant. Brian had been right about their getting a table. Although it is a small restaurant, there are only a couple of other tables occupied. The tables are low on the ground, and people are sat on cushions around them.

"This is fun!" Linda says after the waiter has left them.

"Fun, maybe, but not very comfy," Brian complains. "And I can hardly see the menu!"

"I love the ambience… and the music. It's so relaxing."

Linda ignores the prices on the menu and focuses on trying to understand what the dishes might taste like from the photos of each item.

Brian browses the drinks menu.

"Look at that! £102 for a bottle of Saint-Émilion — that must be good. And £275 for a bottle of Champagne! That's ridiculous."

He orders a more modestly priced bottle of Sake, and Linda suggests they choose a set meal, as neither of them recognises any of the dishes. Each course brought out is new and exciting to Linda. She's never had Japanese food before and begins to ponder on whether their next holiday should be to Japan. The wine relaxes them both, and they chat endlessly about all the possibilities now they have money. Eventually, Brian settles the bill, and they head for home.

It doesn't take long for the taxi to arrive, and the driver helps them to put their shopping bags in the boot.

"Did you enjoy your meal?" asks the driver.

"Yeah, it was lovely, thank you," replies Linda.

"I've picked up a few people from here, and they've all said how nice it is."

When they pull up outside their home, Linda slowly gets out and retrieves the bags. Brian pays the driver with a generous tip as Linda heads inside to put the kettle on.

*****

As the taxi pulls away, Brian notices a small Honda pulling up on the other side of the road with two men inside. As the window goes down, Brian instantly recognises one of them. Sitting in the passenger side is the tattooed thug he'd taken on in the shop at Liam's football match.

"Oi, Brian!" the youth shouts. "The slashed tyres were a warning of what's to come for you and your Yankee wife. You haven't heard the last of this." The youth slowly raises a large knife and turns it to reflect the sun.

Brian is a big man, confident he can look after himself, but being confronted unexpectedly by two men with a knife threatening his family shakes him to the core. Brian can feel his body shaking from head to toe.

The youth continues to stare at Brian, turning the knife, as the driver slowly pulls away. Brian walks quickly towards the house, still watching over his shoulder as they drive away. Once inside, he slams the bolt across the door.

"Would you like a cup of tea, Brian? I've decided on coffee."

All kinds of terrifying thoughts are now going through Brian's mind.

So, it wasn't a puncture; the tattoo man had slashed the tyre with his knife. And he knows that Linda is American and where they live. That dirty scumbag must have followed him after Liam's football match.

Unable to hear what Linda is saying, Brian is just about to phone the police but decides to phone Deano first. Deano can probably find out who the tattoo man is. If he can get a name for this thug, Brian could pass it on to the police. It couldn't be that hard to identify a youth with a tattoo on his face like that.

"Are you listening to me, Brian Jackson? Would you like a cup of tea?" calls Linda once again.

She follows him into the front room.

"Is everything okay, Brian?"

Brian composes himself quickly to avoid worrying Linda, aware of how well she can read his feelings. They are soulmates. They interpret each other intuitively.

"Oh, sorry, love, I was just phoning Deano back. He tried calling me earlier and I missed it. What did you ask me?"

"I've asked you three times. Tea or coffee?"

Deano's phone is ringing in Brian's ear.

"Er, no thanks, love. I'll just take this call."

Brian takes the stairs two at a time to make his call upstairs.

Chapter Nine

Brian closes his bedroom door as Deano answers his call.

"Deano, it's Brian. I really need to speak to you, buddy."

"Sure, what's up? Everything okay?"

"No. Everything's not okay. I think I've got myself a big problem."

"What! What kind of problem?"

"Somebody has just threatened me and my family. Can you come round to mine, please, and I'll explain everything when you get here?"

"Sure thing, mate. I'm only around the corner. I'm on my way."

"That's great. Thanks, Deano."

Brian terminates the call just as Linda joins him in the bedroom, holding a mug of tea in one hand and coffee in the other.

"So what's happening? Is Deano okay? Does he want to know when you're going back to work? I suppose they get loaded with your share of the work."

Brian feels a bit calmer now that Deano is on his way round but doesn't want to worry Linda.

"No, he never mentioned that. He's doing a marathon run for charity, and he's looking for sponsors. He's popping round to tell me about it."

"Gosh, that doesn't sound like Deano. Or not the Deano you keep telling me about. Turning over a new leaf, is he? Did you tell him about the money? Is that why he's singled us out to sponsor him."

"God, I forgot all about that. No, of course not. I haven't spoken to him until today."

Linda laughs.

"How could you forget it, Brian? It's all I can think about." She sits on the edge of the bed next to him, passing him his mug. She puts hers on the bedside table.

"I don't know," says Brian nervously. "I don't think we should tell anybody about the money just yet. That lottery woman—young squeaky voice—she was right about one thing. We need to get our heads around everything first."

Brian stares out of the bedroom window as the doorbell rings.

"Here's Deano now," says Brian.

"That was quick."

"Yeah. He must have been in the area," stutters Brian, taking a swig of his coffee.

Linda runs down the stairs ahead of him and tries to open the front door, but it's locked. She pulls the bolt across and turns the latch.

"Hi, Deano. Where do you get your energy from?" Linda asks.

"Hi, Linda. Energy for what?" laughs Deano.

"You know, the marathon."

"Marathon?" asks Deano.

Brian stands behind Linda and winks at Deano.

"Your charity run, Deano. Everyone else calls them 'marathons'. Come into the front room, buddy, and let's sort something out."

"Oh yeah," Deano laughs nervously.

"Would you like a cup of tea, Deano, or would you prefer a Brooklyn coffee? My mom sends it over from the States. The taste is to die for. I've got a pot already made."

"Oh, thanks. How can I refuse? It's got to be a Brooklyn coffee, then. Black, no sugar, thanks, Linda."

"Coming right up, Deano."

Linda disappears into the kitchen, leaving Brian and Deano in the hall. Deano follows Brian into the front room.

"What's with the marathon shit?"

"I had to tell her something. She knows nothing about any of this trouble."

"So, what's happened? You sounded pretty shook up on the phone. Not like you, big fella."

"Somebody was outside here earlier, Deano, threatening me with a knife."

Deano stares at Brian in bewilderment as Linda joins them with his coffee.

"There you go, Deano. How are they all managing at work without Brian? Is any work getting done?"

She sets his mug on the coffee table.

"Not a thing, Linda. Without him, we're useless." He smiles at her and picks up his mug to take a sip.

"Not a lot of coughing going on here, though, Brian. Sounds like you're well enough to be back on shift, but don't worry! I won't tell. Enjoying a bit of time with the missus, are you?" It's Deano's turn to wink at Linda now. She blushes and retreats to the kitchen.

"I've got a waterproof jacket and some trousers in the shed," Brian says loudly, hoping Linda will hear, "if you want them for running. Come and have a look at them."

Linda raises her eyebrows in surprise as the two men walk through the kitchen with their mugs and out the back door into the garden. She shuts the door after them quickly to keep the cold out.

Brian lifts the shed door a little off its hinges to free it up to open. Once Deano is inside, he shuts the door. Deano cups his hands around his coffee mug.

"Thanks for coming."

"So, what happened, Brian?"

"I caught a guy attacking the owner of a corner shop near my son's school. He was hitting the guy, and his daughter was terrified. I kind of got involved and knocked him down. Thought I'd taught him a lesson, but the other day, my tyre was slashed, and today, he pulled up in a Honda right outside my front door and threatened me. He knows Linda is American and that I have kids. Kept flashing a knife about."

"Bloody hell, Brian. Thought I lived on the edge." Deano sips his coffee. "How can I help?"

"This bloke, he's tall, bald, skinny, with a tattoo on his face. He's spooked me up a bit. Can you make some enquiries… find out who this piece of shit is?"

Deano frowns.

"I know who it is, Brian. Tattoo on his face. Tall, bald, skinny, stealing from shops. That can only be Juicy. I'm not sure what his real name is, but he comes into our pub."

"He goes to The Feathers?"

"Well, he doesn't drink there, but he comes in occasionally selling all kinds of shit that he's pinched from shops. He's a baghead."

"Heroin?"

"Yeah, a complete addict. He'd kill his own mother to sort out his next fix. You don't want to be messing with him, Brian."

"Right, okay, Deano. We know who he is now. Thanks. I'll phone the police."

"Phone the police, Brian? Are you kidding me? And what do you think the police are going to do? They're hardly going to arrest somebody for the odd threat. They don't work that way, buddy. He'd have to attack you or your family before they'd get involved."

"Attack my family? I don't like this, Deano. Why didn't I mind my own fucking business in that shop? If he comes anywhere near my family, I swear, I'll kill him."

"Brian, I know you can look after yourself, but you need to be very careful here. This Juicy has a few mates, and they all carry knives. You don't want to be messing with this lot. They're desperate people with nothing to lose. I'll tell you the best thing to do. In fact, it's the only thing we can do to nip this in the bud. I'll have a word with Bruno. Nobody messes with Bruno, and I mean nobody. And he has loads of backup."

"Yeah, I've heard of Bruno. I've overheard stuff at work. Yeah, he's got a reputation. I didn't know you knew him, Deano. Look, I just want this tattoo bloke to go away. I don't want any trouble or any more shit, especially for my missus and the kids. I just want this to stop."

Brian pulls out a rolled-up wad of £100 notes from his pocket. Deano whistles.

"Deano, Linda's uncle in the States has left us a little money. If I give this Bruno bloke, say, a couple of grand, can he put a stop to all this? I'll give you a grand, too, of course."

"I don't want your money, Brian. I'm your friend. Friends help each other."

"Thanks, Deano. But I will look after you too. Does two thousand sound about right to give this Bruno bloke to stop these threats?"

"Yeah, I think so. Let me have a word with him first. Put your money away for now. I'd better get going. I've got a bit of running around to do. I'll call when I've spoken to Bruno, okay?"

"By the way, Linda knows nothing about this. I don't want her worrying."

"Of course, this is just between us. I'll be in touch."

Brian grabs the dusty, old, oily and waterproof trousers from a shelf at the back of the shed and thrusts them into Deano's hands.

"Take these and thank me for sponsoring you. I'll take the mugs in."

They make their way up the garden path and back into the kitchen. Linda is chatting to Sandra, and the children are watching TV.

"Thanks for the coffee, Linda. Your hubby's going to sponsor me! A hundred pounds if I do the whole run! Not bad."

Linda looks across at Brian.

"I would have thought you could stretch to a bit more than that, love. How far are you running, Deano?"

"Fifteen miles. Need to train myself up. These waterproofs will be useful."

"Well, I'll sponsor you a hundred too. Good for you. What's it in aid of?"

"Er… addicts. They need all the help they can get."

"Well, good for you!"

Deano leaves, and Brian locks the door after him.

"Why do you keep locking the door, Brian? Sandra and the children couldn't get in. Good that Deano's helping addicts. Perhaps we've misjudged him. Maybe that's why he spends so much time at The Feathers."

Chapter Ten

"That's the kids settled. They're made up with their new iPads."

As he sits down to watch TV, Linda snuggles up beside him.

"I was speaking to Mom and Dad earlier. I told them we were coming over to see them. They can't wait to see the kids."

"I'm looking forward to it myself."

"Right, Mr Jackson, I've got a question for you." Linda snuggles up even closer and takes his hand.

"Oh really, Mrs Jackson!" Brian turns to face her.

"Where the bloody hell are we going to live?"

"How do you mean?"

"I mean, do we continue living in the UK, or shall we move to the States?"

"I haven't really given that much thought yet, but aren't the kids settled here in school? It would be huge to move them."

"What you really mean, Brian, is that you're worried about gun crime in the States, aren't you? Why don't you just admit it? That's why you always call me a crazy Yank."

"What do you mean? I wasn't thinking anything like that, Linda, but now you mention it, you are a crazy Yank."

"Yeah, but be honest! You've said it to me before, many times actually, about the gun crime." Linda sits up. "Guns might be a problem over there, but it's getting just as bad here now in the UK."

Brian looks up to catch her eyes. Oh god! If she only knew what he was worried about. That they were being threatened by a criminal with a knife.

"And as for the kids being settled in school. They are still young enough to make that change, Brian. They aren't even in high school yet. Kids adapt quickly, and there's plenty of soccer now in America for both our kids. It's something we should consider."

"I know, I agree. We need to consider loads of other things, too, now, Linda. Our lives will never be the same again."

"It's not as if your mom is on her own here. She has Billy. He's good to her. And they could always fly out to see us."

"Well, let's just go and see your family first and enjoy a well-earned holiday." Brian gets up. He can't sit any longer. His worries are eating away at him. Maybe being out of the picture in the States is just what they need while Bruno sorts this other matter out.

"Okay, I'll book the flights. No need to wait, is there? We could fly out within a few days, really. That travel agent has everything lined up for us. She was applying for your ESTA and pricing out the tickets. I'll give her a call." Linda jumps up eagerly and retrieves her phone from her handbag in the hallway.

Brian goes to the fridge and pours himself a beer.

"Can we wait a few more days, Linda? What's the rush? We need to tell work and get Mum to look after the rabbits. I still haven't bought a tracksuit to fly out in. Do you want a beer, love? I'm having one."

Linda joins him in the kitchen, holding her hands out either side and shrugging her shoulders.

"Why wait?"

"I want to speak to my mum. We should tell her about our win. And I'd like you to come with me when I do it."

"Well, stop putting it off, Brian. We could have told her tonight."

"Not with Deano here. It was awkward."

"Oh, honestly! We could have invited her to eat with us and told her then. Why are you making such a big deal about it?"

Brian hears the impatient edge in Linda's voice and knows it's obvious he's using delaying tactics, but if she knew what his fears were, it might trigger her migraines again, and then her health would go downhill fast.

"We'll go to see her tomorrow. I can still book the flights, can't I?" Linda pleads.

"Yeah, but I was thinking about researching for a nice house rental near your folks. I need a bit more time."

"Oh yes, I love the sound of that, Brian. I never thought about where we were going to stay. We can rent a house with a pool. Right, forget the flights for now. I'm going to search for properties to rent in Brooklyn. Luxury, here we come!"

Linda sits down at the kitchen table to start googling online. Brian pings a second can of beer open and leans down to plant a kiss on her head while placing the can in front of her.

"No thanks, Brian. Not for me." She pushes the can away from her. Brian picks it up and starts knocking his second beer back, breathing a sigh of relief.

His phone starts ringing.

"Hold on, here's Deano again," says Brian.

Linda, too distracted by properties to rent in New York, ignores him. He wanders out to the hall and into the front room again.

"Is Linda listening?" Deano asks.

"No, it's okay, I'm in another room. What's up?"

"We may have a problem with tattoo-man. Apparently, word is that Juicy really has it in for you. But on a more positive note, Bruno's here in The Feathers if you want to come and speak to him. He'll sort the problem out for you."

"Yes, definitely, Deano. I've got to sort this out. Any chance you could pick me up?"

"Sure. I'll be with you in ten minutes."

Brian returns to the kitchen, where Linda is still busy on her phone.

"What did Deano want?" she asks. "He only left here a couple of hours ago. Can't he live without you?"

"Oh, they're buying a house, and Debbie wants me to take a look at it. He's asked if I'll go with him now because the owner's there."

"That's exciting. But it's nearly nine. It seems rather late. Is Debbie with him? I'll join you if she is."

"No, it's just Deano. Well, the owner is going away tomorrow, so Deano's persuaded him to let me look around tonight. It's not that far."

"Oh, okay. Anyway, about the holiday rental. How about if we rent a house in Long Island? It's not far from Brooklyn. We used to go to the beach there when I was little. Liam and Ruby would love it. There's quite a few here, and they all have swimming pools."

"Sounds great. I'll pick up some booze while I'm out. What do you fancy?"

Linda continues staring at her phone.

"Just get me some Prosecco."

"Right, here's Deano. I won't be long."

Before leaving the house, he takes the stairs two at a time and retrieves a couple of wads of notes from the stash of money he'd hidden inside his trainers in the back of his wardrobe.

*****

Brian feels like he's walking into the saloon of a cowboy movie as he enters The Feathers. It's as though the pianist has stopped playing, and everyone has stopped talking to watch him. Nobody seems bothered about the no smoking indoors legislation, so a blanket of smoke hits Brian as they walk across the room. As the two men make progress across the floor, the audience seems to lose interest and the murmur of interrupted conversations resumes.

Deano brings him to a table in the corner, where quite a diminutive man sits with a steely grimace. Next to him is a huge guy, making Brian feel like a midget. Brian and Deano sit opposite Bruno and his friend.

"This is Brian, who I was telling you about," says Deano. "Brian, this is Bruno."

Brian is surprised at how submissive Deano sounds when speaking to Bruno. It's as if he's in awe of the man. Without changing expression, Bruno looks Brian up and down.

"Deano tells me you've got problems with Juicy," Bruno says.

"Yeah. He slashed my tyre and threatened my family. I've got a wife and kids, and I don't like it."

"Okay. I know him. That's not good, but I can make sure he doesn't bother you."

"Will he definitely listen?" asks Brian.

Bruno looks at Brian, squinting his eyes. Brian wishes he hadn't said anything.

"I just told you, he won't bother you once I've dealt with him."

"That's great, thanks," Brian says, keeping eye contact with Bruno.

"Deano said you wanted to pay."

"Yeah, I've…" Brian puts his hand in his jeans pocket.

"Not out here," Bruno spits.

"No, of course not."

Brian sheepishly pulls a tissue out of his pocket and mimics blowing his nose.

"How much have you got?" Bruno asks.

Somewhat intimidated by Bruno, Brian decides to up his offer.

"Is five grand okay?"

Deano raises his eyebrows and turns to look Brian in the eye.

Bruno says nothing.

"Go to the gents. Wait until Ben says it's okay. Then pay the man. Understood?"

Brian starts to feel nervous. Big Ben gets up and disappears behind a door marked 'Toilets This Way.'

"Yeah, okay," Brian replies and follows Ben.

Ben waits for two people to leave before standing firmly against the door to stop anyone else from coming in.

"Okay, now."

Brian's hands shake as he retrieves the five rolls from his pockets. He begins to feel sick.

"There's five thousand there."

"If you say so," says Big Ben as he puts the money in his inside jacket pocket. He smirks at Brian, then turns to leave.

Brian lets a massive nervous breath of air out of his lungs and runs a cold tap to splash his face. He's not sure who he's most afraid of, Juicy or Bruno and Big Ben. Jesus, how did he get into this situation?

Brian returns to sit next to Deano. Bruno looks surprised and tilts his head on one side.

"Our business is finished," Bruno says.

Deano winks at Brian and nudges his head towards the door.

"Come on, Brian, let's go." Then, turning his head back to Bruno, he says, "Thanks for that."

Bruno takes a slug of his beer and looks away from the two men.

*****

"God, that Bruno bloke is scary, isn't he? And I wouldn't like to mess with Big Ben," Brian says once they are safely back in Deano's car.

"That's what you want, though, Brian, people like that on your side. You can rest assured that you won't be bothered by Juicy anymore."

"Thanks, Deano. Let me give you this. It's a grand for you."

"I told you, Brian. I don't want your money. You're a friend and a good one at that." Deano puts his foot on the accelerator and pulls away.

"Okay, thanks, Deano. But I'm going to look after you. I won't forget what you've done. Can we stop at an off licence on the way? I promised Linda some Prosecco."

"Sure."

When they reach Brian's house, it's already 11 p.m., and he sees Linda shutting the curtains in their bedroom. He feels a pang of guilt for getting his family into such danger. Thank god he's got money to throw at the problem.

"Really, Deano. I can't thank you enough. I won't forget this."

"Oh, get out, Brian. You're getting soft! Let's catch up tomorrow, my friend."

*****

"Got the Prosecco," he shouts up to Linda.

"Shush. You'll wake the kids," she whispers down the stairs. "Bring some glasses up. I've seen two beautiful holiday homes to rent in Long Island, but I can't make up my mind about which one to book. Come and take a look!"

Chapter Eleven

Brian and Linda had enjoyed a pleasant evening of drinking on their bed well into the early hours. Brian wakes up realising how lucky he is not to have to get ready for a working day in the stinky leather factory. Linda is already up, sorting the kids out. He can hear her nagging Liam to brush his teeth. He heads downstairs to make some coffee and set the table for breakfast.

When they are dressed, the children come down, arguing loudly about which channel they want to watch before school. Brian pours two coffees and tells them to go and eat instead. He switches the TV on himself to watch the BBC news. He steps back from the TV and sips his coffee. Linda comes in behind him.
"Coffee in the kitchen for you, love," he says.

"I'm beginning to think you were right about getting a new car. It's ridiculous sending the children in a taxi every morning. What were we thinking? I phoned Charlotte, but she's got to take her two to the dentist this morning, so she can't help. Anyway, we haven't really done our share of the school run for her, have we?" Linda fetches her coffee and joins Brian to stare at the TV.

In shock, Brian suddenly drops his coffee to the carpet as he sees Bruno and Big Ben on the news.

"Oh, for heaven's sake, Brian. Look at the mess you've made on the carpet. Ruby, bring me a damp cloth from the sink quickly and a towel! Hurry, please!" Ruby obeys her mum and quickly brings a dishcloth and towel.

"Don't be upset, Mummy. Daddy didn't mean to do it," Ruby pleads.

Linda laughs and gives her a hug.

"Daddy? What's the matter, Daddy?" Ruby asks, looking up to her dad.

"Shush, sweetheart. Daddy's listening."

"Really, Brian. I'll just clear this up alone, shall I?" Brian grabs the remote from a side table and turns up the TV volume.

"Two men were stabbed in the car park of The Feathers public house last night and are now described as in critical condition at the Liverpool Royal Hospital."

"Bloody hell, The Feathers. That's where Deano drinks, isn't it?" Linda says, standing up now to watch with Brian.

Brian drops himself to sit on the edge of the sofa, staring at the TV.

"A fight involving several men broke out at The Feathers public house at around 11 p.m. Police and paramedics were called out to the scene shortly after. It is believed that the two people injured are known to police, who have not ruled out a gang-related incident. No witnesses have come forward, and police are asking for anyone in The Feathers between 9 p.m. and 11 p.m. to come forward."

"Witnesses?" Linda asks. "Who in their right mind is going to cooperate with the police about a load of gangsters? I hope Deano wasn't there last night! Gosh, look at that, Brian. Doesn't it look seedy inside?"

A reporter recounts where the incident appeared to have started, and the camera pans to a few broken tables and chairs. Broken glass litters the floor and makes a crunching sound as the reporter moves towards the camera.

Brian's phone rings, and he takes it from his jeans pocket slowly. He looks at who's calling.

"What's the matter with you, Brian? First, you drop the coffee, and now you've gone into slow motion. How many beers did you have last night? Are you going to answer that or what? Brian! Answer your phone!"

"Yes, of course. It's Deano," Brian says and walks outside, pulling the kitchen back door behind him.

"Have you seen the news?" Deano rushes.

"Have I seen the news? What's happened? I can't believe it. I thought Bruno and Big Ben could look after themselves? Did Juicy stab them?"

"I don't know. Nobody seems to know anything, or they aren't saying. The CCTV didn't pick anything up, apparently. It was dark, and the attackers had masks on."

"Do you think it was Juicy and his mates?" Brian repeats the question nervously.
"I don't know. I have no idea. Bruno has upset that many people over the years—it could be anybody."

"Well, I'm not waiting around to find out."

"What do you mean?"

"We're going to the States to see Linda's family tomorrow. We were going anyway, but this has just speeded things up. I've just been looking at flights from Manchester to New York, and there's a few flights in the morning."

"Don't run because you're worried about the police, Brian. Nobody will cooperate with them. And I'll tell you another thing… The police aren't bothered about a couple of criminals being stabbed. It's good news for them."

"It's not the police I'm worried about, Deano. I'm going to take Linda and the kids to an airport hotel tonight, and we'll fly in the morning."

"Really. Are you that scared? Well, fair enough, pal. You know what you're doing."

"Deano, could you come down to mine before we leave? We'll probably be away for a few weeks until this trouble has blown over. I need to speak to you about one or two things."

"I've got some running around to do this afternoon, but I'll tell you what I could do. One of the calls I've got to make is Graham's, and he doesn't live that far from Manchester Airport. I'll make this the last call, and I'll stay over at his flat tonight."

"Are you sure, Deano? That would be great."

"Yeah, not a problem. He doesn't live that far from the airport. Once I'm all sorted, I'll get a taxi from his to your hotel, and we can have a few drinks."

"Thanks, Deano. I'll phone you the hotel address when I've booked."

"Okay, Brian. See you later."

Brian walks back into the front room.

"What did Deano want?" Linda asks.

"Oh. About the house we went to see last night. It was well over-priced."

"Has he seen the news? See what I mean about crime in the UK, Brian? God, and The Feathers as well. It isn't that far from us."

"You're right, Linda. This used to be such a nice area, and it's no longer safe. I'm bloody fed up with this place. Let's do what you suggested. I'm happy to book flights. Perhaps we can even go tomorrow?"

"I'm game for that, Brian. What about the kids' school?"

"We can tell the school that somebody isn't well in America — anything really."

"Yeah, we could say it's my Uncle Bert. He's been in that rest home in New Jersey for years.

That way, it wouldn't be like we were telling lies. Oh, there's the taxi for the kids. Liam, Ruby, are you ready? I'll just go and pay."

"Where might we be going, Mummy?" Ruby asks as Linda ushers them both out to the waiting car.

Brian watches through the window and wonders who the driver is. Should he go with them? Then he recognises Ted Burgess. He knows him and waves. Ted waves back as Linda returns to the house.

"I'll tell you what, Linda. I'll book the flights. You pack. We'll pick up the kids from school and check into the Manchester Marriot at the airport tonight. There's a swimming pool for the kids. Then we'll fly in the morning."

"Yeah, love it! They'll love it. They'll be so surprised. I'm so excited, Brian. If you phone the school, then I'll pack our stuff. It won't take me that long."

"Okay," Brian replies.

"Isn't it sad, though, Brian, the way those poor people were attacked outside that horrible pub, and there's us, without a worry in the world and all this money to enjoy! We're so lucky, aren't we, Brian?"
"Yeah," replies Brian, heading to the kitchen to pour himself a coffee.

Chapter Twelve

Linda browses the marble-themed bathroom and all the products laid out for their use: shampoo, conditioner, hand lotion, body lotion, sewing kit, shoe polishing kit, and something in a little white box, which she's about to open when she hears Brian on the phone.

"Hi, just to let you know, we've checked into the Marriott Hotel. What time are you coming? Seven's great. We'll be in the residents' bar by then. We're just going for a swim with the kids… Okay, thanks. See you later."

"Who's coming?" Linda asks.

"Oh, Deano. Funnily enough, he's in the area, staying at his mate's gaff tonight, which is near us here. I told him to pop in for a drink."

"Well, you and Deano can have a drink. Me and the kids are watching a movie on this gigantic bed!" Linda jumps onto the bed, and Liam and Ruby jump on, too.

"Our room has two double beds, Mummy. Not as big as yours, but Liam and I can have one each."

Linda adjusts one of the plump white linen-clad pillows to lean back against the headboard.

"We might even order room service, guys! What do you think?" She picks up a menu from the side of the bed and browses it, running her finger down the list.

"Have they got pizza, Mum?" Liam suddenly sounds interested.

"Pizza, burgers, hot dogs, fish and chips, spaghetti… anything you want. But let's swim first. Get your costumes out of your cases, kids, and get changed up here. There are robes in the bathrooms we can use to go down to the pool. You are coming for a swim first, aren't you, Brian?"

The children run off, squealing through the connecting door to their room, and start unzipping their cases to find their costumes.

"Sure. And great if you're happy to stay with the kids in the room. We can have a good catch-up mano a mano," Brian laughs.

"Don't take anything else out of your cases, kids," Linda calls through the door as the children's voices grow louder in the excitement. "We've got to catch a flight in the morning."

The children quiet down, and Linda overhears Liam talking to Ruby, sounding serious now.

"My class is having a maths test tomorrow, and I'll miss it. Whoopee!" Liam tells Ruby in a serious tone.

"We were due to have Miss Grinthorpe. She's really, really strict, and we all hate her. Last week, she made Jane Spratt stand in the corner for laughing when Tommy fell off his chair. I thought it was funny, too, but she didn't see me laugh. Tommy Grinshaw's always so mean to us. It serves him right that he fell off his chair."

Linda smiles and turns to see if Brian has also heard them. He's sitting on the edge of the bed with his head in his hands. She puts her hand on his forehead to see whether he has a temperature.

"What's the matter, honey?" she asks.

"What? Oh, just a bit of a headache coming on. All the traffic getting here, I suppose, but we've got a great holiday coming up. You go enjoy the pool, and I'll lie here for a while." He stands up to give her a kiss.

*****

"Oh no, it's the Americans," says Deano as he saunters across the darkly lit hotel bar.

"Hiya, Deano," the kids shout before he reaches them.

"So, what time's your flight tomorrow, guys?"

"It's not till eleven, so we can relax tonight. No rush. New York is five hours behind, so we're not getting there too late, either," Linda replies. She's sporting an I love New York t-shirt.

"Wow, Liam and Ruby, how lucky are you two, staying in a big hotel and then flying to New York tomorrow, or will you miss school?" Deano teases.

"We won't miss school, silly," Ruby giggles.

"We've just had a swim in the hotel pool," says Liam.

"And tonight we're eating in our bedroom. We're watching a movie and getting room service, and they have burgers, or hot dogs, or pizza. We can choose. Tomorrow, we're going to see Nan and Grandad," Ruby adds proudly.

"Wow, I wish I was as lucky as you guys," Deano replies, ruffling Ruby's perfectly cut brunette fringe.

"What would you like to drink, Deano?" Brian asks.

"Pint of lager, please, Brian."

"Get the kids another Coke and some crisps to keep them going until we eat, Brian, and I'll have another Prosecco. Wasn't that terrible what happened outside The Feathers, Deano? Those men could have been killed," Linda says.

Brian catches Deano's eyes.

"Yeah, terrible," he replies.

"Aren't you scared of going into that place?" asks Linda.

"To be honest with you, Linda, that's done it for me. Debbie never liked me going in there anyway. I won't be going in there again."

"So tell me about the house you're looking at, Deano. Brian's hardly told me anything yet. You must both be so excited."

"Yes, we are Linda. Really looking forward to it but got a lot to sort out first."

Brian turns to them from the bar and hands Deano his pint.

"You know what, Brian, I'll take these up for me and the kids. Ruby's hair is still wet, and I don't want her ill for the holiday.

Lovely to see you, Deano. I think Brian's going to buy you dinner in the restaurant — don't let him get carried away drinking too much, and we'll see you in a few weeks' time. Give Debbie my love, won't you?"

"I will, thanks, Linda, but before you go, here's some dollars for the New York kids. I picked them up in the post office today."

"Wow, a hundred dollars," says Liam.

"That's fifty each for you and Ruby, Liam, but you can look after it as you're the oldest," Deano adds.

"You shouldn't have done that, Deano," says Linda, glancing up at Brian in surprise.

"I couldn't forget the kids on their transatlantic trip. Enjoy New York, Linda. Have a great time, kids! See you when you get back, guys."

Deano leans down to give Linda a goodbye kiss and ruffles both of the children's fringes.

"Get off!" Liam cringes.

"What do you say to Deano, kids?" Linda says sharply.

"Thanks for the dollars, Deano. That's really cool."

"Shouldn't be too long, love. We're just going to have a few beers," Brian says as Linda takes Ruby's hand in hers.

"Thank you, Deano," Ruby says shyly.

"I know your 'few beers'," laughs Linda. "Enjoy!"

Chapter Thirteen

"I hope you were serious when you told Linda you were done with The Feathers?"

"Honestly, I am, but I think the police will probably shut it down anyway. It's got too rough."

"It's a wonder it wasn't closed years ago."

"I think they only allowed it to stay open because they knew where all the villains were," laughs Deano.

"Do you think Juicy and his mates stabbed Bruno and his wingman?"

"I don't know, but whoever it was will have to go into hiding."

"Well, we'll be out of the way for a few weeks."

"I'm sorry for all this, Brian. I feel responsible for introducing you to Bruno."

"No worries, Deano. You didn't know this was going to happen. Let's have one more here and then move into the restaurant. They've got some huge steaks on the menu."

*****

After their steaks and three further pints, the two men take a seat back in the resident's bar, where Brian orders some bourbon shots. He wants to get into the mood for his holiday, and the drink is helping him put the images of Bruno and Juicy out of his mind. With Linda and the children safely tucked upstairs and enjoying room service, he's beginning to feel more in holiday mode.

"Good job I never brought the car," laughs Deano.

"So, how's things with you and Debbie?"

"Everything's great thanks. We're looking at houses. We can't wait to move out of the flat and buy our own place. The guy upstairs is a nightmare. He bangs about day and night, and it makes Debbie really nervous."

"Where are you thinking of moving to?"

"We've got a place in mind on the edge of Woolton."

"Woolton? That's posh."

"We're saving up for a deposit. She's working all kinds of mad hours in the beauty parlour, and, as you know, I'm trying to cut a few corners here and there."

Brian notices that Deano's voice is beginning to slur. He wonders if now might be the moment to try to give him some fatherly advice.

"Deano, you're a good mate, and I hope you don't take this the wrong way, but why are you involved in that seedy drug world when you have so much to live for?"

Deano looks up at Brian, who worries for a few seconds that perhaps he's overstepped the boundary of their friendship, but Deano smiles at him. He picks up the half-finished shot from the table and knocks it back.

"My involvement is minimal. I drop off small amounts of coke for a few friends when they're out socialising. Most of the time, it's for people at home partying in their kitchens. I would never go into it in a big way, and it's only temporary."

Brian indicates to the barman that he needs two more shots.

"If you lie down with dogs, Deano…"

"Yeah, I know, you get fleas," answers Deano.

"You have a full-time job in the factory, so you'll have no problem getting a mortgage. In fact, mortgage lenders will be queuing up to lend you money. You have a beautiful girlfriend and a great future. You shouldn't throw all that away and put your own and Debbie's safety at risk."

Brian and Deano are both slouching heavily over the bar now, resting their chins on their forearms. The bartender fills their shot glasses and moves away to add the cost to their tab on the till.

"You've no idea, Brian."

"No idea of what?" Brian asks.

"Naah. Can't do it, man. Our problems, not yours."

"Tell me, Deano. Maybe I can help?"

"Naah."

"Tell you what, Deano. You share your secret, and I'll share mine."

Brian turns to look Deano in the eye. He thinks he sees a glimmer of relief in Deano. As though the lad wants to offload to someone and might just relent and tell Deano what he's worried about.

"You know it won't go any further, Deano. What is it?" Brian asks.

"Well, for all it's a shithouse, the factory served its purpose to get me and Debbie the mortgage, but Debbie has set her heart on this particular house, which is priced at £280k."

"But that all sounds like good news to me."

"Except we'd need to fork out a 10% deposit."

"Which means you need to find £28,000."

"Exactly."

"Believe me, Deano, you no longer have a problem."

"Don't you think so, Brian? Wish I lived in your world." Deano wipes his mouth with the back of his hand. "Shouldn't we have some nuts or something? I'm beginning to feel a little squiffy."

"Yeah, you're right. Let's wash all this down with some Champagne. I'm getting parched." Brian beckons the barman again.

"Listen, Deano. Let's move over to a table. Can you bring the bottle and two glasses over there, mate?"

Brian stumbles as he climbs down from his stool, and Deano laughs at him. They settle themselves at a corner table.

"Don't get me wrong, Brian. The factory has got me the mortgage, no complaints there. But Debbie's on crap wages. Mine aren't much better. We've worked it out. It would take us about three years to save up the deposit. Three more fucking years making leather, Brian. But if everything works out okay with my little sideline, I'll be done in three weeks instead of three years!"

"Yes, but if you're unlucky in the next three weeks, Deano, you'll get more than three years in jail, my friend."

"I'm almost there, Brian. Then I'll get a decent job and pack in my illegal delivery service."

"You have your deposit now, Deano. You don't have to wait three weeks."

"You're drunk. I'm telling you, I'll have it in three weeks."

"No, listen. It's my turn to tell you something. If I don't tell somebody this, I'm going to go fucking nuts, anyway."

"You're the only friend I've got, Brian. Do you know that?" Deano slurs.

"I've left the leather factory, Deano," Brian says as the waiter brings their Champagne.

Deano waits until the waiter has opened the bottle and poured them each a glass. When he's returned to the bar, they resume their conversation.

"I don't know where to start... Right, okay. We've won the lottery, Deano. You're the only person to know this. I still haven't told my mum yet. In fact, I don't really know how to tell her. Linda is going to tell her family when we get to the States."

"You what? When?"

"Last Saturday. Seventeen million pounds, Deano."

Deano chokes on his champers.

"Fuck off, Brian! No fucking way! You're not kidding me, are you?"

"Deano, do I look like I'm kidding?"

"Fucking hell, you're not kidding. Jesus Christ. Jesus Christ, Brian. I knew there was something going on with you two, but I couldn't put my finger on it. I'm fucking shaking here, Brian. Look at my hands."

"I've been shaking all week, Deano."

Deano takes a large swig of his Champagne.

"You and Linda must be over the moon."

"I was to begin with. I felt so excited for the first few days, but now I feel a bit scared. It's hard to explain. I do still feel excited, but this trouble with Juicy has kind of taken the shine off things if you know what I mean."

"Yeah. Do you know something, pal? I would think very carefully about who you tell. Fucking hell, Brian. Once you tell people something like this, you can't un-tell them if you don't mind me saying something now. You're a great family man and a decent bloke. But you don't see the seedy side of life like I do. Can you imagine if some of these people got wind of your good fortune? That could pose one or two problems that you really don't need, my friend. Believe me!"

"Yeah, I'm beginning to think along those lines, Deano, especially with all this shit with Juicy. But how do I ask Linda to keep this private? If you think I'm a bit unstreetwise, Deano, God bless her! She's completely innocent. I want to protect her from the dark side."

"And the best way to do that, Brian, is to keep schtum. There are some horrible bastards out there."

"I don't understand it, though, Deano. How do rich people enjoy life without any worries?"

"Maybe you should move somewhere posh like Buckinghamshire? Some poor mush from Liverpool wins the lottery, and they have to watch their back for the rest of their life. Can you imagine everybody on the Facebook school run page gossiping about you?"

"Yeah, I can now that you mention it. Still, what's the harm in a bit of gossip?"

"Unfortunately for us, the risk is the same dodgy people you're running away from. Don't publicise it, Brian. Some poor working-class grafter suddenly comes into a big pile of money – believe me, you'll have problems, and not just with the likes of Juicy. Look out for your family with your new wealth and forget the rest."

"You're right, Deano. I won't tell anybody."

"Good. Don't tell a soul!"

"You're going to have to tell Debbie, though. Otherwise, she won't know where the deposit money has come from."

"Yeah, I suppose I can't keep something like that from my wife-to-be."

"No."

"She's good, though. She'll keep it quiet."

"Right. I've got a long day travelling tomorrow. Send me your bank details, and I'll transfer enough money for you to be mortgage-free, and in a few weeks, when I've sorted out our money properly, I'll send you some funds to live a good life, my friend."

"I can't believe it, Brian."

"Hold on, though! There's a condition to this offer, Deano."

The two men are standing now. Brian puts his hands heavily on Deano's shoulders.

"I know what you're going to say."

"This drug shit, it needs to stop right now, Deano."

"It will, Brian." Deano puts his head down.

"I mean it. Totally pack it in, Deano. You have to promise me, right now, that you're finished with all that shit in The Feathers."

"I promise. I don't know how to thank you. I'm very lucky to have you as a friend."

"And I'm lucky to have you as a friend, too, Deano." The two men hug drunkenly.

"Another thing before you go, Deano. Would you keep an eye on my mum while I'm away? You don't have to go round there all the time, but I might ask you to pop in now and again just to check she's okay."

"Of course. Is she still with Silly Billy?"

Brian and Deano start laughing.

"Yeah, she is. But Silly Billy's a good bloke. But I don't want him telling all his mates. That's one of the main reasons I haven't told my mum yet."

"Yeah. Don't tell Silly Billy." Deano sways against Brian.

"I'll send the money for your house in the next few days. I better get upstairs. Don't forget our promise—no more of that shit, Deano, and I'll see you in a few weeks."

"I promise. Safe journey, Brian!"

Brian heads upstairs, and Deano returns to reception to order a taxi.

Chapter Fourteen

Brian, still dressed, is spreadeagled across the bed as Linda shakes him.

"Hope you're not going to drink that much in front of my family, Brian. Would you like a coffee?"

"Oh, my head! I won't be drinking ever again. Oh god, and I've got all that travelling to do."

"Come on! You'll feel better when you sit up and drink this coffee. We'll go down and get breakfast, and you can sleep on the plane. Quiet, kids! Your dad's not feeling well."

"Dad never feels well after drinking with Deano," Ruby says, looking into Brian's eyes. "Your eyes are all red, Daddy. Have you been crying?"

Brian hugs his little girl and staggers to the bathroom.

"What's up with Dad?" asks Liam, joining his sister in the master bedroom.

"I'll jump in the shower. That'll sort me out."

*****

By the time they reach the airport, Brian is feeling better. He's eaten an enormous cooked breakfast, drunk half a pot of fresh coffee, and half a litre of fresh orange juice. As they queue to check in, Brian warns Linda that he couldn't book first class as there were only economy seats left.

"That's okay. At least we managed to get seats, which was good considering we booked so last minute."

"Yeah, but we've got to sit with the hoi polloi." Brian laughs.

"See, you are an English snob." Linda laughs as she hands their passports to the American airline staff member behind the counter.

"Right, guys! Let's get checked in." She smiles at the children, both absorbed on their iPads. "Right, that's our bags through. We're on our way to JFK! We can relax now. There's a lounge through there, Brian. You can pay to go in. You'll love it, Ruby. They have a help-yourself buffet, whatever you want, and your dad can relax. He can't stay the pace."

Inside the lounge, Brian finds a comfortable sofa to sit on, and the children disappear to explore the buffet. Brian's happy to see Linda so excited about returning home. He watches as she pours herself a Bloody Mary and brings him another coffee.

"I'd go easy on those Bloody Marys. Our flight isn't due to leave for another couple of hours," says Brian.

"That's rich coming from you. Half past two this morning, you staggered into bed, and then you were snoring all night. You always snore when you've had a drink. So, people who live in glass houses shouldn't get drunk," laughs Linda.

She joins him on the sofa and places her drink on the glass-topped table in front of them.

"How have we missed out on these posh lounges over the years? It doesn't seem fair."

The kids return with plates of nibbles and Coca-Cola and sit to watch one of the big TV screens.

"On another topic, Linda. Are you planning to tell your family about our win?"

"Yes, of course. I'll probably wait until they're all together."

"But are we really ready to tell our families? We haven't given it any real thought."

"I don't understand the problem, Brian. First your mum and now my family! Why not?"

"I'm not saying there's a problem—well, not if we keep everything under control."

"How do you mean?"

"Well, I can't stop thinking about it, Linda. We're just about to disclose this unbelievably huge news that we've won seventeen million. And then where do we go from there?"

"I haven't the faintest idea what you're talking about, Brian. Hold that thought, though. I'm getting another Bloody Mary."

Brian ponders on what Deano had said the previous night. He watches her add a dash of Worcester sauce to her Bloody Mary.

"What I'm saying is, once we tell people, we can't un-tell them, if that makes any sense."

"Okay… but it's only my family we're telling. It's not as if we're shouting it from the Brooklyn Bridge."

"We may as well be shouting it from Brooklyn Bridge, telling your family," laughs Brian.

"Oh, we're awake now, are we?" Linda teases. "The coffee is finally kicking in, is it?"

"Look, all I'm saying is, I don't think we should tell them yet, not until we are 100% sure, which, at this moment in time, I'm not, if I'm being totally honest, Linda."

"I think you're overreacting a bit. What are you in doubt about, Brian?"

"I don't know, Linda. But, as I say, once it's out, we can't put it back. In a few weeks, I may feel differently about how to deal with this."

"So, answer me this, Brian? How do we explain to my family the beautiful mansion in Long Island with the super deluxe pool?"

"I was thinking of telling them that it belongs to one of my bosses at the leather factory, and he's loaned it to us. Tell them anything you like."

"Wow! You really are worried, aren't you? You've really given this some thought, haven't you?"

"I'm just asking for a bit of time here until my head can take it all in. I honestly don't think I'm ready to share this news just yet."

"Okay, love. Whatever you prefer, but I think it will be hard not telling them once they see us."

Linda gets up and helps herself to a third Bloody Mary. While Brian's happy to see her in the holiday spirit, he begins to worry that she may be overdoing things.

"According to the board, kids, our gate is open. America, here we come!"

Brian retrieves their hand luggage, and Linda knocks half her drink back quickly before they make their way to Gate 143.

"Remember Dorothy, kids? There's no place like home," she says, clicking her heels together.

"Come on then, guys, that's our flight being called," says Brian, putting his arm around Linda, trying to hurry her up.

*****

Once on board, the kids argue over who can sit nearest the window.

"You can swap seats halfway across the Atlantic," says Linda.

"Did you know, kids, the pilot and co-pilot on any flight can't have the same meal?" Brian tries to distract them.

"Why not?" asks Liam.

"In case there's a risk of food poisoning, if they both ate the same food, they'd both be ill. We need one of them well enough to pilot the plane, don't we?"

"Wow!" says Liam.

"I didn't know that, you clever English snob," says a rather merry Linda.

Liam and Ruby choose different meals to eat at the first mealtime. Liam explains seriously to Ruby that if one of them were ill from the food, the other would be able to look after the ill one. They watch films, and Brian shows Liam how to track the flight's path across the Atlantic. As the kids finally fall asleep from all the excitement, Linda becomes restless.

"God, these seats are so uncomfortable, Brian. We should be upfront, lying back in first class. I mean, what's the point of having all those millions if we can't sit in first class."

The air stewardess walks past.

"Excuse me, can I order a bottle of champagne, please?" Linda slurs.

"Yeah, sure, what champagne would you like?" the stewardess asks.

"I'd like the most expensive one that you have, please?"

"That will be our Dom Perignon, if that's okay?"

"Sure thing," says Linda.

"I won't be long. I'll open the bottle up front to avoid waking your children."

"Thank you," Linda replies, smiling.

"You're splashing out, aren't you?" laughs Brian.

The stewardess returns and pours them both their champers.

"I could get used to this lifestyle," Linda says as she clinks her glass with Brian's and takes a sip.

"I take it you guys are celebrating?" the stewardess comments as she places some pretzels on their tables.

"Well, she is," laughs Brian.

"Yeah, he celebrated last night. It's payback time today," laughs Linda.

"So, what are you celebrating?" asks the stewardess.

"We've just won seventeen million pounds on the National Lottery," replies Linda.

Brian chokes on his Champagne and looks around at Linda, who is giggling uncontrollably.

"She's only joking," Brian adds nervously.

"I know! You'd be sitting up in first class if you had that kind of money," replies the stewardess, laughing as she moves away to answer another passenger's bell call.

"Why did you say that?" Brian asks.

"Well, just seeing the look on your face was worth seventeen million, you fucking handsome English snob."

Brian laughs, too, overwhelmed by how lucky they are and feeling more relaxed now they're on their way.

"I love you, babe," he whispers in her ear.

"I love you too, Jacko. Here's another toast." She raises her glass. "No more worries for us!"

God, I hope not, Brian thinks while smiling and raising his glass to Linda's.

"Here's what I think we should do, Linda. Let's enjoy Long Island, the beach, and regular trips into Manhattan whenever we like. We'll have a great time with your mum and dad and Dan, and also Karen and Tom. Then, in a few weeks, we'll buy your mum and dad a bungalow in Long Island to save your dad from climbing the stairs at the house in Brooklyn. But let's hold off on saying anything yet. Are we agreed?"

"You mean, say nothing to my family, Brian? Does that include your mom, too, or is it just my family in the States getting the silent treatment?"

"Of course it includes my mum, Linda. We don't need to tell anybody our business just for now."

"So, let me get this right, Brian. One of the nicest things to happen in my life, and I can't tell my family? I'll have to explain to my mom when I buy her a new car because I'm not letting her drive around in that old heap of shit any longer. And when we get them a bungalow. We'll have to tell them then, won't we?"

"We could tell people we've borrowed the money."

"Borrowed the money? Is there something you're not telling me, Brian? Why wouldn't we tell family?"

"The consequences of going public and telling all and sundry that we now suddenly have millions of pounds might be difficult. Look, I don't mean that we won't look after our loved ones. Of course we will. I'm just saying that we just have to calm down and be very careful here. Can you imagine if everybody found out that we had so much money?"

"What, you mean begging letters and all that sort of thing?"

"Yeah, I suppose so."

Brian begins to feel deflated. He doesn't seem to be able to convince Linda of the risks. Suddenly, he hears her snoring and laughs to himself as he lies back and gently closes his own eyes.

After a few hours of sleeping as best he could in the somewhat tight space for a six-foot-two, generously built man, Brian is woken by Linda asking if he'd like some coffee.

"I think I had too much to drink," she says with an embarrassed smile.

"I suppose that means I'm driving to Long Island, then?"

"It's only about an hour away, and I'll show you the way."

The plane makes its descent, and the kids are also awake. They swapped midway, as Brian suggested, so now it's Ruby's turn to watch out of the window. Brian explains to Liam that the clocks have gone back five hours, and although they left Manchester at eleven, it's only one o'clock where they are now, and the plane finally touches down at JFK Airport.

"Welcome to the Big Apple, kids, the best city in the whole wide world. We'll see Gran and Grandpa soon."

"Daddy always says Liverpool is the best city in the world, and what do you mean the Big Apple, Mummy?" Asks Ruby.

"Yes, what do you mean, Linda?" Brian laughs as he opens up the overhead locker to retrieve their bags. "Pack up your iPads, kids. Make sure you've got everything."

Chapter Fifteen

Eventually, they manage to get through the queues for customs and immigration. They are welcomed by a hire car representative holding up a placard with 'Welcome, Jackson Family' scrawled across it in thick black felt-tip pen.

"I'm Bill from Hertz, here to walk you to your vehicle. Did you have a good journey, folks? I'm not allowed to carry your luggage, but if you need special assistance, I can call for some."

Brian assures Bill that they don't need special assistance. Bill walks backwards, smiling at them all, and only pauses his monologue occasionally to check behind him to make sure he's not walking into anything. Ruby starts giggling at him, but he doesn't seem to notice. He continues to lure them through the airport concourse until they reach some swing doors.

Whenever Brian tries to answer his questions, Bill nods impatiently, smiles and continues with his babble.

"Your 4x4 SUV is waiting over the road, guys. If you would like to follow me, please!" Bill backs effortlessly through some swing doors and then holds them open until the family are through.

They all step out into the glorious sunshine to see a row of shiny, dark-blue Cadillac Escalades.

"Here are the keys. Are you driving, madam, or is it you, sir?"

"Oh, that'll be me," says Brian.

Bill hands the keys over.

"Yeah, Mum can't drive. She drank too much on the plane," says Liam.

"Kids, eh?" says Linda.

Bill smiles weakly.

"Well, you've certainly brought some beautiful spring weather with you. You have a full tank of fuel, and all your insurance details and paperwork are in the glove box. Do you need any help putting your luggage in the car?"

"Wow, Dad. This car is something else!" Liam squeals in awe as he jumps in the back.

"No, that's okay. Thank you very much," says Brian, squinting at Bill in the sunlight. He opens the hatchback and transfers their luggage, two cases at a time, into the back.

"Have a nice day!" Bill winks at the children and smiles at Linda as he continues his backwards movements away from the edge of the pavement.

"Yeah, have a nice day, Bill," replies Brian as he climbs into the driver's seat.

"Jesus, that man can talk, and did you see the way he never took his eyes off us? How on earth does he walk like that?"

Liam starts giggling. "He was Backwards Bill, Dad!"

Everyone joins in the laughter, excited now they have finally arrived and are starting their holiday.

"And listen to me! I'm only in America for five minutes, and I'm telling people to have a nice day."

"You're becoming a crazy Yank," says Linda, laughing.

"Look, Mum, we're driving on the other side of the road," says Liam.

"That's because we do everything the proper way here, Liam."

"The proper way? Oh my god," laughs Brian. "You can tell your mum's back in town, kids."

"Back in town? You sound like John Wayne there, Brian."

"The heck I do," he laughs, feeling more relaxed now that his family are away from the threats back home.

"I'm phoning Grandma here, kids. Hi Mom, we've just arrived. Isn't the weather beautiful? You're on loudspeaker, so don't call Brian an English snob!"

"Hi Nancy," Brian calls out as he navigates under the overhead traffic lights.

"Hi Nan," Liam and Ruby shout from the back. "We're in a huge car, Nan. You'll be amazed!" Liam adds.

"Wow, it's lovely to know you've arrived. Hi everybody," Nancy replies. "How was the flight?"

"Yeah, it was great, especially with your daughter drinking the plane dry and then snoring rather loudly," laughs Brian.

"Take no notice of him, Mom. I only had a couple."

"A couple of bottles, more like," Brian teases.

"Here's Grandpa."

"Oh no, the Brits are here! Hiya Ruby, Liam. Hi Linda, Brian. Hope you've brought plenty of money with you."

Linda and Brian look at one another and smile.

"Can't wait to see you guys. Take your time driving, Linda, there's no hurry."

"Ha! I'm driving Bob. I'm a lot safer than your daughter at the moment! She took full advantage of American Airlines' generous courtesy bars."

"Take no notice of him, Dad! I'm just so excited to see you all."

"Okay. Here's your mom again, Linda."

"Mom, I need to show Brian which way to go. Can we phone you when we arrive in Long Island? Say goodbye, Kids!"

"Yeah, sure. Keep us posted."

"God, I can't believe the traffic, Brian. It never used to be this busy."

*****

Eventually, they arrive in Long Island. Brian notices that the children's excitement is beginning to fade as their weariness begins to overcome them.

"Oh my god, Brian. Look at these houses. They're all mansions. Online, some of them are selling for three to four million dollars."

"Wow! I've never seen anything like this," says Brian.

"Here's Sundrive Avenue now. This is our road, Kids."

"Oh, look! There's our house. Number 7 for good luck. Look, Linda, there's a boat in one of the neighbours' drives. I wonder if these are all holiday homes or whether people actually live here."

Brian drives up to the house around a circular driveway.

"Is this where we live now, Mum?" Ruby asks.

"No, we're just staying here for a few weeks, honey." Linda shoots a wishful glance at Brian.

Brian climbs out of the car and looks up at the six-bedroomed detached mansion they've hired. He whistles as he opens the back door for Ruby to climb out. He lifts her down, giving her a quick peck on the top of her head as he does so. He feels safe now his family are so many miles from Juicy and his men.

Linda checks her phone and then keys a code into the key safe at the front of the house. Brian and the children follow her between two massive pillars up the steps to the gigantic front door. Linda turns the key, and with a loud click, the door swings backwards to reveal a marble-floored entrance hall with a chandelier and a huge staircase spiralling up the wall on one side. They all follow Linda in and spin around, staring upwards and around.

"Come along, kids! Let's find the swimming pool. It's heated."

Linda looks round at Brian and whispers, "I don't know about you, Brian, but I'm never going back to England ever again."

"I think I'm with you on that one, Linda."

"Mum, can we go in the pool?" shouts Ruby, running back inside to where Linda and Brian are still standing.

"Let's pick up some food and drinks first from the stores we passed by near the beach."

"Linda, I feel like I've won the lottery," Brian laughs, hugging her.

Linda taps into her phone to call Nancy back.

"Hi, Mom, we've just arrived in Long Island. The house we're staying in is beautiful. I can't wait for you to see it."

"I was going to say, Linda. You guys must be pretty tired. We'll let you settle in tonight. Dan is driving us up in the morning as soon as I can get him out of bed. And Karen and Tom are following on."

"Okay, Mom. We need to pop out any way to stock up on some supplies. Just wait until you see this place. It's not too far from the beach that you and Dad used to take us to. Okay, I'll speak to you later. The kids can't wait to have a swim in the pool. God, Mom, wait until you see how close we are to the beach. Speak to you later."

On the way out, one of their neighbours calls out to them.

"Hi guys, are you here on vacation?" He's bald and in his fifties.

"Well, kind of, but we may stay a little longer," replies Linda.

"I'm Rick. Pleased to meet you." He approaches Linda, crossing the lawn that spans across the fronts of the two houses.

"I'm Linda, and this is Brian, my husband, and Liam and Ruby. Are you on vacation?" Linda asks.

"No, I live here now. You'll find most of the people on Sundrive actually live here. I took early retirement as a police officer. Have you been to Long Island before?"

"I used to come here when I was little, but we never used to stay overnight. I'm from Brooklyn, and we used to get the train mostly. I live in England now. My husband is English. We've just flown in today."

"Are you guys off to the beach?" asks Rick.

"We may be later, but we're just going to get our bearings and see where the shops are. Nice to meet you," says Brian as he's about to climb back into the Cadillac.

Rick turns to head back to his front door but then seems to remember something and turns back towards Brian.

"Oh, Brian, if you're staying here for a while, you could join me at the shooting range one day. It's close by."

"Oh, there's a golf range? I could do with practising my swing."

Rick laughs.

"No, I was referring to shooting guns, Brian." Linda can't contain her laughter.

"Oh, ha. I'm not really into guns, but thanks all the same."

"Hey, you never know when you might need to defend yourself. You need to keep your hand in."

"I don't even have a gun, so there's no fear of me becoming rusty," Brian laughs.

"You don't have a gun, guys?"

Linda pulls the front door shut behind her as the children climb back into the car.

"No, as you can see, we've got young kids in the house," she says.

"All the more reason to have one. To keep them safe."

"I take it you have one, then?" asks Brian, with his door still open.

"I've got several," replies Rick.

Brian registers this as potentially useful to know while also feeling a little out of his depth with the situation. He doesn't know Rick and has just found out his neighbour has a gun. He recognises a feeling he's had before when arriving in the US. The sunshine and holiday feeling make him relax, but the differences between the US and the UK sometimes frighten him. He switches the ignition on and looks at Liam and Ruby in the back as they fasten their seatbelts. He suddenly feels overwhelmingly tired.

"Oh well, we must be getting off. See you soon," he calls out to Rick with a wave and closes the car door.

"That's all we need next door, another one of you crazy Yanks playing with his guns."

"You have to remember, guns are a big part of the culture here, you English snob."

*****

The kids are fascinated by the shops. They had been much younger when they last visited and hadn't remembered how huge they were.

After filling the car with food, wine and beer, Brian and Linda take the children back to Sundrive.

"Brian, could you do me a favour, please?"

"Yeah, what's that?" he replies.

Linda leans back against her passenger door to take a look at Brian and smiles.

"Could you please pinch me, as hard as you can?"

"I know—and me," he laughs. "It's just totally unbelievable."

"What's unbelievable, Dad?" Liam asks.

"Oh, just being in America and in this beautiful place." He looks at Liam in the rear-view mirror and smiles.

Back at the house, the kids get their swimming costumes on and head straight out through the bifold doors from the living room into the small family pool. The Long Island spring sunshine catches their splashes, and their laughter echoes through the house. Brian unloads the car and watches Linda unpacking cereals into the cupboards and stacking beers and white wine into the fridge. She places a bottle of Champagne in the freezer and sets her watch on a timer for fifteen minutes. Brian takes one of the beers back out of the fridge and rummages in a drawer for a bottle opener.

"It won't be cold yet, Brian," Linda chides.

"I don't care." He wanders out to the pool.

"Aren't you glad you learned how to swim in school, kids? All those lessons you moaned about, and look what fun it can be!"

The children don't hear him above their splashing and screaming, so he sits on one of the loungers between the pool and the house, and Linda joins him with a bowl of crisps.

"Do you think we should tell Liam and Ruby about our win?"

"No, I don't. I think they're too young to make sense of it."

"And what about my parents? Are they too old?"

"We've already talked about this, Linda. But if you must know, when I phone my mum to tell her that we've arrived safely, I'll be telling her we're staying in a holiday home that belongs to your sister's friend. I don't want Billy telling all his mates in the pubs of Liverpool that we've won millions. It's just not safe."

"So, you want me to take the Fifth Amendment, Brian? This is the bit I don't understand. What's the big secret? Why is it unsafe? What do you think is going to happen? Are you worried about us getting loads of begging letters or something?"

"Believe me, they're the least of our problems."

"Problems? What problems do you mean?"

"Right, okay, Linda. I tried explaining this to you on the plane, but you were falling asleep. Do you remember the trouble I had in the corner shop a few weeks ago when Liam was playing football?"

"Yes, but what's that got to do with anything?"

"Well, that yob was parked outside our house the other day, making threats. He must have followed us after the football."

"So what does that have to do with winning the lottery? You're not making any sense."

"I don't know what it all means, but it certainly shook me up a bit."

"Why do I get the feeling you're not telling me everything, Brian?"

"Okay. I was in The Feathers with Deano the other night, arranging to get this trouble sorted."

"You were in The Feathers with Deano? You were in that dive with Deano?"

"To be fair to Deano, he tried his best to help us out. Okay, it's not a nice place, and he hasn't made the wisest of choices, but deep down, he's a decent person."

Brian watches as Linda's earlier serene and happy outlook turns to one of confusion and concern.

"I know he's your friend, but really, Brian! The Feathers! Honestly! I like Deano myself, but I think Debbie could do better. She hates him going to The Feathers. You mark my words, he'll end up in prison, and she'll leave him. Remember these words, Brian, because I can see it coming."

"You don't understand, Linda. Deano and I talked last night in the hotel bar. He's promised me that he's finished with that kind of life. He only did it to get a deposit on the house they're buying. Anyway, he doesn't have to do that anymore because I'm giving him the money for their house."

"I see. So, you've told Deano about our win? You've trusted Deano, who spends most of his life in The Feathers, but you can't trust my family or even your own mother to know?" Linda's voice is getting louder now, but still, the children continue screaming and splashing. "How do you think that makes me feel, Brian?"

"Linda, you've got it all wrong." Brian puts his hand on her arm. "I probably haven't explained it properly."

Linda's anger suddenly dissipates, and he sees real fear in her eyes.

"Did you or Deano know anything about that incident in The Feathers the other night? Tell me, Brian!" Linda glances over to Ruby, who's calling for her goggles. She goes inside to fetch them and returns quickly, throwing them so they miss Ruby and sink into the water behind her. Liam dives for them, and the children both squeal in delight. Linda drops down onto the lounger again. "That's why you dropped your coffee on the carpet in the living room, isn't it, when you heard about The Feathers on the news? Oh my god, Brian! No wonder you were in a hurry to get away."

"I was worried about you and the kids. I had to protect you."

"Well, I can see that, if this guy was making threats, but… but why the secrecy about the win with our families?"

"Linda, I've dreamt of winning the lottery most of my adult life, and now that it's happened, I've never felt so nervous and confused."

"Can't we just enjoy this wonderful new life, Brian? Whatever that guy said to you, we're here now, miles away."

"Believe me, Linda, it's not such a wonderful and happy life out there. Over the past couple of weeks, I've come across some pretty scary people, and there are many more of their kind around. The last thing I want is for them to know that we have all this money. Look how all those rich footballers get burgled when they're abroad. Some of the players' families have actually been attacked, and that's even with all their hi-tech security and bodyguards."

"Yeah, but that's back in England. We're here with my family now, thousands of miles away."

"And what happens when Rifleman Rick next door and everyone else around here finds out I'm just a leather factory labourer and that you worked in a supermarket? Shall we tell them we've just come into millions as well, Linda? Does everyone need to know?"

Linda knows instantly that things aren't quite right with Brian. His voice has grown loud and causes Liam to glance over.

"Mum, Dad? What's up?" Liam asks, standing by them now and dripping onto his dad as he reaches for some crisps.

Linda laughs. "Dad's overtired. He's getting grumpy. I'll go fetch some Champagne, and he'll soon calm down."

Linda returns from the kitchen with some Coke for the children and the Champagne and two glasses. Brian takes the Champagne off her and starts to open it while Liam gulps noisily from one of the Coke bottles.

"Don't be grumpy, Dad! We're on our hols," he shouts as he jumps back into the pool.

Brian can't help but laugh but then turns back to pour the Champagne into the two glasses Linda has set on a small table between them.

"I'm sorry, Linda. I didn't mean to shout. I don't know what's up with me."

"It's okay, love." She puts her arm on his shoulder. "So, what do you suggest we do?"

"Can we… just for now… get used to having this huge new-found wealth… and wait for the trouble back home to blow over?"

"Of course we can. I don't mean to give you a hard time. You're right. If it's worrying you so much, we won't tell anybody our business until we're good and ready. In the meantime, we're going to enjoy Long Island and its beautiful sandy beaches."

"What do you think about me sending Deano £300,000 to buy his house outright? I didn't want to do anything without running it past you first. He's the only person who knows anything about our win or about the trouble back home, and he's keeping an eye on Mum for me. The money will get him out of that seedy world he's involved with, so it's good for Debbie, too."

"I understand, and I appreciate you asking me before sending it. Yeah, send him the money. It would be nice to think we've changed their lives for the better. I know he's not a bad guy underneath, and Debbie's a good person."

"Okay. I'll send it now. When we see family tomorrow, we'll tell them that my boss owns this mansion, just for now. Is that okay?"

"Yeah, okay. That's fine with me, Brian. I just can't wait to see them." Linda starts laughing.

"What's so funny?"

"You calling that neighbour Rifleman Rick. You make me laugh. I love you, Jacko."

"I love you too, babe."

Chapter Sixteen

Waking up in this unbelievable mansion feels like something out of a dream to Brian. He picks up the remote control to open the blinds, and the sun pours into their bedroom. The bed is so huge he starts calling Linda's name to mimic that he can't find her.

"Would you like a coffee, love?" he asks.

"Yeah, but I'm coming down for it. I'm not lying in bed on a beautiful day like this. Besides, I was going to walk down to the beach before the family arrived. Summer's definitely on its way. God, we won that money just at the right time, didn't we?"

"I know. It's great, isn't it?"

"Did you send the money to Deano?"

"Yeah. I sent it last night. He sent a massive thank you. Doesn't know how he'll ever make it up to us." Brian picks up the clothes he'd discarded on the floor the night before while Linda rummages in their suitcases.

"Ah, that's nice. Right, I'll phone Mom to see what time they're coming. She said that Dan was driving them up. And Brian, please don't discuss politics with him when they arrive."

"Does he still think I'm a communist?" laughs Brian.

"Brian, you know what he's like. He hasn't a clue about politics, God bless him. I know he's brainwashed with all the stuff he gets from social media, but he's still my little brother."

"Linda, don't get me wrong. I think the world of Dan. But why would somebody who hasn't two pennies—I mean two cents—to rub together vote for a billionaire like Donald Trump, who couldn't give a toss about poor people like him?"

"Well, that's up to Dan."

"I know, but every time powerful people like Trump stand in front of the American flag, you get poor patriotic people like Dan, with absolutely nothing in their pockets, standing up and saluting. I don't know if you've noticed, but there aren't too many American flags around here, Linda, and these people really do have money."

"You don't need to explain any of that to me. I studied politics at Liverpool University, remember, until you got me pregnant."

"Dan always cracks me up, though. I mean, his views are so odd for someone so poor. Remember last year when he needed that hernia operation? He had no money and couldn't even afford his health insurance."

"I know! Karen and I ended up paying for it. But that's Dan. He's just so stuck in his ways. Anyway, with our money, he can definitely afford it now."

"I know, but what about all the people who can't?"

"You're preaching to the converted here. One of the main reasons I left the States was because they don't look after their poor people."

"Really? I thought it was because of the mass shootings?"

"Well, yes, that as well. But what's the point in discussing any of these issues with Dan? You know he's never going to change. People like him are too far gone. So please, no politics when he arrives."

"Can I just ask him if he still has the American flag on his bedroom wall?" Brian jokes.

"Yeah, and when you do, I'm going to tell all my family we're millionaires," laughs Linda.

"Okay, you win, no politics."

"I'll get the kids up. I bet you're excited, Linda."

Once dressed, they make their way downstairs, and as they enter the kitchen, Linda's phone rings.

"Oh, hello, Mom. Yeah, we've been up for ages. Isn't the weather beautiful? What time are you guys leaving? Oh, you've just left. That's great... God, Dan was up early? Yeah, it's 7 Sundrive. It's the second avenue behind the beach shops on the front... Okay, see you in about an hour."

"I can't believe it." She gives Brian a big hug and starts searching for the coffee maker.

*****

When Linda's parents arrive, they all run out onto the drive to greet them.

"Look at the size of you two," says Nancy, holding on tight to Liam and Ruby.

Eventually, after everyone has hugged and said hello, they go inside.

Brian forgets how huge Dan is and also what a big heart he has.

"Oh my god, the Limeys are in town," Dan jokes. "How are my two little munchkins?"

"Who are you calling Limeys? Look, kids, it's Uncle Buck. God, you're looking more like John Candy every day, Dan." Brian gives his brother-in-law a huge embrace. "Great to see you, Dan!"

"And you, Brian. Tell me, are you still a communist?"

Linda gives Brian a menacing look.

"If you don't mind, Dan, this is a politics-free zone."

"Not for us Republicans, big sis."

"Yeah, we're on holiday, so no politics," says Brian.

"You mean vacation, buddy? You're not in little old England now," laughs Dan.

"Yeah, I'll have to remember that one."

"Right kids, what's all this I've been hearing about a swimming pool?" Dan asks.

"Come and have a look. Mom, Dad, wait until you see the pool." Linda leads everyone out to the terrace, where she and Brian had arranged the sun loungers the night before.

The full length of the pool stretched out before them as they stepped onto the terrace, and on each side were five sun loungers. Brian had moved a large terrace table near the patio doors so they could bring food out easily.

"Oh my god. Oh my god! That pool is awesome. Your boss must think a lot of you, letting you stay in his place," says Bob.

"Yeah, you should take a leaf out of your boss's book, Brian. You see, capitalism can be very rewarding," says Dan.

Brian whispers to Linda, "And that's coming from your little brother, who's absolutely skint."

"No politics, remember, or I'll tell Dan that you're now a capitalist with millions in the bank," Linda whispers back.

"Yeah, you're right, Dan. You can't beat a bit of capitalism." Brian smiles.

Just then, Linda's sister Karen joins them with her husband Tom.

"Your front door was wide open, so we let ourselves in! Just look at the size of you guys! You're not little anymore," Karen shrieks, rushing over to hug Liam and Ruby.

Brian watches as Linda holds onto her sister for what seems like ages.

"I wasn't expecting you and Tom until after work, Karen," says Linda.

"Tom gets away early on a Friday, and I booked a day's holiday."

"Karen, Tom! Have a look at this pool!" says Dan.

"Oh my god, Linda. It's beautiful. Mom said Brian's boss owns the place? God, wouldn't it be great to have money like this, Linda?"

Brian catches Linda's eye as he hands out bottles of beer. The party wanders around the pool in amazement.

"Watch what you're drinking, Tom. You're driving back, remember," Karen reminds her husband.

"You can all stay the night, Karen. There are six bedrooms, and there's plenty of room. Let me show you guys around the rest of the house."

*****

After the tour of the house, they make their way back outside into the sunshine, and the drinks begin to flow.

Brian and Linda had prepared a buffet while waiting for everyone to arrive. They now bring it out onto the terrace. Liam and Ruby flit backwards and forwards, carrying plates and cutlery to help their mum and dad. When the bread rolls, cheese, meat, fish, crisps and dips, pasta, and salad are all laid out, Liam marches solemnly around the sun loungers, offering all his family plates and serviettes and inviting them to help themselves. Brian brings some white wine and glasses out and a cool box with more beers.

"I'm starving, Mum. Can we start now?" Liam asks impatiently.

"Guests first, Liam," Linda chides.

Dan stands up and proposes a toast. "Welcome home to the Limeys!" They all laugh, raise their glasses and go to explore the buffet.

"Would you like to visit Central Park in the next few days, Liam and Ruby?" Karen asks.

"Yes, please," Ruby replies, with a mouthful of celery and hummus.

"I'd like to go up to the top of the Empire State Building as well. I went there a few years ago, but I can't remember it," Liam says. "I was only young then," he says in as deep a voice as he can muster.

He fills his plate with crisps and mini sausages.

"Well, we can go there, too," says Karen.

"Linda, is that ice cream shop still open on the front?" Dan asks.

"Yes, we passed it yesterday. It brought back so many happy memories."

"Okay, kids, after lunch, we're going to the ice cream parlour. Uncle Buck is going to treat you to some authentic American ice cream, not like that cheap stuff you get in little old England. I'll bring some more booze back as well. Us Yanks are going to show you Limeys how to drink."

"Oh my god. Dan's on the booze. This is going to get messy," says Linda, laughing.

*****

"Mum, the shop we went to sold the biggest ice creams you've ever seen," Ruby tells her mum excitedly when they return. "I had real strawberries and melon on mine and cream and raspberry sauce on top."

"I know, Ruby. I used to go there when I was little."

"Wow, it must have been great living in America when you were growing up, Mum," says Liam.

"It was, apart from Auntie Karen and Uncle Dan stealing all my toys."

"More like the other way around, big sis," replies Dan. "Come on, kids, let's get changed and take a dip." He heads inside to get changed.

"Your boss must be a multi-millionaire," Nancy comments.

Brian throws Linda another searching look.

"Did he give you a raise as well, Brian? Staying here for a few weeks is going to cost you guys, surely?" asks Bob.

"We borrowed some money, actually," Brian quickly explains.

"It's alright to borrow money, but you have to pay it back. In my day, if you couldn't afford it, you couldn't have it," Bob lectures.

"Those days are gone, Dad. Everybody uses their flexible friends now. Live every day like it's your last, I say," shouts Karen.

"No, your dad is right, Karen," says Tom.

"Oh, you're a fine one to talk, Tom. Just look at Linda and Brian! They're skint, but they're living like millionaires for a few weeks. And good for them, I say."

Karen raises her glass to her sister.

Once again, Brian and Linda can't help looking at one another. The children return with their costumes on and jump in the pool. Dan follows, taking a running leap and splashing them all on their sun loungers as his hefty weight hits the water.

As the drinks continue, Linda whispers to Brian, "Dad looks a lot older, and he doesn't look well."

"Don't worry. We'll look after him. Don't you worry about a thing." Brian sits back on the lounger and watches the children splashing around in the pool with Dan. For the next couple of hours, he listens to Karen, Tom, Bob and Nancy and the memories they recall, occasionally wandering around to fill up their glasses or distribute more beer. Bob stands up to clear some empty beer bottles and suddenly catches hold of Brian's arm when he loses balance.

"Dad, you look a bit unsteady on your legs. You haven't even had very much to drink yet!" Linda says.

"He's struggling with his knees, Linda. We don't have a free health system like you guys in the UK, so we have to check whether our health insurance covers things, you know," says Nancy.

"We don't need a free lefty, welfare state. This is the land of the free," says Dan, towelling himself down on the edge of the pool. Brian feels quite a lightweight as he takes in Dan's enormous belly.

Linda sits upright.
No, but if you did have one, Dan, we wouldn't have had to find the $7,000 for your hernia operation last year, and Dad wouldn't be worrying about whether he is covered by insurance for his knees," says Linda sharply.

Brian glares at Linda, and as he tops her glass up, he whispers, "I thought you said no politics! You sound like you're addressing the Senate."

"Yeah, well, he's a right dick! How can he be so stupid?"

"You're talking about your little brother here."

"Okay. I'm alright now. Okay! I'm cool. Not so little anymore, is he?" she giggles.

*****

Different family members take turns swimming with the children as the day passes, and eventually, they order pizza to be delivered for dinner. By early evening, everybody is totally under the influence, happy and content with the haze of a day spent in the sunshine, good company, and well-watered and fed. As the sun goes down, nobody is keen to go inside, but there's a chill in the air, so they retire to the living room, and Brian lights the wood fire, which is centred in the room in a pillar-like structure.

"It's great that we can stay, Linda. It's like we're all on vacation," says Karen.

"Yeah, you're so lucky, Brian, to have such a good boss. How long are you staying?" Nancy asks.

"Well, he doesn't really mind. It's the Easter holidays for the children. We've explained to the school that we may stay a few more weeks, and they've given us permission. So, we're in no great hurry to return home, really."

"I wish I could find a boss like that, Brian. In fact, I wish I could find a job!" Dan says.

"It's not your fault you can't work, Dan. How are you now?" Brian asks.

"I'm not getting any better, Brian. I guess I was just dealt a bad hand getting this emphysema in my late twenties."

Everyone seems to mull this over, and Brian isn't sure what to say. Fortunately, Liam breaks the silence.

"Mum, if it was so great growing up in America, why did you leave?" He grabs another slice of pizza from one of the boxes left on the dining table.

"I went to university in England, Liam."

"Tell Liam the truth, Linda. We kicked her out for being a left-wing troublemaker," laughs Dan.

"Liam, it's nearly time for you and Ruby to go to bed. But when you're older, I promise you I will explain the politics of this country. And believe me, it's not as nice as the ice cream you had earlier. Now, say good night to everyone."

"Can I bring you up to bed, guys?"

"Yes, please, Nan," they chorus.

Chapter Seventeen

"Brian, I can't believe you let me argue with Dan last night about politics, especially after me telling you not to go there," says a slightly hungover Linda.

"I wouldn't worry about it. You weren't that bad. But God love him, he's still the same."

"No, Brian, he's got worse," laughs Linda. "Somebody's already up. I can hear movement in the kitchen. I bet it's Mom and Dad. They're always up early. It definitely won't be Dan. He lies in bed all day, lazy swine. And Karen will be dead to the world. She drank more than me!"

Brian's phone starts vibrating.

"Who's contacting you now Brian?"

"Hey, that's strange. It's a text from Debbie asking if we're awake. Something's got to be wrong."

"Well, you'd better phone her."

"Yeah, I will. Give me a chance!"

"Hi, Debbie. Is everything okay?" Brian listens to Debbie's response, frowning.

Linda shuffles over the bed to lean close to his ear and listen too.

"What? No way! Why? When? Oh my god! I don't believe it!"

"What's up? Are they okay?" asks Linda, interrupting Brian's questions, unable to hear Debbie's half of the conversation.

"Where are you now, Debs? Calm down. Take it easy… Take your time… I know, love, I agree with you. Right, please listen to me. You can't do anything at the moment and we'll find out more today… I know he is. You don't have to tell me that.... Okay, love, phone me back later when you have more news. In fact, phone me anytime. Okay, Debs, but try not to worry. Bye."

"Deano's been arrested, hasn't he?" Linda holds Brian's gaze.

"How did you guess that?"

"Either he's had an accident, disappeared, or been arrested for Debs to call us like that."

"What an absolute dickhead! He's been arrested for possession of drugs. He promised me all that shit was finished. Jesus!"

"You're right. He is a dickhead." Linda leans back against the pillow and sighs.

"What an idiot. I guess we'll know more later today. Debbie's going to phone back later. Poor girl. You said he'd end up in jail. I just can't believe how stupid he is. God, what a fool! Poor Debs."

"There's nothing we can do about it now. Let's go down and get some coffee." Linda grabs some clothes from the wardrobe and heads for their en-suite bathroom.

*****

Nancy and Bob are playing Uno with their grandchildren at the huge breakfast bar in the kitchen. Ruby and Liam's legs dangle from the high breakfast stools, making them look younger than their age. Brian swings Ruby off the stool and manoeuvres himself onto the stool with her on his lap. She giggles and snatches her cards up quickly to stop them from falling to the floor.

"Nan keeps losing." Ruby giggles.

"Ruby keeps cheating," Liam chides.

"I knew it would be you two up," Linda says to her mom and dad. She gives her mum a hug.
They all banter for a while while Linda makes them some coffee.

"God, I can't believe how beautiful this house is. Puts our little abode to shame. Some people get all the luck, don't they? Is he nice, Brian's boss?"

"I know, Mom. Some people are very lucky. Yes, he's okay. Hey, kids, do you fancy breakfast down by the beach?"

"Whooppee!" Ruby shouts, jumping off her dad's lap.

"Sounds great," Nancy replies enthusiastically. "It'll be like going down memory lane, Linda, won't it? Like when we came on holiday when you were little."

"Let me give the others a shout and see if they fancy coming," Linda says.

"No need to shout us," Karen says, walking into the kitchen. "Tom and I have already showered in our posh en-suite. Don't you think it's sinful that somebody can have all this wealth? Your boss is one jammy guy, Brian."

"Absolutely," says Nancy. "I couldn't agree more. Don't bother asking Dan about breakfast. He'll be in bed for a good while yet."

"I know, Mom. You're right," Linda laughs. "He was never an early riser."

"Right, we'll let Dan have a sleep. Let's go then, guys. We can walk down, it's not far. Kids! Get your shoes on quickly if you're hungry!" Brian rounds everyone out of the house.

*****

At the beach, they find a diner that Linda remembered from her childhood. It had no doubt changed hands a few times in the meantime, and Bob didn't remember it. Inside was bright with red booths and gingham tablecloths. Their waitress introduced herself loudly with glee and ushered them to a booth for eight overlooking the shore. The tide was just turning, and dog walkers were chatting on the beach, occasionally throwing sticks for their mutts or pebbles into the waves. The sun was catching the white froth on the turning waves, and Brian sighed with contentment as he watched Linda and her family peruse the menu cards excitedly.

"Some people certainly know how to live," says Tom. "Karen, we'll have to move out to Long Island."

"Fat chance of that happening on your wages in an engineering workshop and mine as a teacher," Karen scoffs.

"God, if you stay in your boss's mansion for a few weeks, Brian, you'll find it hard going back to your little old house in England." Tom laughs.

"Who says we're going back, Tom?" Linda asks, looking at Brian.

The waitress arrives carrying two plates of huge omelettes in each hand. She flawlessly lays them in front of Bob, Nancy, Linda and Tom. The children have chosen pancakes with maple syrup, which arrive shortly after. Brian and Linda have chosen the full-cooked breakfast with hash browns and grits.

"Poor Dan is missing a great breakfast," says Bob as they all tuck into their food.

"He could do with losing a bit of weight, though," Nancy adds.

"Is Christine still on the scene, Mom?" asks Linda.

"She comes and goes, but to be fair to the girl, I think Dan enjoys shooting pool at his local bar with his buddies too much," Nancy replies.

"Yeah," says Karen. "And I'm not so sure about some of his buddies there either." She leans away from Ruby and Liam, who are sitting on her left and across to Brian and Linda. "Me and Tom called in to have a drink with Dan a few weeks ago, and most of his friends were in and out of the toilet powdering their noses, if you know what I mean," she whispers.

"God, it sounds like The Feathers," Linda remarks under her breath to Brian.

"I bet you guys don't have such problems in the little old village where you live back home," says Tom.

"Tom, we don't exactly live in a 'little village in England', and to be perfectly honest, I think that kind of thing goes on everywhere in today's society," Brian replies, beginning to feel a little peeved that everything to do with England is described in the diminutive.

Once they've all finished eating and drunk too much coffee, Brian beckons their waitress for the bill.

"Let me get this?" says Tom, pulling out his wallet.

"Not a chance, Tom. You're our guests, and besides, we've saved enough money already by not paying for our accommodation for the next few weeks," Brian explains.

"And some accommodation it is!" Karen adds.

"Shall we go back and see if Dan's up yet, kids?" Karen asks the children.

"Can we wake him up?" shouts Liam.

"Shall I bring him something back to eat?" asks Nancy.

"No, it's okay, Mom. I'll make him something when he wakes up," Linda says.

Chapter Eighteen

When they arrive back at the house, Dan is already up and sitting by the pool with a bottle of beer. Brian notices that there are already a couple of empty bottles by the sink.

"Would you like something to eat, Dan?" Linda asks.

"I'll wait a bit, if that's okay, sis, thanks."

"Did you have a good sleep?" Brian asks.

"I did, but I think all that alcohol may have helped. Which reminds me, Brian, you'll have to come down to Spud's bar. You'd love all the guys in there."

Karen, Tom and Linda all look towards Brian.

"Well, Dan, I'm hoping to see a bit of Manhattan and New Jersey with Linda and the kids. But thanks, anyway."

"I'm only talking about a couple of games of pool. You don't have to stay all night. Come on, Brian, won't my big sis let you out? What do you say? What about a weeknight?"

"We'll see. Maybe just for a couple of beers," Brian replies, not wanting to make a big issue of turning down Dan's invitation. Linda has her back to Dan and throws her eyes upwards.

The family join Dan by the pool, one by one. After a while, Linda brings Dan a burger with fries and salad. Brian wonders if she's feeling guilty about having attacked Dan's politics the night before, but he's glad Dan's going to have something to eat. He doesn't want him to get too drunk again; it seems to take the edge of the family's delight at being together.

"Wow, sis! I might move in here for good," laughs Dan.

"That would be great, Uncle Dan," says Ruby. She's changed back into her swimming costume and steals one of Dan's fries before taking a running jump into the pool.

"Ruby, what have I told you about not eating in the pool? You could choke!" Linda turns back to Dan.

"Yeah, the children would love that!" she says to Dan.

Brian lies down on a free sun lounger and contemplates Linda's family again. Her parents seem worried about Dan's lifestyle, weight, and the people he hangs out with. Tom and Karen seem okay but are sometimes quiet. Nancy is Nancy, as usual, always filling the gap in any conversation. He watches as Linda and Nancy burst out laughing at some private joke. He loves to see Linda happy with her mum. He gets up again from the sun lounger and heads to the kitchen for another bottle of bubbly. Why not? Everyone's having fun. With the sunshine and laughter, the late morning blends into midday and early afternoon as they all enjoy another extended drinking session, and Linda and the children occasionally bring nibbles out.

"Our life would be idyllic if we could stay here every weekend," says Karen.

"Yeah, I could certainly get used to this," says Tom.

Linda browses the vinyls on the shelf in the living room next to an old player. She pulls out a Frank Sinatra record and carefully lays it on the turntable. Brian creeps up behind her and grabs around her waist from behind.

"Feel like a smooch, do we?" he jokes.

"Get off, you oaf," she laughs. "Help me turn this up. We need music by the pool."

"Oooh, really complicated. Look, there's a control deck here... Let me see, it must be the button that says, 'Pool Side'. Shall we try that one?"

Linda elbows him painfully in the ribs.

"Oof, that hurt." Brian mimics pain and bends over.

"There you go. Here's old blue eyes just for you," Linda says, sliding the patio doors from the living room to the terrace open.

"Oooh fun. Let's take a look at what other music your boss likes," Dan says, rushing inside to take a look and dripping water all over the living room carpet.

*****

It's late in the afternoon, and the kids are swimming in the pool when Brian's phone rings.

"Excuse me, let me take this call," he says, heading back inside.

Tom raises his eyebrows.

"Hope that's not your boss telling you he's got us on CCTV, and Dan's making too much of a mess plodding water throughout the house," Karen teases.

Brian smiles back at Karen. He feels a little sorry for her. She seems to have put on a lot of weight since they last saw her, and she's aged considerably. She has a sad air to her that he can't quite put his finger on. Perhaps she's just fed up with their lives, struggling to make a living and not having much fun.

"I hope he's not phoning to say we're in the wrong villa," Tom jokes, grabbing a handful of pretzels.

"Or one of the neighbours telling you to turn Frank Sinatra down," laughs Dan.

Brian catches Linda's eye. Linda isn't laughing; she's probably guessed that it's Debbie. He goes through the door to the kitchen and pulls it closed behind him for privacy.

"So, what's happening, Debs?"

"I was hoping you could tell me, Brian. I just phoned the police station, and they told me he was released hours ago without charge. I've been unable to sleep all night, worried sick, and he hasn't even bothered to let me know that he was released. I've tried ringing him, but he won't answer. I bet he's back at one of his mate's houses snorting coke. The selfish bastard. We were just about to buy our first proper home. It's just outside Woolton Village, one of the nicest parts of Liverpool.

I've worked my fingers to the bone, trying to save up for this deposit."

Brian hears Debbie's voice crack.

"I know you have Debbie. Can I ask you something personal, Debs?"

"Sure, what is it?" Debbie snivels.

"Did Deano mention my helping you out?"

"What do you mean… helping us out?"

"I gave him some money to help you buy your house."

"Sorry, buddy," Tom butts in, sliding the doors back open. "Nancy wants a top-up, and the wine's in the fridge." Tom's tall and athletic body seems to reach the fridge in one step.

"Wait a minute, Debs, I just need to help my brother-in-law with something. You'll need to open a new bottle, Tom." Brian passes Tom the bottle opener from the breakfast bar. "Sorry, Debs. Go on."

Tom takes the bottle of wine and opener and shuts the door again behind him.

"He never tells me anything. I don't know anything about any money, Brian," Debbie continues. "It's very kind of you, but I don't understand. Why would you give him money? We've almost got all the £28,000 we need saved up."

"This is awkward to explain, Debbie. I know you nearly had enough, but I offered Deano some help."

"Brian, sorry, but can I speak to you later? My mum is ringing me."

"Yeah, no problem, Debs. Speak soon."

Brian can see Linda watching him from by the pool. She gets up, slides the patio door back open and moves closer to him to talk.

"So what's happening with Deano?"

"Well, fortunately, he was released without charge. He mustn't have had much stuff on him, but Debbie's not too happy. He hasn't gone home or even let her know where he is."

"I told you, Brian, she'll end up getting rid of him, and I wouldn't blame her. I suppose at least the police let him go."

"Something doesn't sound right, though, Linda."

"What do you mean?"

"Deano hasn't told Debbie we gave them £300,000."

"What? That's strange. Did you tell Debbie?"

"Well, not really."

"Not really? What does that mean?"

"Well, I wasn't sure how to explain that we suddenly gave him three hundred grand. She would probably find that a little odd, don't you think? And if Deano didn't mention it, I couldn't really get into the whole money thing. Anyway, fortunately, her mum was calling her, so she said she'd call me back later."

"So, are you going to tell her?"

"I don't know. I don't know what I'm doing anymore. What if the police had taken a look at his bank account? They'd have seen the money I sent him. Oh my god. They'll think I'm involved in drug peddling, too."

"Don't be silly, Brian. We won the money legitimately, which we can prove. And all you've done is try to help a friend. There's no law against that. So, don't worry about that."

"I've just left the country, too, which will surely look odd."

"If you were up to anything underhand, you wouldn't be transferring the money via a bank. You'd be dealing in cash. And why would you do anything underhand anyway when we have all those millions in the bank?"

"Shhh. Not too loud. You don't want your whole family hearing."

"Hearing what?" Tom returns with the white wine to replace it in the fridge. "And who's this 'Debs' person, Brian? My brother-in-law's not having an affair, is he?"

Brian is non-plussed, not really sure what to say to Tom. All of a sudden, he feels tired and wonders if they'll get any time without Linda's family with them all the time. He longs for a few hours with Linda, just shooting the breeze and watching the kids in the pool.

"Don't be daft, Tom. Debs is the wife of a colleague. Brian's just helping them out a bit at the moment."

"Only kidding, Brian," Tom says, slamming the fridge door shut and picking up a huge bag of tortilla chips to take outside.

"Wait, Tom, there's guacamole and salsa dips to go with those." She quickly places serviettes and sauces on a tray and passes it to Tom, who heads out with his goodies back to the pool.

"God, he gets on my nerves sometimes," Brian says.

"You're just jealous because he's still young and fit-looking," Linda teases.

"I'm young and fit-looking," Brian whines, looking Linda in the eyes, mimicking that he's offended. "I can swing for anyone given the chance, but then, maybe that's not always a good thing." He grabs a beer from the fridge and sits down at the breakfast bar. He twists the cap off and takes a swig.

"About Deano's money, Brian. There's nothing we can do right now," Linda whispers softly.
They head out to the pool and join the others.

*****

After another hour, Brian begins to feel that salsa dips aren't quite filling the spot. He and Tom head off to the local Food Bazaar, where they buy steaks and giant langoustines for the BBQ. Tom tries to pay for the food, but Brian doesn't let him, so Tom heads to the liquor store and meets Brian back in the car with a case of beer.

When they return to Sundrive, Linda already has a salad ready, and Bob has set up the BBQ by the pool. As the evening begins to chill, Liam, Ruby and Dan head inside to get dressed.

"Brian, we were just saying while you were gone, everyone in this neighbourhood must be millionaires," Dan says when he returns in his shorts and sweatshirt and pops another beer can open.

Once again, Brian and Linda can't help looking at one another.

"They probably are. This is a very affluent part of Long Island," says Brian.

"Sure thing," says Dan proudly. "This is the land of opportunity. The richest country in the world, with the richest people."

"So what happened to you then, Dan?" Karen asks. "If we're meant to be the richest nation in the world, Dan, why are there people dying of hunger on the streets?" Her tongue has loosened with the white wine.

"Good question," agrees an equally tipsy Linda. She lies down on the lounger next to her mum. "I'm going to have to slow down on the booze."

"Yeah, well, a lot of those people are just too lazy and don't want to work," says Dan.

Linda sits bolt upright. "Dan, I could respect and understand your conservative republican views if you had any fucking money, or any common sense for that matter. But you haven't got a pot to piss in, and for some weird reason, you're happy for this country to continue as it is. The likes of Trump are laughing at people like you all the way to the bank!"

A short pause holds the air.

"Okay, that's enough politics, you lot." Bob breaks the silence. "We all have different opinions, and we should respect that. Liam, Ruby! Go set the table inside. It's getting too chilly to eat out here, and these steaks are nearly ready."

"Yeah, I'll come give you a hand," says Nancy, heading in after the children.

Dan staggers into his downstairs bedroom, calling out to them all: "I'm not arguing with you lefties. Good night!"

"I'm definitely with you on this, Linda," slurs Karen, trying to stand up. "Tom and I have been trying for a baby now for three years, and we can't afford any more IVF treatment." She turns to see Dan disappearing into his room. "How does that seem fair in this great rich nation, Dan?" she calls after him.

But Dan has staggered into his room and slams his door shut on them.

Ruby's eyes widen, and she exchanges a glance with Liam, who giggles.

"Karen! I had no idea," Linda glances at Brian. Her eyes are watering.

Bob places the steaks carefully on the dish Nancy has taken outside for them, and they all move towards the long table in the open-plan living space.

"I guess we've all had a few too many today, but it's just been so nice catching up," Nancy fills the silence.

"He's always like that, Mom. I don't know why you make excuses for him. Linda, I would have told you we were trying for a baby, but it's not easy over the phone, and I'm sure you and Brian have secrets. Besides, we were hoping to surprise you all with good news. But there's nothing we can do about it now."

A silence descends on them all again for a few minutes. Eventually, Liam points out that the langoustine is on fire on the BBQ, and they all rush out laughing to salvage the crustaceans.

"They're okay," Bob shouts. "The shells protect them!"

*****

After dinner, Nancy took the children to bed, and then she and Bob retired too. Tom and Karen stayed with Linda and Brian for a last nightcap. Brian had by now realised that the sadness he'd recognised in Karen's face was her disappointment at not getting pregnant. Linda and Karen were in a corner, having a heart-to-heart.

"So, it's actually money preventing you from keeping on trying for a baby?" he asks Tom.

"Yes, but that's just the way it is," says Tom. "I've already mortgaged the house to the hilt. I don't have any more resources. I guess that's it now." Tom knocks his whisky back. "We weren't going to tell anyone, but I guess Karen's had a few too many to drink today, and, well, you know, it gets to her sometimes. Well, it gets to us both most of the time."

Brian feels a pang of guilt for having felt so negative towards his brother-in-law earlier in the day. He and Linda are so lucky to have Ruby and Liam.

"It must be tough for you, too, Tom!"

"Well, yes, but the toughest part is seeing Karen unhappy."

The two men look at each other and then across to Karen and Linda. Karen is blowing her nose into a tissue.

"Maybe it's time for bed, love?" Tom asks tenderly. He stands up and moves over to his wife, pulling her up by her hands. She sways towards him, laughing.

"It's so good to see you, Linda. I miss you so much," she says as Tom leads her upstairs.

*****

Linda picks up her glass and moves into the chair Tom has vacated next to Brian.

"Well, that's it then, Brian! The big secret is over. I'm not standing by watching my baby sister unable to have a family because she can't afford it. We have to tell them our little secret in the morning when they're all sober."

Chapter Nineteen

The following morning, Brian wakes up to find Linda sitting at the end of their bed.

"Are you okay, love?" he asks as he sits up.

"I couldn't sleep. I kept thinking of Karen, unable to have children. God bless her. Why are some people born so unlucky in this life?"

"Are you still going to tell everyone about the lottery win?" Brian asks.

"I told you last night, Brian, I'm not going to let a lack of money stop my sister from having a baby, not when we've got enough for her to have thousands of babies."

"Nor me, Linda. Of course not. We can pay for her treatment, there's no doubt about that. But we don't have to tell her about our win, though, do we?"

Linda stands up and turns to face him.

"Fuck you, Brian! So, it's okay for your drug dealing buddy to know our business. But not my baby sister, who can be trusted, unlike your good friend Deano, who's just wound up in prison!"

Brian moves towards the end of the bed and lowers his voice so nobody can hear. He sits at the end and puts his head in his hands.

"I know, I know. I screwed up, okay? I'm sorry."

Linda sits down next to him and sighs.

"But I think I've got the solution, if you please just give me the chance to explain?" he continues.

"Go on then! What solution?" Linda pulls the cord to her dressing gown more tightly around her waist, elbowing Brian in the ribs as she does so. He flinches but ignores it.

"Sorry. That was an accident."

"I know."

"Go on then. What solution?" she says more kindly.

"Picture Karen and Tom with a toddler running around a new luxurious home, with a family saloon sitting on their driveway. Does that make you happy?"

"Of course. I'd love them to have all that, and we could give it to them now."

"And if Dan and your mum and dad had a lovely pad too, here in Long Island, and they were all looked after, would you be happy for them as well?"

"Obviously, that goes without saying, Brian. We've already agreed we want to do this for them. But we can hardly do it without telling them where we got the money, can we?" Linda walks away from Brian to retrieve the remote for the window blinds. As she opens them, the sun pours into the room. Brian frowns from the light and then claps his hands together.

"Right, hear me out! You must know by now that our lives can never be the same again. Both the little scare back home and this win have made me a little edgy. The last few days, I've given this a great deal of thought. So before you go shouting and swearing at me, give me a chance to explain my idea."

"Okay. I'm sorry for shouting at you." Linda puts her arm on his shoulder. "I love you. It's just so frustrating. They're all struggling, and we could help. We have all this money to solve their problems, but they don't know. What's stopping us?"

"We've talked about this before. Remember the squeaky voice asking us to mull over whether to tell the world? Once it's out, it's out, and there's no going back."

"Yes, I do remember, and then you went and told Deano anyway!" Linda's voice grows louder again.

"Yes, I know. But nobody knows here, and we don't have to tell anyone else. We've won the lottery, and there is a way we can help your family without telling anyone."

"Well, go on! I'm listening. Spit it out!"

Brian notices an impatience in Linda, which is unlike her. Perhaps it's all the alcohol they've been drinking. She's usually so patient, the calm one in the family, even when the children are testing their parents' resilience. He reaches over to the chair for yesterday's t-shirt and shorts and pulls them on.

"Okay, so imagine, we tell all your family. Then Dan gets drunk and tells everyone he knows in the pubs where he spends most of his life. And Tom tells all his mates in that engineering plant where he works. Soon, everyone knows our private business."

"Okay, I see that. But Karen and Tom wouldn't tell a soul if I asked them not to. Particularly as it's going to solve their problem and give them their dream in life—a child. A child, Brian! Imagine if we didn't have Liam and Ruby. Can you imagine what our lives would be like? Anyway, you said that you have a solution. Hurry up! I'm famished and really need a coffee."

"Okay. Why don't we just tell your family that my uncle in England has left us some money? And I'll tell my mum that your family in the States have left you some money. That way, we can still buy them all what they need, but nobody finds out that we've won the lottery."

"Is that your solution, Brian? But suppose I'd like to look after my friends as well as my relatives?"

"Well, I thought about that, too. Here's the clever bit. We can send friends anonymous gifts, like a car, money, etc. They'll never know the gifts are from us. We can be there for anyone we know who needs help. They just won't know it was from us. That way, the people we care about get looked after, and we get to keep our business private. Everybody wins. What do you think?"

"I think it sounds nutty. Inheriting from family is just the same as winning the lottery. You suddenly get loads of money! What difference does it make? The only difference is that the private business you've told them about is untrue! You're crazy!"

Brian puts his hands up to warn her to keep her voice down, but his gesture seems to annoy her more.

"This is what I'm going to do, Brian! As soon as I've had my shower, I'm going to ask Karen to join me for a walk down to the beach. We can have breakfast down there and take a nice leisurely stroll. And while we're out, I'm going to tell her we've won the lottery. Because, quite frankly, if I don't tell somebody, I'll go absolutely fucking nuts myself. So, you tell me, Brian, what do you think of that?"

They stood opposite each other now, looking each other straight in the eye. Brian felt a new fear. Before, he'd been worrying about Juicy and how he could ever be sure he could keep his family safe if they returned to England. Now he was beginning to wonder if winning the lottery wasn't one of the worst things that had ever happened to them. He and Linda never used to argue like this. Now, when they should be happier than ever before, they were always disagreeing over things.

The only moments they'd had to talk with each other over the weekend had been in their bedroom, and he was beginning to feel the strain of having house guests all the time.

"Okay, it's compromise time," he said with an edge of failure in his voice. "I understand that you want to tell your sister. I get that. And you're right. There was probably a part of me that just wanted to share with Deano that night. It's a kind of relief to get the news off your chest to someone. I had exactly the same feeling when I told Deano. But can we at least agree on one thing?"

"What, Brian?" Linda says sharply.

"Just tell Karen, nobody else? That way, we've both just told one person. Will you at least agree to that for now, Linda?"

"Okay, fair enough. And will you just do one final thing for me, Brian Jackson?"

"What?"

"Will you give me a big kiss, you handsome, difficult, nutty, English snob!"

"I love you, you crazy Yank," Brian replies, relieved. Perhaps they are just tired after the travel and all the excitement. Everything is going to be fine.

Chapter Twenty

Linda feels excited at the prospect of sharing their wonderful news with her sister. It isn't quite like when she told her that Liam or Ruby were on the way, but the implications which the news will have for Karen and Tom make it just as important. She pushes her irritation with Brian to the back of her mind. She knows he means well, he's a good husband and father, and she loves him to bits, but he seems to have a separate set of rules for himself and her. She feels justified in standing up for herself when the discrepancies show.

Now, hand in hand, they walk into the kitchen to the aroma of coffee and find Karen and Tom sitting at the breakfast bar. The kitchen, now functioning for a family of nine, has acquired a lived-in air, with open packets of biscuits on the counters and half-drunk bottles of red wine clustered by the hob. Someone has been out to fetch pastries, probably Bob, and damp costumes are hanging over the backs of the breakfast bar stools. A black sack bulges out of the kitchen bin, overloaded with packaging from the takeaways and BBQ meats they've been cooking, and the sink is littered with dirty dishes that wouldn't fit into the dishwasher. Linda clocks the damage and makes a mental note to tidy the place up a little after her walk.

A note of sadness touches her as she ponders on how, when younger, her mum would never have let anywhere get to this state. She would have been busy washing, cleaning, and ordering the rest of them about to get the place ship shape, whether in her own home or Karen's or Linda's. She puts her concerns over Nancy and the problem of the state of the kitchen on hold. Right now, Linda's priority is talking to Karen.

"I'm walking down to the beach if you fancy joining me, Karen? Brian, why don't you make some breakfast for Tom? And if you guys have any energy, and Dan, too, when he's up, you can have a blitz on this kitchen!" Linda says, turning back to wink at Brian behind her.

"Cancel that second coffee, Tom. I'm going for a morning stroll," says Karen, jumping down from her stool at the breakfast bar.

Tom looks around the kitchen and then at Brian. He looks down at the coffee he's just poured and then offers it to Brian, who knocks it back enthusiastically.

"Breakfast first, mate? Clean later?" Brian suggests.

"Good shout," Tom agrees.

"There are eggs, bacon, and tomatoes in the fridge, love. You can cook Tom a full English! Or there seem to be plenty of pastries, too!" The two sisters grab their jackets and head off for the beach.

*****

"How beautiful is this, Linda? Walking down to the beach with my sister. I'm just so thrilled to be with you all here."

"I know, and to think, some people do this all the time."

"So, how's little old England, sis?"

"Okay. Well, I don't know, Karen. The kids seem happy enough in school, but where we live has become a bit dodgy with crime and gangs. And I'm not sure I can stand another British winter. You wouldn't believe how dark, miserable, and cold it gets!"

"Oh, New York was cold this winter. We had icicles on our faces," Karen jokes. "Have you noticed, though, how the older we are, the harder life seems?"

"Oh, I don't know about that, Karen. Life's surely not so bad, is it?"

"Tom and I just seem to work, work, work all the bloody time. I wish I'd done better in school, sis." Karen laughs and pushes her hand through Linda's arm so they can walk arm-in-arm. They both look out across the sand to the sea.

"Karen, you're not seriously going to give up on trying for a baby, are you? Thirty-two is far too young to stop trying."

"That ship's sailed, Linda," Karen looks down at the pavement. "The thought of going through all the IVF treatment again without any guarantees… No, I can't do it anymore. It's not only stressful, it's financially crippling. We've decided to call it a day on that one, draw a line on it."

"But are you deciding based on the cost? It just doesn't seem right."

"Well, yes and no."

"I don't understand. Is there something else?"

"To be honest with you," Karen stops walking and turns to face her sister, "Tom and I have gone through a pretty rocky patch this past year. Things haven't been so good."

"Oh, Karen. I'm so sorry." Linda hugs her sister, and they stay locked together for a minute without speaking. Suddenly, solving all Karen's problems with money doesn't seem so straightforward. Linda feels a little sparkle falling away. She had anticipated their walk as being such a positive moment.

"I thought there was something not quite right with you guys yesterday, but I couldn't put my finger on it."

"You should have seen us a few months ago. We've been living a nightmare. But anyway, let's not go there today. Everything seems so positive with you and Brian here. This break in Long Island is just what we need—and your company. It's like a breath of fresh air seeing you and the children." Karen continues walking and pulls Linda along with their arms linked again.

"Do Mom and Dad know about you and Tom?"

"Good heavens, no. Anyway, I think we're okay now. It was just a blip. Everyone goes through bad times, don't they? The test of a good marriage is whether you can pull through them."

"You 'think' you're okay now, Karen? You don't sound sure."

Karen stops walking again.

"Okay, if you must know, Tom was gambling morning, noon, and night. We nearly lost our home." Karen's voice breaks. "I guess all that IVF saga didn't help matters. It just built up as a stress inside him." Karen wipes tears away from her face.

"Oh my god. How bloody selfish! You were going through all that, and all he could do was risk your home!" Linda's anger is bubbling up again. "I can't believe it, sis. You should have told me. What a bastard!" Linda imagines her sister visiting the clinic for all the IVF jabs and procedures, and meanwhile, Tom is boozing and gambling the nights away. She feels incensed. She takes a deep breath. Getting angry isn't going to help Karen now. She needs to stay calm.

"Look! There's the place we ate at the other day. Let's go in there and get something to eat and drink." It's now Linda's turn to pull her sister along. Together, they go into the café and sit at the same booth as before and watch the tide for a while. When they've ordered, Linda takes hold of Karen's hand across the table and continues the conversation.

"Are things okay now?"

"Yeah, well, apart from the massive gambling bill Tom ran up."

"How much?"

"$60,000."

"$60,000, Karen? Jesus!"

"Shhhh. I don't want everyone to know." Karen looks forlorn.

"I kicked him out last year. He stayed at his friend's house for a few weeks, which didn't really help. His friend's a bigger gambler than Tom is, and they seem to drink themselves silly when they're together. He promised me he would stop gambling, so I eventually let him come home."

"Well, thank goodness he saw sense, Karen. You must see that as a step in the right direction. And you're still together. It's all good, Karen. Try to hold on to that."

"What? We split up last year, and now my husband owes $60,000 dollars, and if I want to try for another round of IVF, we'd need another $15,000. I can't say that I find it easy to see the positive at the moment, Linda."

Linda squeezes her hand and then lets go as the waitress delivers two full breakfasts and coffee. She puts the bill under the salt and pepper pot on the table.

"Can I get you guys anything else?" she asks before moving away.

Karen grabs the bill.

"I'll pay for this. You've looked after us all this weekend."

"Not a chance, Karen, I'm paying." Linda snatches the bill from her sister and tucks it under her purse on the seat next to her. She waits until the waitress has reached the counter before asking, "Why don't you go ahead with another round of IVF treatment, Karen? Life's too short. It often doesn't work the first time. Please don't give up!"

"Why? Have you got a spare $15,000 lying around, Linda, to pay for the next round? Even if we had the money now, we've still got Tom's gambling debts to pay off."

"I've got $15 million, sis. Well, actually, it's £17 million in sterling."

"What?" Karen puts her fork of scrambled egg back down on the plate.

"I said that I've got the money you need, Karen."

"I don't understand. How? This is a joke, right?"

"No, it's true. I can give you the money. For the debts and for the IVF treatment. I'm not joking, Karen. It's true."

"What's going on, Linda? What's happened?"

"We won the lottery."

"What?"

"We won the British National Lottery."

"No way, Linda!" Karen's mouth is open.

Linda smiles at her sister. She sees a flicker of something register in Karen's face. She feels an enormous warmth towards her. Thank god she can do this for Karen right now when she most needs it.

Karen's eyes seem to widen and widen. A smile creeps slowly across her face.

"I wondered why you wanted to get out this morning. I knew it! I knew there was something you wanted to tell me.

Oh my god! Oh my god! I can't believe it. It's wonderful! There is a God, after all." Karen starts laughing and Linda joins her. People sitting at other tables look across at the two women laughing and holding both hands across the table.

The waitress comes over.

"Can I help you? Is there anything you need?"

"No, thank you. We're just great," Linda answers, and the waitress returns to her counter.

"Didn't you wonder about the place we're staying in? It's a palace!"

"But you said Brian's boss let you stay there."

"Brian's boss, my ass, Karen. His boss wouldn't give you a dime, and the owner of a dodgy leather factory in Liverpool certainly couldn't stretch to owning the kind of mansion we're staying in. Anyway, Brian resigned last week. Life's too short, like I said."

"And have you left the supermarket?"

"No, I'm going to continue working my nine till three shifts," Linda says in a deadpan voice. "Only teasing. Of course I've left, Karen. We've both retired!"

"Wow! Retired at thirty-four. Is this some kind of a joke, Linda?"

"I'd never joke about you trying for a baby, Karen. Give me some credit!"

"Oh my god. Now, I know you're serious. Goodness me, Linda, what are you telling me?"

"I'm saying go ahead and re-book that IVF treatment, and we can pay off Tom's debts. That's what I'm saying."

Karen shuffles out of the booth to reach across and give Linda a big hug. Other customers in the café glance across again as both sisters now wipe away their tears.

"Stop crying, Karen, everybody will be wondering what's going on," Linda says, as though she wasn't feeling emotional herself. "God, I'm starving. Let's eat before it's all too cold."

Karen bursts out laughing. "Yes. Me too." She starts tucking into her breakfast.

"Have you told Mom and Dad or Dan?"

"No, not yet. Brian hasn't even told his own mom yet in case her boyfriend Billy tells the whole of the North of England. And Dan—God bless him—would be found dead of alcoholic poisoning in a Las Vegas brothel if he knew."

"Ha, that's true." Karen laughs again.

Linda's so happy to hear Karen laugh. She beckons the waitress over to order some fresh coffee now the others have gone cold and again waits until she has returned to the counter before continuing the conversation.

"I'll tell Mom and Dad later. But when you mentioned not being able to get pregnant last night, I knew I had to tell you."

"Oh my god, Linda. I still can't believe it. So, when was it, what happened, how, where? Tell me everything!"

"A couple of weeks ago, Brian and I were watching TV, having a drink. We'd ordered a takeaway as we usually do on a Saturday night. Brian checked his lottery tickets, and it turned out we had six numbers, the jackpot! And that's it!"

"Oh my god, Linda. What are you going to do?"

"I haven't a clue, Karen. We're still trying to get our heads around it all. But I guarantee you one thing, I'm going to look after Mom, Dad, you and Tom, and Dan. You don't have to worry about anything again for the rest of your lives."

"So, you're not telling people, then?"

"I don't know what to do. What would you do if you won the lottery, Karen? Would you tell everyone?"

"I don't know what I'd do."

"Well, we need to decide. Brian's worried about it, and I'm beginning to understand why he's reluctant to go public. He said something the other day that really resonated with me." Linda pauses and looks up at the sky with her hands on her head.

"What did he say?"

"He said, once we've told people, we can't un-tell them."

"Well, that's pretty obvious, isn't it, when you think about it?"

"Yes, but you have to think about the consequences. I mean, look at all these people sitting here enjoying their breakfasts. We don't know anything about any of them. Imagine if they all knew about our lottery win. I'd get that horrible feeling that they were all looking over at me saying, 'There's that woman who won all those millions.' And I'm not sure if I'd like that. I mean, Brian has a point. This is, after all, our private business, isn't it?"

"Well, yes, it certainly is. And you have to do whatever is best for you. But what about everybody who knows you? How will you keep something like this secret from them? They're obviously going to see massive changes in your life. A beautiful new house, car, holidays, etc., etc."

"I know, I know. I keep saying that to Brian. Just keeping this from you guys this weekend has been really difficult. We've had more than one argument about it."

"So, what are you going to do?"

"Brian has this idea—I think it's a bit crazy myself. It's one of the reasons I'm just so relieved to be talking to you about all this before I go nuts."

"So what's his idea, then?"

"Right, well, you know all our cousins, aunts, uncles, nephews, nieces, and all the friends we have?"

"Yes."

"Well, a lot of these people could do with some help, so Brian suggests we send anonymous gifts to help them out."

"Anonymous gifts?"

"Yeah, like if somebody, say, needed a new car, or help with house renovations, or just some money for something."

"Yeah, it does sound a bit odd."

"I know, I think it is, too. For the last few days, I've been worried that he's having some kind of breakdown. You see, it's not just this lottery money on his mind."

"Well, I'm sure it is on his mind a lot."

"Yes, of course, but there's something else too. A couple of weeks ago, Brian defended a shop owner near us during a robbery, and apparently, he overpowered a thug. You know what he's like. He wouldn't stand there and do nothing."

"I know."

"Well, a few days ago, this thug came to our house with a knife and was making threats."

"Oh my god."

"Yeah, I know. He didn't come inside or anything. Brian just saw him outside. But Brian pointed out the risks of these people finding out we have the kind of money we've won."

"Oh, I see. Yes, I can understand Brian's concerns there. But how do you go about sending gifts, Linda? You'll have to pretend that you've received a gift yourself, so they don't suspect it was you who sent it. But I don't know. It does sound a bit mad."

"Yeah, I know it does. But wouldn't it be nice to help people out without having to disclose your private affairs?"

"I suppose so. But how do you go about sending money to somebody without them knowing who it's from? I mean, I don't think you can send cheques anymore, can you?"

"I don't know, but there must be a way of helping people anonymously. And there's plenty of people who I can think of who I'd love to help."

"Yeah, I can think of two people right now. Me and Tom!"

They both laugh.

"Mom and Dad are staying another few nights. Dan is going back because he has a pool game tonight in his local bar. I think I'll tell them later when Dan has gone."

"I'd be careful about that. Mind how you tell them. It's quite some news, and you don't want to shock them! I'm just getting my head around it myself."

"Ha, I never thought of that." Linda giggles. "The shock would probably finish Dad off. Right, that's settled. I'll say that Brian's uncle in England has left us some money for now."

"Okay, and I won't mention it to Tom until we're driving back. It's going to be fine."

Chapter Twenty-One

It's late afternoon, and Karen and Tom are leaving. Dan is also getting ready to say goodbye.

"Thanks for a lovely weekend, both of you," says Karen. "It was just what we needed."

"Yeah, thanks, guys," says Tom.

"Thank you, everyone, especially you, Ruby and Liam, for trying to teach me how to swim," says Dan.

"You're welcome, Uncle Dan," Liam says seriously. "When are you coming back? I'm sure you'll get the hang of it soon." Liam hugs his uncle.

Karen whispers to Linda. "I'll tell Tom once we're in the car. I'd better drive. I don't want him to crash with the shock." She giggles and hugs her sister. "Careful as you go telling Dad!"

"Goodbye, guys. Take your time driving," says Nancy, placing one arm around each of the children's shoulders as they all wave Tom, Karen and Dan off.

"Fancy watching a movie, Nan and Grandad?" asks Liam. "The TV in the living room is enormous, but you can come and watch the one in my bedroom if you like. You could lie on my bed. It's big enough for all of us."

Nancy laughs.

"Yeah, why not," Bob says.

Brian and Linda go to sit outside for a while by the pool.

"So, Karen must have been pretty shocked when you told her."

"She couldn't believe it, and she's going to tell Tom on the way home."

"Wait until Tom finds out!"

"I've got some bad news, actually. Apparently, she and Tom went through a bit of a rocky patch last year."

"I thought there might be something going on. I had a funny feeling something wasn't right last night. Tom got quite drunk and didn't seem himself."

"Yes, I picked up on that too."

"So, is whatever it was over now — are they okay? What caused it?"

"Apparently, Tom got himself into some heavy gambling, and they owe a shit load of money. She kicked him out at one point last year and only took him back once he'd stopped the gambling."

"Good god. I wouldn't have thought that of Tom! It's an addiction, though. Gambling is definitely a disease. How much does he owe?"

"She said about $60,000."

Brian whistled. "Wow. That's unexpected, isn't it? Well, I suppose we should at least be grateful that we can bail them out."

"Yeah, I told her we'd look after them, and she could start more IVF treatment, but she said that she wasn't sure whether she had it in her to try again."

"I thought Karen looked a bit tired. I think she could do with taking some time off."

"I told her they could have stayed on and that she didn't need to go to school today, but she said there's such a shortage of teachers at the moment that she doesn't want to let them down."

"That's your Karen — always thinking of others."

"I was thinking of giving her and Tom a million, if that's okay with you, honey. Wouldn't it be nice if they were millionaires?"

"Yeah, as long as Tom doesn't lose it all gambling again."

"I think he's learned his lesson," Linda laughs.

"What are we going to do about your little brother?"

"I need to think about that one. We don't want him drinking himself to death. What is it with all these addictions?" Linda sighs.

"Well, talking about addictions, I'm going to fetch a beer. Do you want a glass of white wine?"

"Why not?"

Brian disappears inside to fetch the drinks, and Linda watches the ripples shimmer on the pool as the sun starts to sink towards the horizon.

"Bring my cardigan from the kitchen, will you, please?" she calls out to Brian.

Brian returns, clutching her cardigan under one arm and holding a drink in each hand.

"And what about your mum and dad?" Brian nods up towards Liam's bedroom, from where they can hear what sounds like a Jackie Chan movie blaring out.

"I suppose I'll have to tell them about your kind uncle in England for now."

"I've been thinking about your mum and dad. We're going to have to tell them the truth."

"Really?" asks Linda. "How bizarre! Karen convinced me that it would be better to use the inheritance story that you suggested, and now you'd prefer the truth. Why the change of heart?"

"My mum doesn't really need to know anything for now, especially with her fella Billy being such a wild card. I'm sure he would broadcast it all over Liverpool. But who do your mum and dad see? They hardly go out anywhere."

"I was never worried about them telling anybody, Brian. I know for certain that if I tell them something in private, it will stay private. I was more concerned about them collapsing with the shock, especially my dad. He's not in the best of health."

"Well, if they're going to stay with us a while, I can't keep looking at them and lying through my teeth. We could always play it down if you think £17 million is too much at this stage. And I agree with you. I know they'd respect our privacy. Are you hungry? Shall I get some nibbles?"

Linda takes a sip of her wine. "No, don't go. Let's just decide what we're going to do. I must admit, it would be a massive weight off my mind if we told them. It's so lovely being able to tell such good news. I'll explain that we'll tell Dan when the time is right."

Brian stands.

"Where are you going, honey?"

"I was going to make us something to eat while you tell your mum and dad."

"Nice try, Jacko," laughs Linda. "You're staying with me when we tell them!"

"Okay, if that makes you feel better."

"Yes, it would, thanks."

"Oh, they're coming out now. Don't forget, just play it down, nice and calm."

"Not watching the movie anymore?" Linda asks her mum.

"Liam and Ruby are, but we can't lie on those beds for too long. We get so stiff, particularly your dad. We thought we'd take a little stroll while the children are enjoying the movie."

"Take a seat, Mom. Sit down!"

"God, isn't it so peaceful here," says Nancy. They sit down at the table by the pool, and Linda gets up from her lounger and joins them.

"Can I fetch you a beer, Bob? What would you like, Nancy?" Brian asks.

"Well, we were going to go for a walk, Brian, but why not? I'll have whatever Linda's drinking."

Linda leans a little closer to her parents while Brian gets the drinks.

"I had a good talk with Karen today, Mom. Brian and I, well… we've have had a little change of fortune in our lives."

Nancy and Bob look at each other.

"How do you mean?" asks Nancy.

"Mom, Dad, this house... erm, Brian's boss and us staying here in Long Island. Look, I don't know how to explain this. I feel a bit bad about lying to you, but, well... Brian, will you help me out here?" She looks up at Brian as he sets a tray of drinks and nibbles on the table.

"What Linda's trying to say is..."

"This isn't your boss's house, is it, Brian?" asks Bob.

"No, it isn't, and I'm sorry we didn't explain earlier, but we're not sure about who we should tell, really."

"Have you come into money? Is that what you're trying to tell us?"

"Yes, Dad!"

"Well, that's good news," Nancy says, smiling and sipping her wine. "So, what happened?"

"We won the lottery," Linda blurts out, not wanting any more lies.

"That is fantastic," says Nancy, clinking her glass against Linda's.

"Mom, it's more than fantastic. It's unbelievably out of this world!"

"Yeah, I suppose it is. Do the kids know?" Nancy asks.

"No, we haven't told them yet. They're still too young to understand, really," Brian says.

"I agree with you, Brian," says Bob, "You don't want to spoil them."

"I thought you'd be more surprised?" says Linda.

"Oh, nothing shocks us anymore, does it, love?" Bob turns to Brian and chinks his beer can against Brian's. "And good news is always welcome."

"Yes, good news is always welcome. We're delighted for you both," says Nancy.

"Don't you want to know how much it is?" asks Linda.

"Does it matter?" replies Bob. "It's not really our business, is it?"

"Well, I suppose not, but I wouldn't like to keep anything from you both," replies Brian.

"Are you millionaires then?" asks Nancy.

"Yes, Mom."

"Wow!" laughs Nancy. "Well, isn't that something!"

"We're trying to keep things as normal as possible," Brian explains. "I haven't told my mum yet. Her boyfriend would tell the whole world, and I'm not ready for that yet."

"Good move, Brian. Does Dan know?" asks Bob.

"No, not yet," Brian replies.

"And if I was you, I'd keep it that way," says Bob. "He can be quite immature, and I'd be worried about him knowing something like this."

"We'll be looking after him, Dad. Dan will never be short of anything. But I agree with you. I think he's better not knowing at this stage."

"So our message is really that we'll look after you two, Tom and Karen, and Dan, of course, but we'd like to keep our lives as normal as possible, especially for Liam and Ruby," Brian says.

"You've always been a good family man, Brian — and responsible. And I know how hard you guys have worked over in England, so I'm delighted for you both. I really am," Bob says, standing to pat Brian on the back.

"We've both left our jobs. And if Karen and Tom want to leave theirs too, there will be enough money for them to do so. Dad, you don't have to work in that garage anymore, either," says Linda.

"I only work part-time now, anyway, and I quite enjoy it. But I appreciate the offer, sweetheart."

"Linda and I would like to buy you guys a nice place here in Long Island if you fancy it. I know you used to come here when Linda was little."

"That would be lovely, wouldn't it, Bob?"

"Yes, we could go to Brooklyn on our holidays," says Bob, and they all start laughing.

"If Dan wants to continue living with you, he could, or we could buy him a place of his own. You could all choose what you wanted," Linda says.

"It sounds just wonderful," Nancy responds.

"I don't know what plans you've made, but if I were you guys, I definitely wouldn't rush into anything. I think you need some time for all this to sink in, and I mean—a bit more time than you realise," says Bob.

"I keep saying that to your daughter," laughs Brian.

"Mom, Brian and I need to go to the store to pick up some stuff. Would you like anything brought back?"

"No, thanks, we've got everything here. Why don't you and Brian have a few drinks down at one of the bars? We're getting well looked after here by Ruby and Liam."

"Oh, I like the sound of that, Mom. Come on, Jacko, you can take your wife for a romantic drink."

*****

Linda and Brian leave the house and walk to the beach.

"God, Brian, that was much easier than I expected. I couldn't believe how laid back they were."

"Well, they know we're steady, responsible people. I mean, imagine if it was Dan who won millions. They might have been worried then."

"God, you're so right there, Brian. I'd be worried, too, if it was Dan. But they know that their daughter is married to an English gent." Linda gives Brian a kiss and takes hold of his hand.

"So, I'm an English gent now, as well as a snob," laughs Brian.

Chapter Twenty-Two

"This bar looks nice. The Beachcomber, let's go in here."

"Oh, this is very posh! Can we afford it?" Linda laughs, glancing around at all the linen-clad tables and well-dressed clientele. A waiter escorts them to a table immediately.

Brian orders a beer and a white wine. A tall lady in her late thirties accompanied by a much smaller and older man are standing close by.

"Oh, hello! I thought I heard an English accent." The lady says to Brian in a strong New York accent. Linda looks at Brian and raises her eyebrows.

Brian's senses go on alert. He mustn't be quite as relaxed on holiday as he thought. He frowns at the woman. "Sorry?"

"You're staying in Sundrive, right?"

"Well, yes," says Brian, totally confused.

"I'm Angela Jenkinson, and this is my husband PJ. We live across the road from you. We've seen you come and go a few times."

"Oh, right—neighbours." Brian breathes a sigh of relief. "This is my wife, Linda, and I'm Brian.

"Pleased to meet you." He puts out his hand to shake PJ's hand. The short, elderly man nods at Brian and shakes his hand.

Linda gets up from the table and moves to stand with the group. "Nice to meet you both." She follows Brian's lead and holds her hand out to PJ, who takes it warmly in both of his hands and, without a word, shakes her hand. When Linda holds her hand out to Angela, she turns away to hang her bag over a chair by the table next to theirs.

"We heard there was an English guy on the avenue. You're the latest bit of gossip on Sundrive," Angela laughs as she sits and crosses her legs in her short leather mini-skirt. "So, are you on vacation?"

PJ hovers behind Angela while she makes herself comfortable and then sits himself. Linda and Brian return to sit at their table, and both take a sip of their drinks.

"We are for now, but we're thinking of buying a property here," Brian says.

"Oh, fantastic," says Angela. "A new neighbour!"

"We're not quite sure yet, but my parents are buying a property out here, for sure. They're from Brooklyn. Well, so am I."

"Our gardener is from Brooklyn," Angela comments.

Two waiters arrive with an ice bucket and a bottle of Champagne. PJ asks for two more glasses, which one of the waiters seems to whisk out of nowhere almost immediately.

"You'll join us, of course?" Angela flicks her hand across to Linda and Brian, as though used to bidding people to move around at her will. The waiter quickly runs to pull out Linda's chair and move their table to join Angela and PJ's. The process is seamless. He then pours four glasses of Champagne and carefully positions each one in front of one of the four on the brilliant white table mats. A plate of miniature savoury pastries is set in the centre of the joined tables.

Angela raises her glass and stretches her long arm out towards Brian. "To our new neighbour in Sundrive," she says, clinking his glass.

"Thank you for the welcoming!" Brian smiles at Angela. She's certainly a beauty for her age, but there's a harshness about her manner. He's not sure what to make of her. Linda raises her glass to clink with PJ.

"Well, if you're staying in Sundrive for a while, let me tell you a little about the place. The neighbours are really nice — well, nearly all of them." She smiles at her husband. "Have you met Rick next door to you yet? He's our neighbourhood watch guy. He's a bit strange, but he can be quite useful to have around."

"Yeah, we've met Rick. He's into his guns, isn't he?" replies Brian.

"That's him," laughs PJ. "I believe he has loads of weapons. Why can't he just keep a couple of guns in the house like the rest of us?"

"Yeah, right!" laughs Brian, glancing across to Linda and quickly picking up that she's not happy that their romantic tête-à-tête has been broken up.

"I don't suppose you've met Paulo and Donna, two houses up from us?" asks Angela.

"No, I don't think we've seen them yet," Brian says.

"And you probably won't. They keep themselves pretty much to themselves. We don't know what they've got to hide, but we think he's a mafia baron. Well, they are Italian, after all."

Brian glances at Linda again.

"We see a lot of big burly men come and go. But nobody seems to know what he does for a living. Tell me, Brian, what line of business are you in? PJ's retired, of course, but he was in finance."

"Leather manufacturing," Brian replies quick as a flash. He's not sure why, but he feels he has to compete with Angela in some way.

"Is that international?"

"No, UK-based."

"Nevertheless, your business is obviously doing well if you're thinking of buying on Sundrive." Angela smiles at Brian again.

PJ frowns at her. Brian assumes he has to pull Angela in sometimes. She seems to overstep a few boundaries on the social etiquette front.

PJ turns to Linda now. "How are your children liking—" but Angela cuts in.

"We're having a few drinks with some friends tonight, Brian." For just a fraction of a second, Angela drops her emaciated wrist to the table and touches Brian's left hand as though she needs to get his attention. "Why don't you come over and join us? You could meet some of the neighbours."

*****

"I think Angela has the hots for you, Brian. And she's such a snob."

"She's too posh for me," Brian jokes, "and too skinny and tall."

"I notice you weren't averse to watching her cross those skinny, long legs of hers under the table," Linda teases.

"Come on! Let's see what her friends are like."

"'Our gardener is from Brooklyn...' Cheeky bitch! If her friends are anything like her, I'd rather not meet them, thank you very much. And her husband looks old enough to be her dad, although at least he acknowledged that I existed! He must be the one with the money, poor man. Imagine being married to that!"

"So, I take it you didn't like her?" Brian asks in a neutral voice.

Linda swings her shoulder purse at him in jest, and the two walk arm in arm, both a little drunk now from the Champagne. Angela and PJ had gone on ahead, leaving them to finish the bottle alone but insisting that they joined their soirée as soon as they were ready.

"She was only interested in talking to you, Brian! Can't you see that? She wasn't interested in me or what I did. Even when talking about her neighbours, none of the women were mentioned. She was only interested in what their husbands did."

Brian looks at the house across the road from theirs. As they stand, deciding what to do, a limousine pulls up, and a suited gentleman steps out and offers a hand to his partner, dressed in a bright yellow cocktail dress.

"Oh, Brian, we're not dressed for this — I'll feel ridiculous in this Laura Ashley godet skirt I've had since we got married!"

"Well, look at me. I'm not wearing a suit, am I? Come on! It's just a few drinks with neighbours, not the Oscars. And anyway, Long Island cronies would probably die for a Laura Ashley skirt. It's British and 'cute', not to mention, in your case, an antique!" Brian starts laughing, and Linda thumps him in the arm.

"Well, okay, but only because we've got Mom and Dad babysitting, and I've drunk too much Champagne. Not because I like them."

"Fair enough! Text your mum and let her know we'll be late."

"Yes, they'll have fed the children by now. I'll do that!"

As they walk up the driveway, Brian realises that Angela and PJ's house is almost four times the size of the one they are staying in. They stand under the pillars at the front door, waiting for someone to answer. A young gentleman opens the door.

"You must be the English couple?" he says.

"That obvious, is it?" Linda counters with a smile on her face.

"Not at all, but Mrs J told me to expect you. Welcome, and please come this way."

He leads them across a huge entrance hall, flanked on one side by the largest sweeping staircase Brian has ever seen. Chandeliers hang from high in the ceiling. They are taken through a double door to a huge room, which appears to be entirely open to their pool on one side.

Brian glances around to see if there are sliding doors of some sort but can't work it out. People are standing in small clusters around the room, eating canopées and laughing raucously. Waiters and waitresses are weaving between them with plates of colourful works of edible art.

"Guys," Angela's voice bellows across the room. "You've arrived! Everyone, listen up! I want you all to meet our new English neighbour who lives across the road from me."

"And his American wife," Linda whispers to Brian, as everyone suddenly hushes and turns to look at the 'English' couple.

Brian suddenly feels a sickly feeling of déjà vu. He recalls walking into The Feathers back home with Deano. Everybody there had suddenly turned around, wondering who he was when he entered. Although this is a completely different environment, the situation feels similar in a strange way. All of Angela and PJ's friends are now quiet and still, looking to see who he is. Linda was right, too; Angela behaves as if Linda isn't there. There is something disturbing about the whole set-up.

"Brian's thinking of moving to Long Island. He deals in the leather manufacturing industry and has done very well for himself. Oh, sorry, what is your wife's name again?" Angela asks.

"My name's Linda, and I handle finance for an international supermarket consortium," Linda replies, smiling round at everyone.

Brian smiles at her.

"Well, hello, everyone, and good evening!" Brian is not quite sure what to say. Murmurs of welcome and good evening are voiced in return from the crowd, and Brian feels embarrassed by all the attention.

Angela seems delighted to have the opportunity to introduce Brian to everyone.

"Brian, I'd like you to meet Larry, the lawyer. Everybody needs Larry from time to time."

"Pleased to meet you," says Larry with smiling blue eyes.

"Larry the liar, no doubt," jokes Linda, as they move on to the next person for Angela to introduce.

"And this is Grant, who is our real estate expert. When you need a property, this is the guy you go to. And here are Martin and Philip, my next-door neighbours."

"Please to meet you guys," say Martin and Philip in unison. They look alike and could be twins, both dressed immaculately in smart black trousers and casual designer sweatshirts.

A waiter offers Brian and Linda Champagne flutes.

"And this is Brandon, Dr Brandon Philips, to give him his correct title. One of the best physicians in the business. You don't want to know what he charges, he's that good," Angela quips.

"So how much you charge defines how good you are?" Brian whispers to Linda.

She pokes him in the ribs. "Don't start me off, Brian. We'll be kicked out. They haven't introduced us to their shrink yet," laughs Linda.

"This is Tim. He's the best psychotherapist there is. I've regularly offloaded my stress to Tim, but book early, guys. He's in big demand."

"Oh, I bet she has. And I bet he's in big fucking demand with this lot," Linda whispers. "Although she doesn't look stressed to me."

Eventually, Angela leaves them with a couple who have only recently moved from Manhattan out to Long Island. The husband works on the stock exchange, and the wife is a model. Linda asks if they have any children, hoping to find something they have in common.

"Oh god, no! That would ruin my career. I have to keep under 45 kg, you see."

Linda watches the model eye the canopées enviously as they pass by. She grabs the largest and stuffs half of it in her mouth. "Ah, well, yes. It certainly destroys your figure," Linda laments.

"I don't think so, darling. I love you as you are," Brian says, putting his arm around Linda.

Brian soon realises that this couple aren't interested in them at all. The husband waffles on about options and how he's just made a client $10 million in a day through the right choices.

"You've just got to be brave, you know, take the risk, put your neck on the line."

"Well, really lovely to meet you both. We'll have to head back and check on those kids, you know," Linda says.

"Yeah, great to meet you both," Brian smiles, trying to remember their names, but they've turned to join the next group already.

They seek out Angela and thank her for the hospitality, and then a waiter materialises from nowhere and escorts them to the door.

"For heaven's sake, as though we couldn't find the way ourselves?"

"Perhaps they're frightened we'll steal the silver," Linda laughs.

"What a hard hour of socialising that was."

"Don't ever call me a snob again, Linda. I've just met the snobbiest bunch of people I've ever met in my life!"

"So you're in the leather manufacturing business. Good for you, Jacko."

"I wasn't going to give them the satisfaction of looking down at us. They're so prejudiced. The poor guy up the road is labelled a mafia hitman just for being Italian! Anyway, what about you? Finance in an international supermarket consortium? What's that when it's at home?"

Linda starts giggling.

"Wait until Angela finds out you work on the till in a supermarket near the kids' school," says Brian.

"Or that you're a labourer in a factory," Linda guffaws. "God help them! They'll be so disappointed."

"Hey, I'm a multi-millionaire now, if you don't mind, and I'm networking with stockbrokers and models."

"Yeah, and what fun that is!" laughs Linda.

"Oh, and we'd better get a couple of guns in the house, like the rest of our neighbours," Brian says sarcastically. "Honestly! It's unbelievable."

As they cross over, they catch sight of Rick.

"Oh my god, here's Rick. We're meeting them all tonight," whispers Brian.

"Hello Linda, Brian. Summer's on its way at long last," says their neighbour.

"Hi, Rick. How are you?" Linda smiles at him.

"I'm fine, thanks. I've just picked up my new Glock 19, 9mm handgun. It comes with fifteen rounds."

"You sure are into your guns, Rick," says Brian. He wonders whether to mention that Angela spoke well of him but thinks twice when he realises that Rick wasn't invited to Angela's soirée.

"Yeah, well, it takes all sorts in the world, doesn't it? I can't believe that you've never had a gun."

Linda laughs nervously. "We don't do guns in England, Rick."

"Yeah, but with all due respect, guys. You're not in England now."

"Well, Rick, we've left the in-laws babysitting, so we must be going, but nice to see you." Brian ushers Linda towards the house.

"Good night, guys." Rick waves.

"Don't you just love Sundrive, Linda? We've got Rifleman Rick next door, Affluent Angie across the way, and the mafia up the road. Only in America, Linda, only in America!"

Chapter Twenty-Three

Brian watches the children through the terrace doors while he sips his third coffee of the morning. They are playing with water pistols, and Ruby is definitely losing. Linda has made some bacon sandwiches for everyone to help themselves, and Brian has already eaten three.

"So, did you guys have a good time last night then?" Nancy asks as she joins them in the kitchen.

"It was a very interesting night, Mom. We met some of the residents of Sundrive who live here full-time. Here, help yourself to one of these before Brian eats them all."

"Wow! Imagine how wonderful it would be to live here all year round," Nancy comments, placing a sandwich on a side plate.

"I'm not so sure, Mom."

"How do you mean?"

"They're a bit too pretentious for my liking. They were literally throwing their wealth at us. I can't imagine them eating bacon sandwiches with us for breakfast."

"Who was it that once said, 'People are so poor, all they have is money?'" asked Bob, pouring himself a coffee and grabbing two bacon sandwiches. "Their loss if they can't enjoy a good bacon sandwich, that's what I say!"

"It was Bob Marley, Dad. And I think you've just described our neighbours perfectly."

"Were they friendly, though?" Nancy asked.

"Well, yes, but a bit too friendly, if you know what I mean. We were invited back to Angela and PJ's house across the road. Well, Brian was invited, I should say. She took quite a fancy to him."

"Your daughter is just being sarcastic, Nancy." Brian joins them all at the breakfast bar. He leans over to take the last sandwich, but Linda slaps his hand before he can.

"I haven't had one yet, Brian! I think Brian was quite flattered by Angela Jenkinson and all the attention she showered on him. She seemed to enjoy telling all her friends there was an English man living opposite her."

"They don't sound like my kind of people. I just hope you two don't end up like them, all rich and snobby," Bob laughs. "Never could stand flirtatious women, either. Rich and flirtatious is a terrible combination. Shallow is what they are!"

"Brian might become one of the gang, Dad, but money would never change me." Linda walks around the breakfast bar to give her dad a hug from behind.

"As she stands there in her £1000 dress, Bob," laughs Brian.

Bob raises his eyebrows and sweeps a glance up and down Linda's dress.

"What about you and your designer shirts, Brian," Linda retaliates.

"Anyway, when you two are finished squabbling, are you still driving me and your dad back to Brooklyn this morning? I've got loads of washing to sort out."

Nancy sips her coffee but keeps her eyes on Linda, waiting for a response.

"Yeah, but there's really no need to go back just to do the washing, Mom. There are two gigantic washing machines here in the utility room."

"I know, love, but I need to go back anyway and make sure that Dan hasn't burnt the house down."

"God, he's twenty-nine years old, Mom. He's not a child anymore," laughs Linda.

"I know. I just get a bit worried about him, especially with his emphysema."

"You mean you worry about his drinking? Whenever Dan has a hangover, you pretend you're worried about his emphysema," laughs Linda." You can always bring him back here. We've got plenty of rooms. Anyway, we'll be buying you a nice place of your own in Long Island soon."

"Yeah, especially now that Linda has as much money as all her pretentious neighbours," adds Brian.

"Don't you think Brian should be a comedian, Mom? Isn't he just so funny for an English snob?"

"Do the kids still want to stay at our house for a couple of nights, Linda? We were going to take them to Central Park. You and Brian can have a couple of days to yourselves," says Nancy.

The children suddenly appear through the terrace doors.

"Oh yes, Central Park," shouts Liam.

"Yes, please," Ruby adds.

"Yeah, that would be nice, Mom. I know Karen wants to take us all into Manhattan as well."

"Well, when you're ready then, Bob?" Nancy looks up to her husband.

"You're best driving to Brooklyn, Linda. I can't get used to being on the opposite side of the road," says Brian.

It takes just over an hour to drive to the east side of Brooklyn. Linda parks the car outside the house that her parents have rented for almost forty years. Brian had forgotten how old and decrepit it was. Perhaps their luxurious holiday home in Long Island has set his standards higher now, but Bob and Nancy's home has definitely seen better days. The sooner they buy them somewhere else, the better.

Dan greets them as they all walk through the door.

"Hello, Uncle Buck. Why are you lying on the sofa?" Ruby asks. "Are you ill?"

"It must be his emphysema, playing up again," Linda says under her breath.

"We're staying here for a few nights," says Ruby. "We've brought our pyjamas and everything."

Brian smiles at Ruby's excitement. It's so lovely to see the children enjoying their holiday.

"That's fantastic, kids," says Dan. "Hey Brian, why don't you come to my bar for a drink and a game of pool? You'll love Spud's. It's one of the best Irish bars in the whole of New York."

"I thought you weren't well, Dan?" Linda queries with a smile on her face.

"Oh, I'll be okay once Mom has made me something to eat."

Linda catches Nancy's eye, and they exchange a smile.

"Yeah, why don't you go, Brian? I could pick you up later when you're ready," Linda offers.

"Are you sure you don't mind?" asks Brian.

"Not at all. I can't wait to show Liam and Ruby where I grew up. The last time we were in Brooklyn, they were too young to understand."

"Okay. Do you know where Spud's bar is?"

"Of course I know, Brian. I'm New York born and bred, aren't I? It used to be O'Sullivans', didn't it, Dan?"

"That's the one, sis."

"Me and the kids can drop you guys off now."

"Hey, Mom, don't bother making anything to eat. Brian and I will get something to eat in Spud's." Dan dashes to his room to get dressed and reappears within minutes.

"Right, let's go then! Hope you've got plenty of money, Brian," Dan says, laughing. "Only kidding. It's my treat today, Brian. You gave us all a great weekend in Long Island, Buddy."

*****

"Brooklyn is much busier than Long Island, Mum, isn't it?" Liam says, gazing out of the car window.

"Sure is. There's our old school there, kids."

"Don't mention that place to me," says Dan.

They are soon at Spud's, and Linda pulls in by the entrance.

"See you later, guys. Just don't be getting too drunk or discussing politics, you two!"

Brian walks round to the driver's side and leans through the window to give Linda a kiss. An Irish tricolour flag hangs over the entrance, and scenes of Ireland and memorabilia cover the walls at the entrance. Brian is shocked at how dark the pub is once they are inside. He'd forgotten this about American bars.

"Hi Dan!" the barman calls over. "You're early. It's only two! You don't normally come in till five. Are you having the usual?"

"Yeah, cheers, Joe. Would you like to try a Guinness, too, Brian?"

"Sounds good to me, Dan."

The two men head over to sit at the bar while Joe pours their drinks. Each has a perfect head on it.

"The black stuff always reminds me of the Emerald Isle back home, Brian." Dan takes a swig.

"I didn't know you'd been to Ireland, Dan. Linda often says she'd like to go."

"Well, I haven't actually been there, but I keep imagining how it would taste if I was there."

"Oh right," Brian shakes his head, laughing.

"Joe, this is my brother-in-law, Brian. He's an Englishman in New York, so look after him!"

Joe nods at Brian.

"Your other brother-in-law, Tom, came in last night, Dan, just after you left, actually. He looked like he'd had a good win on the horses or something. He was buying everybody drinks, and when I say drinks, I mean my best Champagne!"

"Oh my god! That means Tom is gambling again. Karen won't like it."

Dan turns to catch Brian's eyes. Brian doesn't like the sound of it either and now wonders if it was a good idea telling Karen and Tom about their win.

"I don't like Tom coming in here," Dan whispers, "especially when he's had a skinful. I know I drink too much, but I know most of the people in here, so I feel safe. Tom tries to buy friendship a bit too much for my liking."

"You must have just missed him, by the sounds of it."

"Right, come on then! US versus UK on the pool table while it's quiet, Brian."

"I haven't played pool for a good while, Dan, so go easy on me," laughs Brian, climbing down from his bar stool to follow Dan. Brian enjoys playing, but it doesn't take long before Dan beats him. By the time their game is over, the bar has filled up quite a bit, and there's a steady hum of conversation.

"To be fair, Brian, you played quite well, considering you haven't played for some time. Let's get a seat. I'll order something to eat before Joe gets too busy. You've got to try Joe's burger and fries."

"Sounds great."

Joe soon brings their food over and two more pints of Guinness.

"So, are you staying at Dan's place then, Brian?" Joe asks amicably as he shuffles items around on the table to make room for their food.

"No, I'm staying in a holiday home in Long Island with the wife and kids, actually."

"Fantastic! I love Long Island, especially this time of the year," says Joe as he removes the menus and tucks them under his arm.

"You want to see where he's staying, Joe — big swimming pool, the lot. He's living like a millionaire out there!" Dan takes a bite of his burger.

"You must have all come into money then?" laughs Joe. "Tom was spending money last night like he was a millionaire. He looked very pleased with himself." He removes the empties from the table and heads back to the bar.

Alarm bells ring for Brian. He can't help but feel worried that Tom knows about their lottery win. He tries to tune back into what Dan is talking about but finds it hard to concentrate.

"Yeah, he's definitely back to his gambling by the sounds of it," Dan continues. "I don't know if you know, Brian, but Karen kicked him out last year because of his huge gambling problem."

"Yeah, I did hear about that, if I'm honest. Must have got pretty bad!"

"Karen would go nuts if she knew he was in here last night and gambling again," Dan says.

Brian isn't sure whether Tom is gambling again, but he obviously came into some money, and Brian doesn't like the sound of that.

"He's a good man at heart, but that gambling has screwed him up big time."

"I can imagine," says Brian.

"Hi Dan," a couple of new arrivals call out.

"Hi Kieran! Hi Sean! How was work?"

"Couldn't get much done today, to be honest, Dan. We've been waiting all day for building materials."

"This is Brian, my brother-in-law. He's over on vacation from England."

"Hi Brian, pleased to meet you, buddy," Kieran says.

"And you guys," Brian responds, watching them as they walk over to the bar.

"You have some nice friends, Dan."

"Everyone in here is cool, Brian. Although there are one or two guys you have to watch. That's why I don't like Tom coming in here, especially when he's had too much drink."

Brian's phone starts ringing.

"Sorry to interrupt your drink with Dan," Linda speaks fast, "but I need to pick you up now. If you can, give Dan some kind of excuse. Tell him our house alarm is going off or something."

"Why, what's going on?" asks Brian.

"Everything is okay, so don't worry. I'll be there in a couple of minutes, and I'll explain then." She rings off.

"Dan, I'm really sorry about this, but that was Linda. She said the house alarms are going off, and the Long Island police have turned up to check things out. She's coming to pick me up now. Sorry, buddy! Can we do this again?"

"Sure, no problem, Brian. I'll have a game of pool with the boys. See you soon, and let me know if everything is okay with the house."

"I will. It's probably nothing, but you know what Linda is like." Brian picks up the rest of his burger to take with him and goes to wait outside.

Chapter Twenty-Four

Linda pulls up outside Spud's Bar, and Brian gets in the car.

"So, what's the big emergency, Linda? It's Tom, isn't it?"

"Yeah, how did you know?"

"The barman inside just told Dan that Tom came in last night drunk as a lord and was buying everybody Champagne. I take it everything's not okay then?"

"No, it's certainly not. He hasn't been home all night. How disrespectful is that? I've just spoken to Karen, and she's had enough. I'm sorry, Brian. I should have listened to you and not told Karen about our win, especially when she has an idiot of a husband like him. We could have still looked after them without telling them."

"I suppose you had to tell your sister, Linda, so don't go blaming yourself."

"Ha. It's not all bad news, though."

"No?"

"Fortunately, I haven't put the money into their account yet, and thank god I didn't. That dickhead would have probably lost it all in Vegas by now if I had. I'm going to see to it personally that the money just goes into my sister's personal account, and he doesn't see a cent."

"Does he know you haven't sent the money yet? According to the barman, he was splashing out like a millionaire last night."

"I've no idea, but I do know this. He'll soon be back in touch with Karen once he's run out of cash."

"So let me just get this right. I'm not defending Tom, but he was out celebrating becoming a millionaire. We expect him home with his tail between his legs when he's run out of cash, especially when he realises the money isn't in their joint account. So, what's the massive problem? Why the emergency pick-up?"

"What's the massive problem? Are you kidding me, Brian? Any normal husband going out for a drink might occasionally be a little late coming home. And that's okay. But when Tom goes out, he stays out for about a week! And when he does eventually return home, it's usually followed by a huge gambling bill. That's not fair on Karen, who works very hard. Anyway, she's not putting up with it anymore."

"I don't blame her."

"As for the emergency pick-up, I was going to ask you to go and speak to Tom. Karen said he sometimes goes to this bar called Flintlocks. It's full of men, usually gambling and getting drunk. There's no way I'm walking in there. I think he'll listen to you, Brian, if you remind him he's on the verge of throwing everything away."

"Why would he listen to me, Linda? I'll try and speak to him, but there's nothing I can do if he won't listen."

"Well, at least we can say we tried. It's either that or Karen's just going to kick him out. I don't want her to be on her own."

"Okay, I'll give it a try. Do you know where this Flintlocks is?"

"I've got an idea where it is. I think it's a couple of blocks up from here. Can you put it in Maps on your phone?"

Brian fiddled around with his phone for a minute or so and then started giving Linda directions. After a few wrong turns, they found Flintlocks.

"Oh, here it is. That was easier than I thought."

Brian smiled at her with his eyebrows raised. She seemed to have forgotten about the three wrong turnings.

"Okay, wish me luck!"

"Just remind him that they can do anything they want now with all the money they have, so why would he waste it all on gambling."

"Let me just say it my way, Linda. I'll just have a quick drink with him, but I can't promise anything."

Linda pulls up by the bar, and Brian jumps out. He goes into Flintlocks and has to take his sunglasses off, it's so dark in there. He asks the barman if Tom Nichols has been in, but he'd apparently left drunk an hour earlier, so Brian returns to find Linda still parked at the kerb.

"I take it he wasn't there then?" asks Linda.

"Well, he was in earlier and apparently left after being drunk."

"Well, that's it. She's right. She should kick him out. He's never going to change. Well, at least we tried. I should stay with her. She's in a state."

"Why doesn't she just come and stay in Long Island with us for now?"

"I asked her to come up and stay with us, but she wants to be there personally when Tom decides to return home. She's changed the locks and wants to tell him it's over, and he's not welcome in their home anymore."

"Yeah, I can certainly understand that. I'd want to tell him as well. So I wonder where he is now?"

"Who knows? Probably at a racecourse, a dog track, or just sitting in a bar somewhere. He may even have flown to England to be with your mate, Deano."

"God, I forgot about Deano. What a pair of dicks the two of them are. It's the likes of those two clowns that give us cool men a bad name." Brian laughs.

"I'm not laughing, Brian."

"No, of course not. Sorry."

"Once he turns up and she's told him it's all over, I'll bring her up to our place."

"Okay, I may as well get a cab back to Long Island. I told Dan I'll have another drink with him another time."

"That's good. It saves me driving back again. And I can get back to Karen. There's a taxi rank on the next block."

"You certainly know your way around here, don't you? Do your mum and dad know about Tom?"

"No. I didn't want them to worry about Karen. Especially as they're spending some quality time with the kids."

"Ah, yes."

"So, how was your drink with Dan?"

"Oh, it was good. He's very well thought of in Spud's, Dan is. I tell you one thing. He's a mean pool player. He absolutely thrashed me."

"Ha, I'm not surprised. He gets enough bloody practice. He's in there every day." Linda laughs. "Do you know something? We often complain that Dan drinks too much, and he probably does. But he's a regular stand-up guy. Okay, he goes to Spud's every day. I know he has a friend in Christine, but they don't live together or depend on each other for anything. But Tom, on the other hand, is a married man, for Christ's sake, who was trying for a baby with Karen not so long ago.

Wouldn't you think he'd appreciate the financial security we've just offered them? He's an absolute idiot. I should have listened to you. I should never have told Karen about our win. It certainly hasn't helped the situation."

"I suppose when somebody has an addiction like Tom's, it doesn't matter what your financial situation is. At the end of the day, it's an illness. Just remember one thing. You told her for the right reasons and tried to help them both out. Who knows, this could even be a new start for Karen."

"I'm so lucky to have a husband like you, Brian. I love you so much."

"I love you too."

Linda pulls into the curb by the taxi rank. A taxi behind her honks, but she ignores him.

"Here we are. Jump out quickly. They think I'm stealing their custom! As soon as Karen's spoken to Tom, I'll drive up, but it may not be until tomorrow. Try and have a nice rest whilst the kids are at Mom and Dad's. You've worked really hard the last few weeks." Linda laughs sarcastically.

"Nearly as hard as you," Brian teases back. "I may have a swim. It's still early enough."

"Give me a kiss then, you English snob. See you later, Jacko. I love you."

"Love you too, you crazy Yank."

*****

Brian gets a taxi almost straight away. The driver quizzes him on the UK and tells him he's visited Buckingham Palace with his wife and daughter. Brian explains that he lives quite a distance from Buckingham Palace, to which the driver responds that Long Island isn't so bad.

On arriving in Sundrive, Brian gives him a generous tip. He heads into the house and grabs a cold beer from the fridge. Knocking it back, he runs upstairs to put some shorts on. The sun is shining, and a cool swim is just what he feels like, but just then, his phone rings.

"Oh, hello, Dan. Yeah, everything's fine, thanks. I think the house alarm just malfunctioned. I'll get it checked out, but thanks for asking. Okay, and don't stay in Spud's too long. Bye, buddy."

Brian sets his half-finished beer on a table and is just about to lie down when he hears the doorbell. He pads through the kitchen in his bare feet and opens the front door.

"Hello Angela."

"Well, if it isn't my handsome neighbour, James Bond. We're having another get-together at mine tonight. Would you and your wife—oh, what's her name again—like to come over?"

"It's Linda."

"Yes, of course. Well, if you aren't doing anything, I've got some other friends popping over who would just love to meet you, Brian."

"Well. It's a bit difficult at the moment, as my wife may be staying the night in Brooklyn."

"Oh really, Brian?" Angela raises an eyebrow and lets a slow smile creep across her face. "Well, there's no need to be here in this big house all alone. You should come over and enjoy yourself. I've told all my friends about this tall, handsome English guy across the road. They simply can't wait to meet you, Brian."

"To be honest with you, it's a bit difficult at the moment, Angela. Maybe another time, perhaps?"

"Why? Is everything okay, Brian? I'm a good listener if you ever need to talk. And it would always remain private—just between us."

"Yeah, everything's okay. Just a few family problems."

Angela puts her arm on Brian's shoulder.

"Look, we've all been there, Brian. PJ and I live virtually separate lives now. Well, he's much older than me," Angela laughs.

"Oh no, you don't understand, Angela—"

"I'm a woman, Brian. I understand a lot more than you think. Look, if there's anything you need while your wife's away, and I mean anything, don't hesitate to knock. That's what friends are for."

Angela gives Brian a hug.

"Yeah, okay. Thanks, Angela."

"Hopefully, we may see you later then, Brian. Don't forget, that's what friends are for. Goodbye for now." Angela winks at him as she turns away.

"Goodbye, Angela."

Brian closes the door slowly and looks at himself in the hall mirror, brushing his hair to one side. He can't help but feel flattered by her words, "tall, handsome, English guy." He turns sideways on and tries to suck his beer belly in. Perhaps he should get a little exercise. He returns to the pool and walks down the steps at the shallow end.

He's not as good as the kids at swimming but can do the basics. He swims up and down quickly, getting out of breath. As he's swimming, he reflects on how lucky he is at the transformation in their lives. After a while, he sits on the steps with his feet still in the water, taking in the evening's last rays of sunshine. After about an hour, he goes to fetch another beer. He feels relaxed and falls asleep.

A couple of hours later, his phone wakes him.

"Hello, Linda. How's things?"

"Were you asleep? Did I wake you?"

"You did, actually. I was well away. And you sound like you've had a drink."

"Karen and I have had several drinks, if you must know, Jacko."

"So, what's happening? Has Tom been in touch?"

"He most certainly has. The cheek of him. He turned up here, as expected. He tried opening the door, but of course, his key no longer works. Then he started knocking on the window. When he saw me, he looked very embarrassed."

"Ha! Serves him right. What did Karen say to him?"

"She told him to sling his hook and never return to the house again. He told her she couldn't do that as it was his house too. Karen told him to get himself a good lawyer then."

"I don't blame her."

"He mentioned the money from us."

"I thought he would. What did Karen say?"

"She told him he wasn't capable of living with that kind of money. They'd be skint within a week. He walked away shouting that his lawyer would get what he was entitled to."

"So, I take it you and Karen are coming back to Long Island now that she's sorted Tom out?"

"No, I'm going to stay here with Karen tonight. I'll bring her up in the morning."

"That's not what you said earlier. You promised that if Tom showed up, which he did, you and Karen would come up here."

"For god's sake, it's only for one night. We're having a girl's night. We're in her local bar at the end of her block."

"Oh, I see. So you're out at a local bar while I sit here on my own in this big house in Long Island. I should have accepted Angela's invitation to go over to hers tonight, then."

"What did you just say? Angela asked you over to hers?"

"Well, we were both invited, actually. But I told her you might be staying in Brooklyn."

"Both invited? I'll bet she couldn't even remember my name. Thanks for telling her I wasn't home tonight!"

"Well, it's true, isn't it? You aren't coming home. What else am I meant to say?"

"She has the hots for you, Brian, and you know that only too well! And now you've gone and told her that your wife won't be home tonight! Are you playing the neglected husband here or something?"

"And what are you playing at, Linda? A marriage guidance counsellor for Karen?"

"Marriage guidance! How dare you!"

Brian takes a deep breath. He's not sure how this argument escalated so quickly.

"I didn't mean it, Linda. I'm just disappointed. I thought you'd be coming back tonight."

"This is my very upset sister we're talking about here, Brian. Her marriage is over, and I'm trying to help her. I'll tell you what! Why don't you go over to see your fake girlfriend? Have a nice night, Brian!" Linda hangs up.

Brian tries phoning her back but only reaches her answer voicemail.

"Linda, stop being childish and answer, please. What the hell was all that about? You shouldn't drink if you can't take it. Please answer. Let's not leave it like this tonight!"

The third time he phones and she doesn't pick up, he throws his phone down on the sun lounger and fetches another bottle of beer.

Chapter Twenty-Five

It's about 8 p.m., and Brian is sitting alone in the back lounge, flicking through the TV channels. Even with all the channels available, he can't find anything of any interest to watch, and he's lost count of how many beers he's drunk. He's bored. He tries Linda's phone again, but it's still switched off.

The doorbell rings. An inset pops up on the TV screen, showing the feed from the CCTV camera at the front door. He can see it's Angela again. He notices that she's very photogenic. She looks younger than he expected. Before opening the door, he quickly checks himself in the hall mirror and fixes his hair parting.

"Hello, Angela. Can't stay away?" he jokes.

"Hi Brian, I was wondering if you and your wife fancied coming over?"

"Well, she's not here, Angela. She's staying at her sister's tonight. I mentioned she might not be back today, if you remember."

"Yeah, I noticed the car wasn't there and wasn't sure if she got a taxi back. Look, Brian, I'm here as a friend. Is everything okay with you guys?"

"It's been a strange kind of day. Come in, Angela."

She follows Brian into the house.

"What a delightful home, Brian. You should buy this place. We need more people like you in Long Island."

"Yeah, it's a beautiful house. Would you like a drink?"
"Ooh, yes, please. I'll have a dry white wine."

Brian opens the fridge, hoping Linda's left some chilling. He finds an open bottle of Chardonnay. It's probably cheap compared to Angela's usual tipple. He opens the glass cupboard and wonders which glass would look most elegant. He chooses a tall-stemmed, tulip-shaped one, fills it two-thirds, and hands it to her.

He grabs the bottle opener and levers the top off another bottle of beer. For a fraction of a second, he wonders whether to fetch himself a glass now Angela's here but decides not to bother and takes a swig before sitting on the sofa.

"Please take a seat, Angela."

She comes to sit a few inches away from him on the sofa and turns towards him, leaning in.

"So what's the problem, Brian?"

"Well, I don't know how this happened, but me and Linda have fallen out over a situation that had nothing to do with us, really. Her sister's having a few problems with her husband, and Linda and I have somehow found ourselves caught up in it. I understand she wants to help her sister, but there's a little bit more to it than that."

"Has your wife stopped to think of you, being here, without really knowing anybody?"

Angela's comments give Brian a sense of self-righteousness. This is exactly what triggered his anger. How selfish of Linda to expect him to stay on his own here while she's having fun in bars and drinking cocktails.

"So, when you say there's a little bit more to it?" Angela probes further.

"Well, we tried helping them out financially. They don't have much money, and to make matters worse, he has a massive gambling problem."

"I'm sure somebody with your intelligence, Brian, already knows that certain people just can't be trusted with money."

"Well, it sounds like you've just described Karen's husband, Tom, perfectly!"

"Take you, for instance. You're a successful British businessman. What does your brother-in-law, er, Tom, do for a living?"

"He works in an engineering workshop in Brooklyn."

"On the factory floor!" Angela gasps and raises her eyebrows.

"Yes."

"God, he sounds like one of those factory manual workers. He definitely doesn't work with his brain like you then? As I say, some people shouldn't be allowed anywhere near money."

"That sounds a little unfair! What do you mean?" Brian smiles to hide his amazement at her statement.

"Well, take Rick, your neighbour. I think he was awarded a handsome financial compensation after a bullet wound in the shoulder cut his police career short. He's obviously exaggerated his medical problems, of course! He looks fine to me. Anyway, what does he do with all that money? When he's not playing with his guns, he drinks morning, noon and night. When you speak to him, you can tell straight away that he's never had money before. Your brother-in-law will be the same.

As I say, Brian, some people are just not meant to have money. They can't cope with it."

Brian looks at Angela with an embarrassed smile. Angela would be shocked if she knew that he was a factory labourer, fortunate enough to come into a big pile of money and that Linda worked on the till in their local supermarket! Nobody was newer to money than they were. Angela might not be so interested in them then.

"Your wife may think she's helping out, but you belong in a different class to your brother-in-law. I thought you Brits knew all about the class system, Brian?" Angela laughs.

"Oh, yeah," Brian joins in the laughter nervously.

"Seriously, though, how could people like him ever know how to deal with money if they've never had it before? Your uncouth neighbour, Rick — do you know, he came to a party at mine one evening, and he told everybody that he'd just come into a load of money. I was so embarrassed! He won't be invited again. Anyway, I'd better be getting back to my guests. Would you like to come over and meet them, Brian?" Angela moves closer to him on the sofa.

Brian stands up quickly.

"I won't tonight, Angela, if that's okay."

"Okay, sure, but I don't like leaving you here on your own." She sets her wine glass on the coffee table.

Brian notices that she hasn't touched it. Probably not good enough for her.

They walk to the door, where Angela turns around and puts her arms on Brian's shoulders. She's quite tall, and Brian's not sure whether she's looking down at him.

"I really don't think your wife should be leaving you here on your own. I know she's helping her sister, but you don't know anyone here. Well, I want you to know, Brian, that you do know somebody now. I regard you as a dear friend, and if you ever need to talk, I'm always here. Never forget that. We need more wealthy, successful people like you in this country, unlike Rick and your brother-in-law. They don't move in the same social circles as you and I."

"Thanks, that's very nice of you, Angela."

She gives Brian a quick kiss on the cheek and hesitates as she pulls away, looking him straight in the eyes.

Brian hastily opens the front door, not sure where to look.

Angela pulls out a card from her jacket pocket.

"If you change your mind about coming over, or you ever need to talk to someone, here's my business card. I'm not trying to advertise my stocks and shares company here, but my personal phone number is on there. I only give this card to people close to me." Angela places her card on the hall mirror shelf.

"Thanks, Angela."

As Brian closes the door, he looks into the mirror again. He feels very pleased with himself and speaks to his reflection: "Wealthy, successful people like you… You're part of the rich set now, Jacko, or as they say back home, 'the upper class'."

His phone rings, and he's pleased to see that it's Linda.

"Hello, how are you doing?" she asks. "I'm sorry about before. I was just a bit upset about Karen. It's all kind of got to me."

"That's okay. I understand. I'm so glad you rang. Are you still in the bar?" Brian walks slowly back into the lounge.

"No, we're back at Karen's. We've brought back something to eat. So what are you up to, Jacko?"

"I'm watching TV."

"Well, at least you never went over to Angela's without me. I'm sorry as well for calling her your girlfriend. I guess I just don't like other women eyeing up my handsome English guy. I know you'd never give her a chance."

Brian thinks it best not to mention that Angela has just left. He picks up the glass of white wine and knocks it back before placing the empty glass in the dishwasher and fetching himself another beer.

"So, are you bringing Karen up to Long Island tomorrow?"

"Yes, I've persuaded her to take some time off from school. She's been through a lot lately."

"Yeah, she could do with a break. Do you know something, Linda?"

"What?"

"I suppose when you think about it, some people are just not meant to have money."

"Well, definitely not Tom," Linda replies.

"I don't mean just Tom. I mean people in general who aren't used to it."

"I don't understand, Brian?"

"Well, if someone isn't used to having money, how do they know how to deal with things if they suddenly come into it."

"A bit like us, you mean?"

"Well, I'd like to think I'm a bit better, at least a bit savvier with money."

"A bit better, Brian? I've never heard you speak like that before."

"You know what I mean, Linda!"

"No, I don't really. I hope you're not really turning into an English snob. Who do you think you're better than, Brian?"

"Well, don't you think we're better than people like Tom and Karen?" he asks.

"No, I don't. I think he's got a gambling problem, and he's an idiot. But fundamentally, we're no better in any way than Karen and Tom are. There's no class system in the US like you Brits have."

"I never used to think about this, really, Linda, but I'm beginning to understand why there are different levels in society. Some people just don't understand the concept of money."

"Wow, what have you been watching on TV, Brian? I've never heard you talk like this! Where is this coming from?"

"Well, maybe it's taken our recent good fortune for me to realise it."

"Look, Brian, you and I have fortunately fallen on our feet with our recent good fortune, and I'll be eternally grateful for that. But I don't think I'm any better than or belong in a separate class from anybody else. And I'm a bit surprised to hear you come out with something like that!"

"I'm not saying I'm better than anybody, Linda."

"Well, it certainly sounds like that to me, Brian."

"All I'm saying is that I can understand why there are different sections of society."

"Well, we can talk tomorrow. Karen's just served the food. We'll see you tomorrow. Oh, and I'd stop watching whatever you're watching if I were you. I love you, even though you really are becoming an English snob!" Linda laughs.

"And I love you, you crazy Yank. See you tomorrow."

Chapter Twenty-Six

Brian is woken by Linda's phone call.

"I hope you're not still in bed, Jacko. Me and Karen are on our way and should be there within the hour. And I hope the house is tidy."

Brian can hear the smile in Linda's voice, so he knows she's only teasing him.

"It's ten o'clock. Of course I'm up!" He jumps up out of bed, grateful that she phoned to warn him of their arrival.

"Karen thought you'd still be in bed."

Brian can hear them both laughing.

"Well, she was wrong, wasn't she? See you both soon," he replies.

Perhaps he should cut down on all the beers. He wonders how many he had the previous evening and makes a mental note to count the empties.

He races down to start clearing the rubbish, including all the beer bottles. There are nine. He tries to remember what time he started drinking.

It wouldn't seem so bad if they were stretched out over the evening. He can't remember spilling beer on the floor, but his bare feet stick to the kitchen tiles, so he quickly wipes them over with the mop. He inspects each room for more rubbish and then jumps into the shower to freshen up. His timing is perfect. Just as he's finished getting dressed, he hears Linda and Karen park up.

"Told you he was up, Karen," Linda says as they join Brian in the kitchen.

"Hi Karen," Brian says as he gives Linda a big hug. "Sit down, girls, and I'll make some coffee."

"Thanks, Brian. Not had any yourself yet, then?" teases Karen.

"Have you spoken with your mum and the kids?" Brian asks Linda.

"Yeah. Mom said they all had a lovely day yesterday in Central Park. Dan and his friend Christine are taking them to the Statue of Liberty today."

"I wouldn't have minded going there myself. I'm getting a bit fed up with hanging out by the pool," Brian says.

"Well, me and Karen are looking forward to taking it easy by the pool. I can't be bothered moving anywhere today."

"Have you had something to eat?" Brian asks.

"Yeah," the women respond together, laughing.

"What's so funny?"

"We just reheated that leftover takeaway from last night. It always tastes better the next day. We'll grab some lunch later."

"Well, I'm going to walk down to the beach for breakfast."

"Why don't you just make some toast, and I'll prepare us all something nice for lunch in a couple of hours?"

"No, I'm going now. I'm absolutely starving, and I can't be bothered making anything. I'm going to treat myself to a nice, sit-down breakfast. Do you need anything bringing back, ladies?"

"No, I'm okay. I'm just going to chill by the pool while the kids are away," Linda says.

"And I'm fine, thanks, Brian," Karen adds.

"Okay, see you both soon. Don't forget the sun cream."

*****

Brian walks down towards the beach. With the kids at their nan and grandad's and Linda spending another day with her sister, he begins to feel at a loose end and a bit left out. In the Beachcomber restaurant, he chooses the best table overlooking the sea. A waitress with two long plaits and designer-torn jeans brings him a menu and some coffee. There's hardly anyone there, and it's a gorgeous day. He browses through the menu and feels a tap on his shoulder. He looks around, and Angela is standing there in her shorts and T-shirt.

"Oh, look, if it isn't Daniel Craig. What are you doing here all alone? I saw your wife's car in the drive, so I assume everything's okay?"

"Oh yeah, she stayed by the pool with her sister, Karen. They're both suffering the effects of a hangover, from what I can tell. There's lots of giggling going on but little energy to do anything."

"Do you mind if I join you? PJ's out golfing with friends, and I'm alone today."

"Please do, Angela. It would be nice to have the company."

"Well, as I said before, Brian, I'm always here if you need to talk. Are you having something to eat?"

"Yeah." Brian picks up the menu again as the waitress arrives. He notices there's a chain hanging across the back of her jeans and wonders whether she can sit comfortably in them.

"Can I have a full breakfast and some more coffee, please?"

"And I'll have the waffle with maple syrup, please, and the apple and cinnamon tea."

Angela turns to Brian. "I'm quite the sweet tooth."

"Well, you certainly don't need to worry about your figure, Angela!"

"Thank you."

"I take it you've been out walking?"

"Yeah, I like to get my ten thousand steps in every morning. I was just on my way back to cook something to eat, and then I saw my handsome English neighbour sitting all alone. So is Karen staying with you guys now?"

"She sure is."

"Great, your wife is looking after her sister, but I just hope she doesn't forget about you, especially as you hardly know anybody here."

"Even the kids are visiting all the sites in Manhattan," says Brian. "We haven't been anywhere yet."

Brian feels a little guilty whining when his own hangover is pretty painful, too. He has to admit that he's no saint himself.

"Poor Brian." Angela catches his hand but then pulls away as the waitress refills Brian's coffee and places a tall glass of apple and cinnamon tea in front of Angela.

The smell of cinnamon reaches Brian's nostrils and seems to ease his headache a little.

Chapter Twenty-Seven

Meanwhile, back at Sundrive, Linda goes up to change into her swimsuit and brings the sun cream down with her so Karen can use it too. She rummages in her handbag for a scrunchie for her hair and looks around for a mirror. She heads for the downstairs toilet, which is in the hall by the stairs, but as she pulls the door open, she hears Karen shout.
"Sorry! Forgot to lock it. Be out in a minute."

Linda stands in front of the hall mirror. She's putting a little weight on with all the eating and drinking they've been doing since they won the lottery. She'll have to pull the reins in. She wonders if Brian has noticed. She stands sideways and pulls her tummy in. Not good at all. Perhaps she should buy one of those chiffon blouses to wear over her swimsuit.

"Admiring yourself, are you?" Karen teases.

"Absolutely not! Look at me! I'm double the woman I was a year ago. When did I pile all this on?"

Linda takes hold of her tummy to emphasise her concern to Karen.

"Don't be silly. You can only be a size 12, surely? Compared to most of my friends our age, you're petite!"

Linda opens the suncream and puts the lid on the shelf under the mirror. She passes the tub to Karen and notices a business card next to the lid on the shelf. She picks it up. Displayed right across the middle in bold print are the words Angela Jenkinson (Stocks and Shares). She wonders why Angela's card is there and then remembers Brian mentioning that Angela had invited them over last night. She must have left her card when she called. A little odd, but the woman is a little odd!

Linda's head is pounding, and when she looks closely in the mirror, she can see her hangover isn't doing her forehead wrinkles any favours. She is tired and a little exhausted from all the emotional support she's been giving Karen. She wants Karen to see that she can cope without Tom and that her choice to cut him out of her life is the best way forward, but hiding her own worries about how Karen might feel when the anger has died down is draining. She isn't sure this is the best solution after all. One minute, Tom and Karen are trying for a baby, and the next minute, Tom isn't part of her life at all. Whatever they all think about Tom, everything has happened very quickly. Relationships are strange. She fleetingly pictures herself and Brian and feels lucky.

But just as quickly, her mind returns to Angela. Had she come into the house? If so, how long did she stay, and what happened while she was there?

"I'm having a coffee. Do you fancy one?" Karen interrupts.

Linda picks the card up again.

"I said, do you fancy a coffee?"

"Er, what?"

"For heaven's sake! What's the matter with you? For the third time, do you want a coffee?"

"Er, no thanks, Karen. Sorry."

"Is everything okay? What's that you've got there?"

Linda quickly tries to compose herself. Karen has enough going on in her life at the moment.

"No, I'm okay. I'm just feeling a bit delicate from all that booze."

"I'll tell you one thing, Linda, this house is much cleaner than mine. You've got a good husband in Brian."

"Yeah." Linda places the card back on the shelf, smudged now with sun cream.

Karen walks out to the pool with her coffee, and Linda follows her out. Seeing Angela's business card has — for some reason that she can't quite understand — cast doubt in Linda's mind. It's as though a cloud is hanging over her. She's not usually the jealous type, but now it seems strange to her that Brian was so adamant about eating at the beach and in such a hurry to leave the house. She feels a certain frustration that their lives are never quite free of worry. Once they got the lottery money, she thought all their problems would be over, but it was as if new, bigger problems had come with the money, like Deano's problems, Karen's problems, and now she was starting to think her husband might be straying. She'd never felt like this before. What on earth was happening?

"Karen, I'm just going to the store to pick up some soft drinks. We haven't got much left in the fridge, and I feel I should take it easy on the booze for a day or so."

"But you're all togged up for the pool, and you've put sun cream on now! Wait an hour or so. What's the rush? I'll come with you later."

"It's okay. I'll put a dress on over this. I'll drive, and it'll only take a few minutes. I can get some salad for lunch, too. You enjoy the sun!"

Linda can hear that her voice is shaking. She hopes Karen won't notice. Perhaps it's the hangover.

"You do sound shaky, but I doubt it's a hangover. You were okay driving this morning. I don't feel poorly, and I had more than you, but then I'm probably used to it. I can tell you, living with Tom, it's hard to avoid."

"I'm okay. I won't be long." Linda heads upstairs to get dressed again.

*****

Driving down to the beach, Linda can't believe she's doing this. In their eight years of marriage, she has never once had any reason to doubt her husband. But her sixth sense is telling her that something is not quite right.

She parks across the road from the Beachcomber restaurant she suspects Brian would choose, and her suspicions are confirmed. This is the up-market bar where they first met Angela and PJ. She's shocked to see Brian sitting comfortably at a sea-view table with Angela. She can see them both clearly. Her whole body starts to shake. She sees them laughing and joking. She feels a sharp stab of jealousy, something she's never experienced before in her entire life.

She sits there just looking at them eating their breakfast, hands occasionally wrapped around their hot drinks. Angela sets her drink down and reaches across to touch Brian's arm, and they both burst out laughing. At a certain moment, Angela seems to turn to look out at the street. Linda hopes she's parked far enough away for Angela not to notice or recognise the car, but Angela continues her conversation with Brian. Brian seems to be beckoning the waitress over and ordering something.

She rings Brian and breathlessly watches him answer his phone. He stands up and walks away from the table.

"Hi Linda, everything okay?"

"Will you be long?" she asks.

"Will I be long? I've only just left the house, you crazy Yank."

"Would you bring some cold orange juice back with you, please?"

"God, I thought you were going to say Tom had turned up or something. Is that all you want, some orange juice? Yeah, I'll bring some back."

"How long will you be?" Linda asks again.

"Well, I was going to go for a walk after I'd eaten. You're not in that much of a hurry for orange juice, are you? Must be a really bad hangover if that's the case!"

"Well, yes. Can you bring the juice back first, please?"

"God, Linda! You mean you want me to go to the shop, come home, and then come back. That's ridiculous. You're behaving so childishly. It's not like you. What's the matter?"

"Don't bother, then, if it's too much to ask!" Linda shouts. "I'll drive down and get it myself."

"Okay, okay! I'll bring it. Now, can I finish my breakfast, please?"

"Will you be long?"

"About twenty minutes."

"Thank you." She hangs up.

Linda continues to watch Brian and Angela laughing together. She instinctively feels that they must be laughing at her. She can't believe this is happening. All these years, they've had disagreements, fallouts, and even some really low times, but never anything like this. Angela's long locks rest in voluptuous curls on her shoulders, and she looks young and fresh in her T-shirt. Linda looks at herself in the rear-view mirror and sees the dark rings that her hangover has produced under her eyes. Her hair is limp and unwashed, and she didn't bother to put any makeup on before she set off this morning. She sees her husband in a new light. He's happy, laughing, and he's with someone else. It shakes her to the core. When did this start? What happened last night?

Linda's hands are shaking as she flips her seatbelt loose. She pulls the key out of the ignition and opens the door. She'll confront them. But as she steps out of the car, her phone rings. It's Debbie. She can't take it now. Her head's not straight. She needs to sort her own life out right now.

She selects the 'busy' response to ignore the call, but it immediately starts ringing again. She ignores the call and is getting out when her phone starts ringing again. She suddenly realises it's the middle of the night in England and there may be something wrong. Plus, she doesn't want the phone to ring when she walks over to confront Brian and Angela.

This time, she answers it.

"Hi, Debbie. Do you mind if I phone you straight back? I'm just shopping at the moment."

Debbie doesn't respond, and all Linda can hear is crying from the other end of the line.

"Is everything okay, Debbie? Hold on! I can't hear you properly." Linda gets back into the car and closes the door. That's better, I can hear you now. What's the matter, honey?"

"Linda, I'm sorry to trouble you," Debbie sobs, "I tried phoning Brian last night and this morning, but he's not answering."

"Oh yeah, he's a bit busy at the moment, Debbie. So, what's happened, love?"

"I don't know where to start. You think you know somebody, Linda, and then everything changes."

"Yes, I know what you mean, Debbie." Linda looks across to where her husband is still sitting with a woman who has made it very clear that she's interested in him.

"I haven't heard from Deano for almost a week. Not even a phone call. I've had the estate agent on the phone. We need to pay the deposit by Monday, or we'll lose the house. I'm worried sick."

"And I take it Deano has the money?"

"Yes."

The two women fall silent while Linda works out what to do.

"Debbie, are you still there? Can you hear me?"

"Yeah. I'm still here."

"What a time for Deano to disappear. God, what is it with men!"

"This is the man I'm meant to be marrying. I'm having his child, and I don't even know where he is! What am I going to do, Linda?" Debbie breaks down into loud sobs.

"Debbie, did you just say that you're pregnant?"

"Yes," Debbie replied quietly.

"I didn't know."

"I didn't know myself until last night."

"Well, well, that's wonderful news, Debbie. Congratulations! I wish things were better for you right now, but this is lovely news, isn't it?" Linda hears Debbie sniffing still. "Look, Debbie, I'm sure everything's going to come right, you'll see."

In her head, Linda was hoping she was right and Deano would turn out to be an okay guy, although her confidence in men right now wasn't very strong.

"I don't know what to do. I've always thought Deano was a good bloke. Had this happened earlier, I'd have been happy, Linda. But now, I'm not sure."

"You know the sad thing about betrayal, Debbie? It never comes from an enemy. But will you please listen to me very carefully?"

"Yeah, of course."

"I've got something very important to tell you."

"Oh Linda, Deano hasn't run off with another woman, has he? Is that what you're going to tell me?" The sobbing starts again.

"God, no. Well, I bloody hope not, Debbie. But you need to know this. It's about the money for the house."

"Yeah, Brian told me that you guys helped with the deposit. I can't thank you enough."

"Debbie, it wasn't just the deposit. You are under the impression that Brian sent Deano £28,000. Is that correct?"

"Well, yes. Isn't that what happened?"

"No, Debbie. He sent Deano £300,000 to buy your house outright so you would be mortgage-free."

"He sent Deano £300,000?"

"Yes. We've recently come into some money, and we wanted to help you out. Plus, Brian was convinced it would help Deano to get back on the straight and narrow."

"Oh my god! Oh my god, Linda. I had no idea. You don't think he's disappeared with the money, do you?"

"I've no idea, but I hope not. I'm not feeling very charitable towards men at the moment, but in all fairness, we need to hear what Deano has to say."

"You're right. I need to know what's going on."

"But I just want to reassure you, Debbie, that everything will be okay. Either way, I will personally see to it that you still get your house. And that's my promise to you. When do you have to pay the deposit?"

Debbie is crying again. "By Monday."

"We'll give Deano another few days, but if we haven't heard from him by then, I'll send you the money. So, there's no need to worry about the house. But I'm afraid I can't help you with Deano."

Some movement in the restaurant catches Linda's eye. Brian and Angela are standing up.

"Debbie, I'm going to have to go. Can I phone you later?"

"I don't know what to say, but thank you, Linda."

"Okay, I'll have to go, Debbie. Speak to you soon."

Brian and Angela begin walking away from the restaurant and towards Sundrive. Brian seems to have forgotten the orange juice and walks past the store with Angela.

Linda drives home the long way round to avoid their seeing her. Once inside, she goes upstairs and peeks out of their bedroom window. Brian and Angela are just entering Sundrive. They arrive outside Angela's house and continue talking for a few minutes. Then Angela gives Brian a quick hug and waves goodbye. Linda quickly runs downstairs and pretends to be making some coffee as Brian enters the house.

Chapter Twenty-Eight

Linda hears the front door, and Brian joins her in the kitchen. Her hands are still shaking as she sips her coffee.

"Oh yes, I'll have a coffee, please," Brian asks.

"How was your breakfast?" Linda asks. She stands up and moves across the kitchen to pour him a coffee.

"It was okay. Why are you sitting here alone?"

"I just feel a little tired, you know. The restaurant was only 'just okay'? Was it busy?" Linda offers him his coffee.

"It was pretty quiet. We're in for another warm day. Is Karen by the pool? I wouldn't mind a dip myself."

Brian opens the fridge to get some milk and takes the mug of coffee from Linda. He grips it around the edge so she can let go of the handle.

"Ow, that's hot!"

"Sorry. So, you didn't have to wait long for a table?"

"No, not really. So, you and Karen are relaxing today, then?"

Brian pours some milk into his coffee and returns the milk to the fridge, slamming the door as he does so. He takes a sip and carries it outside. Linda follows him out.

"Yeah, we're taking it easy today," she answers deadpan.

The way he keeps changing the subject worries her. Why is he being so evasive? Why not mention that Angela was there?

"I bet this is better than being at work, Karen?" Brian says.

"Oh, you can say that again, Brian."

"Oh, I forgot the orange juice, Linda. Sorry, it totally slipped my mind."

"Just as well you went out to get some, Linda," Karen laughs. "Did you go to the breakfast café we went to?"

"Er, no. I went to the beach breakfast bar on the front."

"The posh one? Where all the rich people go?"

"So, you're taking some time off work, Karen?"

Linda begins to feel irritated as Brian avoids the questions. He must have something to hide. He chose to go to the beachcomber bar where Angela hangs out, where they first met her.

"Yeah, I'm taking the rest of the week off. We should have gone down to the restaurant with you, Brian, instead of letting you eat on your own." Karen says.

Brian looks up at Linda, but when she looks back at him, he quickly looks away.

"I don't know why you'd want to go there. It's full of pretentious people," she challenges.

"So, how are the kids?" Brian changes the subject yet again.

"I told you earlier. They're fine. Karen and I popped in to see them on our way here. Dan and Christine are taking them to see the Statue of Liberty today. By the way, Dan saw Tom in Spuds Bar last night, and he was pretty drunk. He said he wouldn't let Karen leave him broke while she had all that money. Dan asked, 'What money'? So, I had to tell him, Brian."

"Yeah, better coming from you, I suppose, than him hearing Tom's drunken version."

"I told him we were just waiting for the right time to tell him."

"Was he surprised?"

"Not as much as I thought he would be, although he's happy we're going to look after him, too. He understands us not wanting everybody to know, but he's worried we'll need to watch Tom as he's not a happy man. He's right, too. Tom's got a gambling and drinking illness that none of us are qualified to help him with."

Karen's phone begins to ring.

"Speak of the devil. Here's Tom ringing now," says Karen.

"Are you not going to answer it, Karen? He's only going to keep ringing," warns Linda.

"I've got nothing to say to him. I've said all I want to say."

"Karen, if you've really had enough of him, why don't you just give him some money and pay him off? We've certainly got enough money to do that," suggests Brian.

"That's no use," snaps Linda. "He'll only lose it all and then come back looking for more. Karen needs a good lawyer now to put a proper end to this." Linda can't believe that Brian is suggesting giving money to a gambler. What is the matter with him?

"Yeah, but how long will that take?" asks Brian. "Just give him half a million and explain that once that's gone, he won't be getting any more."

Linda takes a deep breath and sighs.

"I know you mean well, Brian, but Linda is right," Karen says. "He would definitely just spend it and come back asking for more. I want to cut off ties with him once and for all. I need to for my own well-being. You and Linda giving me this money is an opportunity for me to start a new life."

"Karen, if you want him to stop bothering you every few minutes, just call him back and tell him your lawyer is looking after everything," Linda interrupts.

"Do you know something, sis? You're absolutely right! I'll calmly explain the situation to him, from one adult to another." Karen ties a sun wrap around her waist and takes her phone with her inside.

Linda looks at Brian and wonders what to say. She remembers Debbie's call.

"By the way, Debbie phoned earlier. She tried ringing you several times."

"I know. I can't be dealing with her and Deano at the moment, Linda. She's only going to tell me that he's still missing. I shouldn't have given him any money."

"The poor girl was distraught when she phoned me. It was the middle of the night in England. She's about to lose the house. That's why she was trying to call you."

"Well, that's Deano's fault, Linda, not mine!"

"Exactly, Brian. Deano's fault, not Debbie's."

"So? What am I supposed to do? Organise a national search party for Deano?" Brian raises his voice and throws his arms in the air.

"She's pregnant, Brian," Linda says sharply.

"She's pregnant?"

"Yes, she's pregnant. And she's got a few days left to pay the deposit on the house. And your mate has selfishly gone missing."

"Well, that's unfortunate, but why should I feel responsible for their problems? Like I said, some people should never be allowed anywhere near money."

"Their problems, Brian? The only person I can see with the problem here is Debbie. Your friend, who has disappeared with the money, doesn't have a care in the world. So, it's not their problem. It's poor Debbie's problem. And where did 'some people should never be allowed anywhere near money' come from? You didn't used to believe that! I don't know what's happening to you, Brian, but you're not the person I used to know. I never thought I'd say this, but this money is really changing you."

"Am I supposed to feel bad just because I have money and other people don't?"

"Oh my god! Just listen to yourself, Brian. Do you know who you're beginning to sound like?"

"Who?" he asks.

"Angela and PJ across the road, who look down on people who haven't as much money as…"

"Hold on!" Brian interrupts, but Linda is livid now.

"I haven't finished yet. Here's big, rich Brian sitting by the pool in a big, beautiful mansion in Long Island, and there's Debbie, now pregnant in her little flat in Liverpool, worried sick that she's going to lose her little terraced house that she's worked so hard for." Linda is standing now, leaning over Brian in his lounger.

Linda glares at him. Doesn't he feel anything for Debbie?

"You don't like Angela and PJ, and the only reason is because they have money. But you don't really know them, so you're prejudiced!"

"I know he's old enough to be her dad and that she's out looking for her next fix in her sad, rich, fake life of hers!"

"Wow, you really don't like her, do you?"

"I don't really know her, Brian. I only met her the other night, just like you did. But if I'm being totally honest with you, no, I don't particularly like her. From what I've seen of her so far, she comes across as a very false person with far too much time and money on her hands."

Karen coughs from the kitchen and then returns to the pool area.

"Well, that was a big mistake. He was still drunk, and he didn't listen to a word I was saying. I tried explaining that the lawyers are sorting everything out."

"Well, at least you told him," Linda says, sitting back down on her lounger.

"He said he owes a lot of money, and he's coming out to Long Island to get his share."

"Well, let him try calling here! He'll be sorry," says Brian.

"He sounded very angry. I've never known him like this before." Karen sits back down on her lounger.

"Well, he's bound to be annoyed. He's just realised he's going to be missing out on all that money," says Brian.

Karen frowns and picks up her coffee mug from next to the lounger.

"Actually, it's getting a bit warm for me out here. I'm going to sit inside for a while." She collects Linda's and Brian's empty mugs and takes them inside.

Linda takes a deep breath.

"Poor Karen. Tom must owe loads of money to all kinds of people. Stupid man," says Linda.

"I told you that we shouldn't have told family, not until we had things in place. The lottery woman told us too, old squeaky voice. But you! Oh no, you wouldn't listen to me or her!"

"I wouldn't listen to you? It was you who told Deano, remember? So don't be putting all this on me, Brian."

"And another thing — I'm fed up with having to deal with all these losers."

"All these losers? Who do you think you are, Brian?"

"I'm a millionaire, Linda! That's who I am, a millionaire. And it's time I started living like one."

"And don't you think I want to enjoy life as well? But before I can do that, I've got one or two people to look after, like, in case you haven't noticed, my sister. And I'm going to take her to see a good lawyer this afternoon."

"I thought you said you were relaxing by the pool today?"

"That was before Tom phoned and threatened to come out here to Long Island."

"In case you have forgotten, Linda, I don't know anybody in this country, and I've had enough of sitting here waiting for you."

"There's nothing stopping you from coming with us, Brian."

"I'm not going to see any lawyers, Linda. I should be out enjoying life, buying a big boat or a helicopter, or skiing down a mountain or something, instead of dealing with other people's problems."

Linda stares at the man she thought was her husband. A frown creeps across her face.

"Other people's problems?" she shouts. She doesn't care if Karen hears her. The anger is just boiling up inside her. "I can't believe you! This is my younger sister we're talking about here, Brian. She needs me right now, and if you can't understand that, then we've got real problems."

"Well, you go and look after her then," Brian bellows. "Oh, and take care of Debbie and Deano as well. And if Tom does turn up here making threats, just call the police because I'm not getting involved anymore. I'm going out." Brian storms out of the house, slamming the front door behind him.

Linda follows after him out into the hall. She looks on the shelf for Angela's business card, but it's gone.

Chapter Twenty-Nine

It's early afternoon, and Long Island is experiencing a warmer climate than usual as Brian walks along the beach in his T-shirt, shorts, and sandals. He doesn't really know where he's walking but needs to get away from the house, which is currently filled with doom and gloom.

His wallet, containing his bank cards, is tucked inside his shorts pocket. He knows the bank cards aren't just ordinary bank cards. The cards he now walks around with daily are worth millions of pounds. This knowledge gives him an incredible feeling of being able to do whatever he likes, something he has never experienced before in his life. He contemplates flying to Vegas or perhaps travelling down to South America and sailing along the Amazon. He could buy a fleet of luxurious sports cars. He'd always wanted one, and now he could buy several. Yet, for some strange reason, now that he can afford to do all these things and more, something is holding him back.

He finds himself walking into the Beachcomber Bar. It's still early and quiet. He approaches the bar and orders a bottle of beer. He brings his bottle to the rear of the bistro overlooking the picturesque beach.

He retrieves Angela's business card from his wallet and stares at it for a couple of minutes, unsure whether to call her. She told him to phone her if he ever needed to talk. After a short deliberation, he decides to phone her.

"Hello, Angela, it's Brian. Hope I'm not disturbing you."

"You'll never disturb me, James Bond. Is everything okay?"

"I was just wondering if that offer to talk was still open?"

"I told you, Brian, whenever you need to speak to me, I'm always available. Are you at home? I'll come over."

"No, I'm in the Beachcomber."

"Can you give me ten minutes?"

Brian takes another swig of his beer. Although he's grateful for the company, he wishes it was Linda coming to join him. Why can't Linda just take some time to enjoy all this with him? Looking out at the beautiful beach whilst waiting for Angela, his thoughts are suddenly brought back to Liverpool, working 12-hour shifts in a factory and struggling to pay his mortgage.

He was never sure then what to do with his life. Despite now having £17 million in the bank, he's still not sure what he wants to do. His mum, Sandra, pops into his mind. Oh my god, he thinks. All of Linda's family now know about his win, but his own mother still doesn't know. He decides to put this right before Angela arrives and dials her number.

"Hello, Mam, how are you?"

"Wow, that's strange. I was just going to phone you, Brian. I just said to Billy, I haven't heard from our Brian and hope he hasn't run off with some rich American woman." Sandra laughs.

"Rich American woman?" Brian frowns, feeling that his mum can see his every move.

"I'm kidding, son. What rich American woman would be interested in a factory worker from Liverpool? Ha, ha. Only kidding again. They'd all be queuing up for my son. Best son in the world, lad. I'm great, thanks, son. How are Linda and the kids?"

"We're all great. I was just out having a walk, and I thought I'd give you a call."

"So, are you all having a nice holiday? Where are you again?"

"We're in Long Island. It's about an hour from New York. It's really nice here. In fact, I'm looking at a beautiful beach with a cold beer in my hand."

"Bloody hell, Brian. It's alright for some."

"We're thinking of staying out here a bit longer. You and Billy could come out and visit us. Talking of Billy, how is he? Is he still a big moaner?"

"Ha, yeah. He's just gone to pick up his arthritis tablets. When he comes back, we're meant to be buying a new car today. Well, it's not that new, but it's better than that old banger we're driving around in. Billy saw it advertised yesterday. It sounds like a good bargain."

"How much is it, Mam?"

"I think it's advertised for £3,500. But Billy's hoping to get the price down a bit, maybe to £3,250."

"So, has Billy left the house, did you say, Mam?"

"Yeah, he's just gone."

"Mam. I've got something to tell you."

"Is everything okay, love?"

"Yeah, don't worry, everything's fine. Just don't buy that car, Mam."

"Oh, you're not going to start giving me advice about cars again, are you, Brian?"

"Mam, I was going to tell you when the time was right, but me and Linda have come into some money. Well, it's quite a bit of money, actually. I wasn't sure how to tell you. But why don't you and Billy buy a brand new 4x4 or whatever you like? I'll send you the money for it."

"What the hell are you talking about, Brian?"

"Linda has already told all her family over here. So, it's only fair that I tell you and Billy. We won a good few million on the lottery, Mam. We're going to buy you and Billy a bungalow. It will definitely help Billy with his arthritis."

"You're not joking, are you, Brian?"

"I'm deadly serious, Mam."

"Oh my god, Brian, you really are serious! When did this happen?"

Brian could hear the incredulity in his mum's voice.

"It was only a couple of weeks ago. I wasn't sure how to tell you."

"Oh my god. I don't know what to say, my love. That's fantastic news."

"Mam, I only ask you and Billy one thing, please?"

"You don't want us to tell anybody."

"Exactly, Mam. We don't need everyone knowing our business. For some reason, it only seems to invite trouble."

"Okay, I'll tell Billy not to mention it. Oh my god, Brian. So, what do you and Linda plan to do, love?"

"We're not sure yet. We're still getting over the shock ourselves. As I said, we may stay here for a little while. You and Billy can come over if you like."

"Brian, I still can't believe it."

"Mam, I'll send you some money today. I mean serious money."

"How much were you thinking?"

"I don't know. Why don't I send you a million, Mam?"

"Oh my god, Brian, a million?"

"Why not? You're my Mam, aren't you? Promise me you'll be careful and keep this to yourselves?"

"I may need a glass of Billy's Scotch! Only kidding. I'll be okay, but I still can't believe it, Brian."

Brian can see Angela approaching.

"Mam, I'll have to go. Tell Billy, after you've resuscitated him from the shock, that I said hello, and I'll speak to you later. Love you, Mam."

"Love you too, son."

Brian puts the phone down, feeling ecstatic. That sense of helping someone you love is an unbelievable feeling.

"Hello, Brian, busy man on the phone, I see," Angela says, twisting to show off her profile in a skin-tight silk dress as she leans in to kiss his cheek.

Brian notices how beautifully svelte and cool she looks.

"I was just on the phone to Liverpool."

"An international business call. You're such a highflier, Brian."

"What can I get you to drink, Angela?"

"I'll have a fresh orange juice, please."

Angela takes a seat opposite him, leaning forward so Brian catches a glimpse of her cleavage. Brian beckons a waiter over and orders her drink and another beer.

"So, is everything okay?"

"I don't want to burden you with my problems."

"That's okay."

"Well, Linda is taking her sister, Karen, to a lawyer this afternoon. Karen's husband is a drunk and a compulsive gambler. But I feel that doctors and solicitors should be dealing with all this, not Linda. I didn't bring my family to the US for all of this. We came for a holiday. I was hoping we could all enjoy life here for a while. I understand Karen is her sibling, but this sort of thing is for professionals to sort out, not us. And I've got the money to pay for all the help Karen needs."

"As I've already said to you, Brian, Linda needs to understand that you're a stranger, all alone here. I hope you don't mind my saying, but I think your wife is being selfish. She's certainly not thinking of you."

"I don't understand why she needs to go with Karen to see a lawyer. Karen has decided she no longer wants to be with Tom. Fair enough. All she has to do is to start divorce proceedings with her lawyer. That's why you pay lawyers—to handle all the stress."

"I don't know if you've noticed, Brian, but I don't entertain any kind of stress in my life. Is your job stressful?"

"I've retired, Angela. I'm no longer working."

"You've retired at your age? God, you must have been successful, Brian. Well, that's almost me. I'm retiring at the end of the year. If it was up to PJ, he'd work until he collapsed. He has absolutely no concept of fun whatsoever. God, he's so miserable."

"I don't understand, Angela. If he's so miserable, why are you with him?"

The waiter arrives with a tray and sets their drinks on the table. He places a bowl of pretzels between them, and Angela reaches out for one.

"Isn't it obvious, Brian?"

"You mean you're with him for the money?"

"We're only here once."

"Ha, that's most definitely true."

"Every time I speak to my shrink, I come away thinking, I'm going to enjoy life to the full. I was hurt once, and I promise you that will never happen to me ever again, whether in love or in business."

"So, were you hurt in love or in business?" Brian asks. He then realises that perhaps he's offended her. They hardly know each other but seem to be sharing some quite personal confidences.

"I'm so sorry, Angela. It wasn't my place to ask that or to ask why you're with PJ. I don't know what came over me." He reaches out to take a handful of pretzels and puts a couple in his mouth.

"Brian, we're neighbours, and I hope, by now, something more? No, I've never been in love, so I'll let you work that one out." Angela leans towards him and takes a sip of her orange juice.

Brian laughs.

"You know what a hedonistic person is, don't you, Brian?"

"A person seeking constant pleasure."

"Of course you know. You're a self-made, successful British businessman. We're so alike, you and I, Brian."

Brian is quite impressed with this. He warms to her praise and begins to feel relaxed. He knocks back his second beer.

"I hope your wife appreciates you. Maybe we should match her up with PJ?" Angela smiles, and Brian smiles back at her.

"Do you know, Angela, it's definitely time to have fun. I really enjoy your company. You make me feel so happy."

"What a lovely thing to say, Brian. Us hedonistic people should stick together!"

"You're so right, Angela. Life is all about happiness, isn't it?"

"Brian, you're a successful businessman. You don't need me to tell you to look after number one."

"I must admit, I'm beginning to think like that."

"Beginning, Brian? You need to think a lot more like that. As I've said, we're only here once."

"You're so right, Angela!"

"I'd say that it seems your wife is neglecting you. Would you like me to be your guide around the Big Apple? We could go into Manhattan for the rest of the day if that appeals to you?"

"I'd love that, Angela. I really would. But I'm not really dressed for it."

"I wouldn't worry about that. You look fine to me, but we could always pick something up for you."

"Yeah, of course."

"If you wait here a couple of minutes, I'll fetch my car."

"Okay! Thank you, Angela. That would be just great!"

Brian orders another beer while he waits for Angela.

Chapter Thirty

Karen enters the kitchen, fixing her hair back in a bun.

"Is everything okay with you and Brian, Linda? I heard most of that argument."

"Oh, it's just him. He can be so childish at times."
"He's right, though. I don't need you to come with me to see a lawyer. You two need some time together."

"Does he expect me not to look after my little sister?"

"Oh, come on, Linda, I already feel bad enough being here without you guys falling out."

"It's not your fault, Karen. Brian can be very selfish when he wants to be."

"Linda, the last thing I need right now is to see you two squabbling, and I certainly don't want you bickering over me. Anyway, where's he gone?"

"I don't know, probably down to The Beachcomber bar."

"Right, I'm going down there to fetch him back."

"Just leave him, Karen. If he wants to sulk, let him sulk."

"No, I'll go and explain that I don't need you with me today. I can manage just fine on my own. I may not be able to make an appointment today in any case."

"Honestly, Karen, believe me, money talks. You'll be able to get an appointment if I talk to them. I want to help you, and I shouldn't have to explain everything to Brian all the time. After all, you are my sister."

"I appreciate that, but we've got enough trouble on our plates with me and Tom without my causing a rift between you and Brian. I'm going to find him now and bring him back. And that's the end of the matter, Linda. I won't be long. Bye."

To Linda's surprise, Karen grabs her handbag and leaves, letting the front door swing shut behind her. Linda sighs and goes out to sit by the pool. She suddenly feels terribly sad. Lying back on a sun lounger, she closes her eyes and tries to work out what on earth is going on in her life.

*****

Linda must be tired because she dozes off immediately and is woken by footsteps approaching. She opens her eyes to see Karen looking rather forlorn, standing in front of her.

"Well, where is he?" Linda asks.

"Erm, he wasn't in the bar," Karen replies. She rummages in her handbag and retrieves her phone.

"He wasn't there?"
"No, he wasn't."

"What's wrong, Karen?"

"What do you mean?" Karen turns away from her sister's gaze and drops down on the adjacent sun lounger. She kicks her shoes off and lies back.

"Okay, Karen, it's me you're talking to now. You've got to be honest. I think I know what's going on. He was sitting in the bar with a brown-haired woman, wasn't he?"

"No, Linda," Karen answers just a little too quickly for Linda to be able to believe her.

"I can see it in your face," Linda responds. "Tell me the truth, Karen. Was he with a woman with long brown hair?"

"No, he wasn't in the bar, Linda. And who is this brown-haired woman you're so worried about anyway?"

"It's our neighbour, Angela. I saw them having breakfast together earlier. She's been after Brian since we moved in. And Brian is stupid enough to be flattered by her false advances. God, I hated that woman from the moment I met her."

"Well, he wasn't in the bar, Linda, and I can't believe that Brian would do something like that. Why didn't you mention this if you saw them together?"

"I wouldn't have believed it either, but then again, two weeks ago, he didn't have £17 million in the bank."

"I don't understand. What does the money have to do with anything?"

"Since we won the lottery, he's been acting strangely. First, he was totally obsessed with not telling anybody, and I mean absolutely nobody, including the people closest to us. Then, he started talking as though he thought that he was better than everyone else, which, as you know, is definitely not Brian. And now, he wants the trappings of a millionaire lifestyle. The money has definitely changed him, and not for the better."

"Well, I suspect anyone would change a bit if so much money suddenly became available to them, don't you think?"

"Yeah, I suppose that coming into a load of money might change most people. I accept that. But Brian has changed in a weird way. It's hard to explain, Karen, but it's like he's had some kind of breakdown."

"I thought the lottery people helped with the sudden transformation of lifestyle that comes with a big jackpot win. Aren't they looking out for your well-being?"

"Well, to be fair, they did try to warn us. The woman who came out to confirm our win left leaflets, and all sorts of information, and people we could get in touch with. But you know Brian, he likes to do things his way."

"Why don't you just phone him? Tell him you're not going with me today and ask him to come home. Please phone him, Linda!"

Linda looked at Karen and frowned. It was odd how worried Karen seemed. Perhaps her break-up with Tom was colouring her view of Linda's marriage. Or perhaps Karen was right.

After all, Linda had been shocked when she saw Brian with Angela. The image of Brian and Angela laughing after he'd hung up on her call replayed in Linda's mind.

"Okay, I'll phone him," Linda relents.

She tries Brian's number three times, but each time, it goes to voicemail.

"He's not answering."

"Text him! Maybe he's not getting his voicemail messages."

"Why are you so worried, Karen? None of this is your fault, and besides, he's probably just walking it off. You know what he's like."

"I've brought all my problems to your door, and it sounds as though you've got enough of your own to sort out right now."

Linda looks at Karen pensively. She can't help but feel that Karen is hiding something. She probably did see Brian with Angela and just doesn't want to be the messenger of bad news. Suddenly, she feels sorry for Karen. With all her problems of not conceiving and breaking up with Tom, Karen is still worried about her big sister. Linda reaches over to give Karen a hug.

"It's only a tiff we're having, Karen. You mustn't worry. Look, I'll text him now." She taps into her phone and then reads her message aloud.

"'Hi Brian, I'm not going to town to see a lawyer with Karen—I'm still at home. Can you phone me, please?' How's that, Karen? Let's see if he replies."

Karen's phone starts buzzing.

"Now what? Oh god, I could do without this. It's Tom ringing," Karen says. "Tom, I've told you my lawyer will be in touch."

"Let me speak to Tom, please, Karen." Linda grabs her phone and puts it on loudspeaker so Karen can hear.

"Hello Tom. It's Linda here. Karen has already told you. She's had enough of your gambling and has nothing more to say to you. She is now putting everything in the hands of her lawyer. Once everything is sorted, you will be given a fair settlement, which I'm sure you'll be more than satisfied with. But in the meantime, you're just going to have to wait!"

"You listen to me, Linda. I don't have time to wait. I need money right now. I've got people on my case who want what I owe them.

They know that my wife has the money, so they want to know where she lives. You need to send me money now, Linda! DO YOU HEAR ME!"

Linda switches the loudspeaker off and holds the phone against her ear. She keeps her voice neutral and paced.

"So, as I've said, Tom, you will receive a very fair settlement..."

"Listen, Linda! These people aren't to be messed with, and they want to find Karen. I can't protect her anymore. She won't be safe if I don't pay them off!"

"You're the one that needs to listen, Tom. Explain to these people that if they try to come anywhere near Karen, we're phoning the police." Linda hangs up.

Karen's phone rings repeatedly, but Karen and Linda ignore it.

"I feel so bad, Linda. I'm so sorry I've brought all my problems to you."

"You've done nothing wrong, Karen. Tom's compulsive gambling has caused all of this, so please stop blaming yourself.

In fact, why don't you leave the lawyer today and join me down at the beach? We can have something nice to eat before Dan drops the kids off."

"Sounds good to me."

It doesn't take Linda and Karen long to get changed. As they leave the house, Linda points out Angela's house. Linda notices how Karen fiddles with her handbag strap. She still feels that Karen is unusually quiet and suspects she's hiding something that's troubling her.

"Wow, that's worth some money. It's huge," Karen says, gawping at Angela's house.

"She must be out. Normally, her blue convertible is parked out front."

Karen turns away from Linda. A bird taking a dust bath by the side of the road seems to have caught her eye.

They stroll down to the beach, walk into The Beachcomber, and order two iced teas. Linda doesn't feel the joy and excitement she felt the first time she was there with Brian. All the fun and anticipation they had shared seemed to have disappeared.

"Oh look, there's Angela's husband," says Linda.

"Which one?" asks Karen, scanning around all the seated customers.

"The old guy sitting over there with the white baseball cap."

"God, he does look old. So how old is this Angela?"

"I would say late thirties."

"He must be touching seventy. I take it he has all the money, then?"
"What makes you think that?" Linda says, laughing. "Stop looking at him, Karen. He'll know we're talking about him."

Linda leans towards the window and glances up and down the beach hopefully.

"We might see Brian if he's gone for a walk on the beach. We can wave him over to join us."

"Linda…"

"Hold on, Dan's ringing me," Linda interrupts.

"Hi Dan… Okay, yeah, that's great… We'll see you then. Bye."

"What time will they be here?" Karen asks.

"In about an hour. What were you about to say?"

"Oh, I can't remember, er… I know… I was going to ask if you'd like to live here permanently."

"I don't think so. I'm not too impressed with all these rich people leading shallow lives. I don't know if I could handle them on a daily basis. There's something very false about them all."

Linda looks at her phone.

"He hasn't even read my message," she tells Karen.

Karen checks her phone, too. Linda suspects she's afraid that Tom will ring again.

"You're jumpy, Karen. What's the matter?"

Karen starts crying. "I thought it was just Tom and me having problems. I'm worried about you and Brian now, too."

"Karen, I told you. It's just a tiff. So what if he sat in a bar with a new neighbour to have a drink? I trust him. I guess I'm just irritated by the woman. It's no big deal. Stop worrying about it, Karen. It's nothing. I over-reacted."

"Linda, I texted him too after I went looking for him. I was worried and wanted him to come home. So he hasn't answered your messages or mine. Where is he?"

"He'll be on the beach somewhere, like I said. For heaven's sake, Karen. It's nothing! You're more worried than I am!"

"That's because I saw him, Linda," Karen blurts out. "He was with a woman just like you described."

"Honestly, Karen! I'm a little surprised you lied to me about this."
"I didn't. They weren't just sitting in the bar together. The truth is, they drove off together. Once I realised you suspected something with this woman, I was scared. I didn't know what to say."

Linda looks up and holds her sister's gaze.

"Was it a blue convertible?"

"Yes."

The two women are quiet for a moment. Linda feels a greater sense of shock than when she saw Angela and Brian laughing together.

Shock that Karen was so worried that she hid the truth from her, shock that Brian would go off with Angela without a word, that all of a sudden, their close and loving family life was falling apart.

"This is all my fault, Linda. I'm so sorry. I should have gone to see the lawyer on my own. I should have told you what I saw as soon as I got back. I'm so stupid. I'm sorry." Karen gets a tissue out of her bag, wipes her eyes, and blows her nose. "I was so looking forward to our having some time together, and I've even ruined that."

"You haven't, Karen. Being with you is very special to me, and nothing can spoil it. And stop blaming yourself for everything. None of this is your fault. Brian's just being very selfish. Come on, let's go home. I couldn't eat anything now, and the kids will be back soon."

Linda stands up and looks around at all the nodding heads and laughing faces and feels an anger inside her. However much money she and Brian had, they would never be as fickle and false as the people she'd met at Angela and PJ's that night.

On the way out, Linda stops by where PJ is sitting with a few of his friends.

"Hello, PJ."

"Hello, it's Brian's wife, isn't it?" he says without standing up.

"Yes, and my name is Linda." Linda can hear an edge to her voice, which betrays her irritation. "And what about your wife, Angela? Is she not around today?"

"No, she's gone shopping, I think."

"Yes, so I understand."

"Sorry?" PJ frowns.
"Oh, she didn't tell you? Well, my husband didn't tell me, either. They've gone out together, apparently."

"Who is this woman, PJ?" asks one of PJ's well-dressed friends, protectively.

"She's a neighbour. Well, she's staying across the road from us."

"I don't know when you last spoke to Angela," Linda continues, "but I haven't been able to contact Brian for at least two hours."

PJ stands up, appearing a little embarrassed in front of his friends. He drops his napkin on the table.

"What's all this about, Louise? Angela goes out with loads of guys. Why are you making such a fuss? If you don't mind, I'm having a few drinks with some business clients here, and we'd like some privacy."

"It's Linda, not 'Louise' or 'Brian's wife'. My bloody name is Linda, for Christ's sake. And I'll tell you what this is all about. Your bored wife is out to destroy other people's lives, and she doesn't care whose.
Oh, and by the way, she thinks my husband is a high-flying businessman, whereas, in fact, he's a factory labourer who happened to win the lottery two weeks ago. Oh, and I worked on the till in our local supermarket, which I'm very proud of. We somehow ended up here with the likes of you shallow people. I must be going, but I hope you have better luck getting in touch with your wife than I'm having trying to contact my husband. Wonder what they're up to! Goodbye!"

Linda ushers Karen out of the door.

"Oh my god, Linda. I've never seen a group of men go so quiet in all my life! Are you okay?"

"Not really, Karen. But I'm looking forward to seeing the kids."

Chapter Thirty-One

Linda is still fuming as they return to the house. She parks up in the driveway and looks for the front door key in her handbag.

"Did you hear what PJ said, Karen? Angela goes out with loads of guys! I bet she does! What a pair of weirdos!"

Linda eventually finds the key and unlocks the front door just as Dan arrives with the children. Linda's heart leaps when she catches sight of them.

"You're here early," she calls out, rushing to hug Ruby and Liam.

"I think they missed the swimming pool." Dan laughs. "They couldn't get here quickly enough!"

"God, you guys look tired. Looks like you've been going to bed too late at Nanny and Grandpa's."

Linda pushes the front door open so the kids can run ahead of her.

"They fell asleep on the way here," Dan explains. "They're probably full of energy now!"

"Have you eaten? Would you like something to eat?" Linda asks.

"No, Mum, I'm having a swim," Liam shouts over his shoulder as he heads upstairs to change. Dan brings their bags in and sets them down in the hallway.

"Me too." Ruby follows Liam upstairs, bolting up the stairs two at a time.

"We had some fries and burgers before we left," Dan says.

"At least they've been eating healthy whilst in Brooklyn," Linda replies sarcastically.

"Where's Brian?" asks Dan.

"He's gone out," Linda snaps.

Dan looks across to Karen, who shrugs her shoulders.

"By the way, Mom and Dad know that you guys have split up, Karen."

"Well, they had to know eventually. I think they've known things weren't right for a while."

"Tom called to the house earlier. Mom wouldn't let him in because he'd obviously been drinking, and I have to say, he was in a right state.

I didn't let him in. I didn't want the children to see him like that! Apparently his contacts are getting impatient for him to repay his gambling debts. I've never seen him like that. He was really frightened."

"I know. He's been on the phone to me, too," Karen replies.

"They're pushing him to tell them where you and Linda are."

"I don't know why he expects Linda to bail him out. He's just passing the buck like he always does when he owes money. Tomorrow, I really am going to get the divorce rolling."

"I spoke to him too," Linda adds. "I told him we'd phone the police if anybody came to threaten us." She takes a beer out of the fridge and passes it to Dan.

"You need to be careful, Linda. I know some of these people Tom owes money to. Believe me, you don't want to be messing with them. They're not nice people."

"God, where's Brian when you need him?" Linda retrieves her phone from her bag and looks at the screen. "Nothing."

"Yeah, where is Brian?"

"Brian and I had an argument. He walked out in a sulk."

"Okay, so? We all have arguments," Dan reassures Linda.

"It's a little more than that, to be honest. He's getting a bit fed up with sitting around here. I think he was expecting to do something exciting now we can afford it. But I guess Tom's problems got in the way."

"I can sympathise a little. After all, he doesn't know anyone here, does he?"

Linda looks at Dan despairingly.

"Well, apart from that woman over the road."

"What woman?" asks Dan, raising his eyebrows.

Linda turns her back on Dan and takes a bottle of white wine out of the fridge. Her nerves are on edge, and she can't believe that Brian still hasn't phoned her. She pours two glasses and hands one to Karen.

"Her name is Angela; it's their neighbour. I saw her picking Brian up in her car earlier." Karen takes the glass from Linda and swallows a large gulp.

"She made it crystal clear from when we first met her that she had ideas about Brian. And he's stupid enough to be flattered by her attention." Linda takes a sip of wine.

"That doesn't sound like Brian." Dan frowns.

Linda indicates to Karen and Dan to be quiet while the children run through in their swimming costumes. Linda hears them splash into the water and is glad that at least they are having fun.

"He hasn't read any of my text messages," she tells Dan, "and he knows we're both trying to contact him."

"So, what's going on, guys? I thought you two were so close. The golden couple, always loved up." Dan raises his arms in the air to show his confusion.

"So did I. I don't want to sound like I'm making excuses for him, but I honestly think winning this money has changed him. And shallow Angela over the way hasn't helped."

"I'll phone him. He may respond if he thinks it's something to do with the children," Dan suggests.

"It can't do any harm." Karen looks hopefully at Dan.

"Just switches to answer machine... Hello Brian, it's Dan. I've just arrived with the kids at yours. Listen, we all have arguments—that's life. But we could do with you back home now, buddy."

Linda's phone begins to ring.

"I'm not answering that; it's one of those withheld numbers." She puts her phone back down on the breakfast bar.

"What if it's Brian returning Dan's call? He may not be able to use his own phone. I'd answer it just in case, Linda. Maybe he's using Angela's phone," Karen suggests.

"Okay, I'll answer it... Hello?" Linda puts the phone on loudspeaker.

"Is this Linda, Tom's sister-in-law?"

"Who's this?"

"Your brother-in-law owes us $300,000, and we need the money now."

"And what does that have to do with me?"

"Tom told us his money's tied up with you."

"I don't have a cent of Tom's money."

"Well, then, you need to help him out. The debt has to be paid today."

"My sister is starting divorce proceedings with Tom. Once everything is sorted out, he can make his own arrangements about paying whatever he owes you. Now, if you bother me or any of my family again, I'm contacting the police. Goodbye." Linda hangs up.

"That wasn't the wisest move, Linda. You don't know who you're dealing with," Dan says.

"I don't care. I'm not paying off his gambling debts, Dan."

"You don't know these people, but they most certainly know all about you."

"Yeah, well, Tom has obviously given them my phone number."

"Yeah, and I can guarantee he's given them your address as well." Dan's voice is getting louder.

"So, every time Tom loses a fortune, we have to pay it off? And where will that end?" Linda shouts.

The phone rings again, and they all stare at it.

"I'd answer that, Linda."

Linda frowns and glares at him; she doesn't feel Dan is giving her the best advice, and he seems more afraid of the caller than she is. She hesitates for a moment and then answers. She switches the phone to loudspeaker again. The three of them stare at the phone, waiting for the caller to speak.

"Listen to me very carefully. I'm going to say this only once. We know that you won the lottery, and you have millions with which to pay off Tom's debt. And we can be with you within minutes."

"You don't need to be with me within minutes. I have nothing to do with Tom or his gambling. If you contact me or my family again, I'm calling the police."

"You should never underestimate people, Linda. That's very disrespectful. Right now, I'm watching your children swimming in the pool. Do you really believe that the police can protect you?"

Linda runs out to the pool and shouts at Liam and Ruby to come inside. Karen follows her out and helps the children scramble out. Ruby starts crying. Linda gives each of the children a towel from the storage box and ushers them upstairs to get changed.

Dan picks the phone up.

"This is Dan, Linda's brother. This debt has nothing to do with Linda."

"Yeah, we know who you are, Dan. How's Spud's Bar? We look after the place and make sure it's well protected, so we know all about you."

"Okay, Tom owes you money, but Linda isn't going to subsidise his gambling."

Linda grabs the phone from Dan.

"You think you can threaten my children and my family?!" she screams. "If I was you, I wouldn't be around here when the police arrive." She hangs up.

"You shouldn't have done that, Linda," says Dan again.

"Dan, what's the matter with you? If we give them what they want, every villain in the state of New York will be queuing up for their cut. We can't live the rest of our lives like that!"

"But, Linda, think about it! They're already watching the house. For all we know, they're listening to us now. They could have the house bugged. They couldn't care less about the police, and they've probably got most of them on their payroll anyway. You're naïve if you think they care about the police."

"The children are getting changed, and I've suggested they watch a movie in their bedroom. They're pretty shaken up, Linda. You need to calm down! Where did you put the bags, Dan? Ruby wants her puppy teddy."

Dan points to the hallway. Linda ignores Karen and walks into the living room while she waits for the police to answer her phone call.

"She's phoning the police, but I think she's making a big mistake, Karen," Dan says.

"No, I agree with Linda," replies Karen. "How can you ever stop these people if you succumb to what they want? There's no alternative. We have to get the police involved."

"The police are on their way. I've told them someone is trying to get into the house, and it's an emergency."

Karen drops down onto the sofa next to Linda. "I can't believe that Tom has caused all this trouble. I'm so sorry!"

"I'll stay here with you until Brian gets back," Dan offers.

"Thanks, Dan. I'll try him again. Where is he?" Linda dials Brian's number and puts her head in her hands while she waits for him to answer, but once again, the call switches to voicemail. The three siblings sit in the living room for a few moments. The music from a Walt Disney movie reaches their ears. Linda can't help but wonder at the irony of being in this beautiful house, with the sun shining, the pool glistening, the children lying on their beds watching a movie, and yet not one of them is happy.

"Is Ruby okay, Karen? I should go up and see her."

The doorbell rings, and they all look at each other.

"Look, it's the police," Dan says, pointing to the CCTV feed on the television screen. "Karen, you go and check on the children. Keep them upstairs."

Linda goes to the door.

"Good afternoon, is it Mrs Jackson? We received a call to come out to the premises?"

"Yes, I called."

"I'm Police Detective Paul Whenner, and this is Police Officer Ingrid McBride."

"Thank you for coming. Please come in."

The two police officers walk into the house. They both wear holsters with guns and take off their hats as they enter. To Linda, they seem enormous in the hallway. She ushers them through into the living room.

"This is my brother, Dan. My sister is looking after my children upstairs. My family are being threatened, you see. Please... sit down."

The officers ignore Linda's offer to sit. One of them starts exploring the living room and looking out through the windows to the garden and pool. The other stands in front of Linda.

"Okay, so is everyone safe at the moment, Mrs Jackson?"

"Yes, we're all okay at the moment, but—"

"So, they tried to get into your house?"

"Well, not exactly. But they phoned and told me that they could see my kids in the swimming pool. They've been watching us."

The officers exchange glances. McBride slides open the patio doors from the living room to the pool area and starts checking around the pool. Linda turns around to see what she is doing and then back to the officer who is speaking to her.

"But nobody has actually tried to gain access to your property?" Whenner continues.

"Well, no. Let me explain. My brother-in-law is a compulsive gambler and owes them money. They're threatening me and my family unless we pay it. I told them that I wouldn't pay, and it was his debt, not mine."

"Who are these people? Do you have their contact details? We can warn them not to threaten you again."

"I don't even know who they are. They just phoned demanding the debt be paid."

"Have you got their number?"

"No, it was a withheld number." Linda sits down herself now, beginning to feel exhausted from it all.

"Look, with what you've told us, this is really difficult to follow up. You have CCTV, so I suggest that if anybody calls, you don't open the door, and you call us straight away. We'll be patrolling the area anyway, so it won't take us long to reach you. The main thing is to make sure your property is locked and secured."

"But they said they were watching us. They must be nearby."

Officer McBride returns and joins the conversation.

"There's nobody outside and no clear eyeline to indicate visibility from off the grounds. They were probably just trying to frighten you."

"But they knew the children were in the pool," Linda argues.

"Could be a lucky guess?"

Linda frowns at McBride. She feels the officers are not taking the danger they are in seriously.

"I can assure you, there's nobody outside. If anyone was watching the premises, we would have seen them when we arrived. Look, they may have just been trying it on. You've done the right thing by not agreeing to pay them, though."

"Okay, thanks for coming round," says Linda, disappointed, although she isn't sure what she expected them to do. She sees them out and then returns to sit with Dan.

Her phone starts ringing again, and she grabs it, hoping it's Brian.

"It's that withheld number again." She looks across at Dan. "I wish they'd called while the police were here."

Dan reaches over and takes the phone. He presses to answer and switches the loudspeaker on.

"Now that was a very stupid thing to do. I told you the police couldn't help!"

"The police are patrolling the area, so you'd better be careful," Linda shouts back. The caller hangs up.

Chapter Thirty-Two

"Wow, this is a fast car, Angela."

"I just love driving with the roof down in the sunshine. The breeze you feel is superb. So, shall we visit Manhattan, then, Brian?"

"Sounds great, Angela."

"Is there any particular place you'd like to see?"

"Well, I've already done most of the tourist places. Unless there's somewhere you can think of."

"I've got just the place in mind. I don't think you'll be disappointed." She glances across at him with a seductive smile.

"Sounds good to me."

"Do you like Fleetwood Mac?"
"Who doesn't?" replies Brian.

Angela plays Little Lies at high volume, and they both chant, "Tell me lies, tell me sweet little lies," holding each other's gaze for a few seconds.

Brian feels his phone vibrating and takes it out of his pocket. He decides to ignore it.

"Is it Linda?" Angela asks.

"It's her sister, Karen, actually."

The text message from Karen arrives on his screen. He reads it out to Angela.

"Well, if she wasn't going to the lawyers with Karen, she should have told me earlier. Talk about being messed about. Anyway, it's too late now. I'll speak to her later."

"Good on you, Brian. I hate it when people mess me about. Do you like Italian food?"

"I don't think I've ever had a proper Italian meal."

"There's the Highgrove Hotel. It has a beautiful skyscraper restaurant overlooking Central Park and most of Manhattan. I've been there a few times." She looks at him again. "I can guarantee you won't have tasted anything like it before."
Brian smiles and looks away nervously. He's not sure going to a hotel with Angela is such a good idea, and he's irritated now he knows that he could have spent the day with Linda. He puts his phone back in his pocket, which reminds him that he's wearing shorts.

"Angela, I've just thought. I can't walk into a classy restaurant in these."

"No problem. There's a designer store on the way, and you can change in the hotel before our meal."

"Fantastic! Just what I need. This is exactly what I'm talking about, Angela. You certainly know how to enjoy life."

"We only live once!"

*****

As they enter Harcross Designer store, they are greeted immediately by a tall, dark gentleman, immaculately dressed and obviously known to Angela.

"Good afternoon, madam, and hello to you, sir. It's so nice to see you again, madam."

"Oh, Si, can you look after my dear friend here? He's going to need a complete outfit, the works, please. You know the score!"

"Of course. Yes, certainly, madam. Shall I put it on madam's account?"

"No, I'll pay on my card, if that's okay?" interrupts Brian.

"Certainly, sir."

Si looks Brian up and down and then starts measuring him and shouting orders at his assistants, who bring different items for Brian's consideration.

"These shirts are nice, Brian—oh, and I quite like these boxer shorts," Angela evaluates each item, standing just behind Brian and brushing against him each time she reaches out to feel the fabrics.

"Oh yeah, they're very nice," says Brian, feeling her leaning in against him.

"This is a great store, Angela. I take it PJ shops here?"

"Good heavens, no!" Angela laughs. "Si comes out to the house with a team to sort out PJ's wardrobe. I only come to the store with special friends." Angela holds his gaze for just a moment too long.

After half an hour of choosing clothes, Brian feels he has what he needs. He pays the assistant but declines the offer of a receipt.

"You're very laid back, Brian. I admire that! It's cool!"

By the time they are back at the car, the traffic has become hectic, and Brian feels a shadow creeping over his day as they enter Manhattan. He should have been with Linda today. They should be here together. Something seems all wrong.

"As an English guy, what do you think of the Big Apple, Brian?"

"I think it's an amazing city. It has everything."

"I absolutely love its magical feeling. I've travelled all over the globe, and I consider New York the best city in the world."

"Well, you obviously haven't been to Liverpool, Angela."

Angela strokes Brian's hand lightly with one hand and starts laughing.

Brian looks round to see what he has said that is so funny.

"No, I haven't, actually. The home of the Beatles? You'll have to take me there one day, Brian. Do you think I'd like Liverpool?"

"I know you would, Angela. It's a well-known fact. Everyone who goes to Liverpool always goes back."

"Well, here we are at the Highgrove Hotel. The valet will park for us." Angela jumps out of the car, leaving the keys in the ignition, and instructs a porter to collect the bags of new clothes from the boot.

"Brian, would you like to order us a drink in the piano bar? I'll sort out everything at reception."

"You don't have to do that, Angela. I'll pay for our meal."

"You're such a typical English gent, Brian. No, this is my treat for you. It's my way of welcoming you to New York. I don't know what it is about you. You're special to me."

"Thank you, Angela. I consider you a good friend, too. What would you like to drink?"

"Just get me a fresh orange for now, please."

Brian orders a beer and fresh orange juice. He's thirsty and drinks quickly. He orders another, and after about ten minutes, Angela joins him.

"Right, that's everything sorted." She sits down and picks up her drink.

"This is a lovely hotel, Angela."

"It's one of the best in town."

"So, do you come here with PJ?"

"Are you joking?" laughs Angela.

"Oh," says Brian quietly.

"Now, let's take your clothes upstairs, but you don't need to change now. I was going to suggest a walk in Central Park while the sun's still shining."

"That sounds great. Lead the way!"

Brian follows Angela to the lift and is amazed by the chandeliers and the huge, polished marble tiles in the enormous lobby. The lift is manned, and they are politely asked which floor they would like. The room that Angela has booked is actually a suite of rooms with a balcony overlooking Central Park. Brian wonders if Angela's or PJ's money has paid for this.

"You can change when we get back," Angela calls from the bedroom as she hangs Brian's new clothes up in the wardrobe.

*****

As they stroll through Central Park, Angela quizzes him on his previous visits to the US.

"I take it you've been to the Dakota Building, where John Lennon was shot?"

"Yeah, coming from Liverpool, I had to do it. In fact, I've been twice."

"There's a little bar up this way, Brian. There's always fantastic live music there. We can work up an appetite over a few drinks."

"You're definitely speaking my language now, Angela." Brian smiles but wonders how many beers he should have and quite what he needs to work up an appetite for. He begins to feel increasingly uncomfortable in the situation he's got himself into.

"Here we are."

"It's quite busy for a late afternoon."

"Yeah, it's usually full of tourists having a great time here in the Big Apple."

"This side of New York reminds me of Liverpool."

"So, tell me, where did you meet Linda?"

"I met her in Concert Square in Liverpool. She was studying at Liverpool University, and we just hit it off, I guess. What about you? Where did you meet PJ?"

"He was my boss. In fact, if the truth be known, he's still my boss."

"And I suppose you guys just hit it off as well?"

"No, Brian. At no point in my life have PJ and I ever hit it off," Angela speaks seriously, without any emotion whatsoever.

"Oh, erm…" Brian doesn't quite know how to react.

"I've told you, Brian, I'm a hedonist. My goal in life is fun, fun, fun. In simpler terms, PJ pays for my fun."

"What if he ever left you?"

"How could he ever leave me when we've never really been together?"

"But I thought you were married?"

"Only on paper, sweetheart, only on paper. And I've absolutely no worries because I know where all the bodies are buried."

Brian chokes on his beer. "You what?"

"Don't worry, it's just a figure of speech. What I mean is that I have all the knowledge of his corrupt business deals with well-known people. It wouldn't be in PJ's interest to upset me."

"If you don't mind my saying, Angela, you lead quite an extraordinary life."

"And I wouldn't change it for the world, Brian."

After a couple of hours and a few drinks later, the bar atmosphere is bubbling. Brian and Angela are dancing with a crowd of holidaymakers to 'What a Feeling' by Irene Cara. As the music eventually slows, Angela wraps her arms around Brian's neck and leans in to kiss him.

"I'll get us a drink," Brian suggests.

"Why don't we get a drink back at the hotel?" Angela gazes into his eyes.

"Okay, we'll do that!" Brian smiles.

They are soon back at the hotel and return to the piano bar.

"A bottle of your best champagne, please," Brian orders.

"Brian, let's have it up in the room."

"Why not!" Brian thinks of the balcony and the views.

As soon as they are in the room, Angela leans in to kiss Brian again but is interrupted by a knock on the door. A waiter has brought their champagne upstairs. This gives Brian a few moments to think. He feels quite drunk now and isn't sure what to do. On the one hand, he wants to have some fun, but on the other, he feels everything is going too fast and not quite the way he intended. The waiter opens the champagne and pours two glasses. He then seems to slide out of the room as elegantly as he arrived. Angela retrieves her phone, and Brian wonders if he should drink some water before starting on the champagne. He can't remember how much he's had to drink, but he knows it's probably too much.

"It's PJ. Let me just get this, Brian, in case it's important."

Angela takes her call out onto the balcony.

Brian thinks twice about drinking water and decides to have the champagne after all. He wanders into the bedroom and browses his new clothes in the wardrobe. This is the life he expected as a millionaire. He could get used to this lifestyle. He makes himself comfortable on the bed and looks in the mirror opposite.

He raises his glass to his reflection. Surely things couldn't get better than this?

Angela seems to be having a lengthy chat out on the balcony. Brian suspects it's an important business call, so he goes to top up his glass while waiting and then returns to the bedroom. He begins to feel better after a couple of glasses of bubbly. Eventually, Angela joins him but with a sour grimace.

"Everything okay, Angela?"

"No, everything's not okay!" she snaps. Brian notices that she doesn't look quite so exotic when she's not smiling. In fact, she doesn't look attractive at all.

"What's the matter?"

"Your wife visited The Beachcomber earlier with her sister and was extremely rude to PJ while he was entertaining business clients."

Brian sits up on the bed.

"Oh, I'm sorry. What can I say? She shouldn't have done that. I'll speak to her about it."

"These are important clients, Brian."

"I said I'm sorry, Angela." Brian doesn't like the side of Angela he's seeing now.

"And are you sorry for lying about being a successful businessman?"

"Pardon?"

"I believe you were a factory labourer before winning the lottery, Brian? And your wife worked on the till in her local supermarket?"

"My wife told PJ that?"

"And she was extremely rude."

"She must be very angry with me, then." Brian isn't sure why, but he feels relieved that Linda is bothered about his behaviour. Perhaps he does mean something to her after all. He begins to feel ashamed for resenting her spending time with Karen.

"She's not the only person angry with you, Brian. I've never felt so embarrassed in all my life!"

"I don't understand. Why would you feel embarrassed, Angela? I thought it was PJ she was rude to."

"How will I ever be able to show my face again if my friends learn that you're just a factory labourer? I don't like anybody taking me for a fool, Brian. The shame of it! Really? Are you too thick to see that?" Angela spits the last words out.

"The shame of it?" Brian gets off the bed and stands up. "The shame of it? Now, hold on, Angela! Yeah, okay, I shouldn't have said I was a businessman, but I wasn't trying to make a fool of you. And why should I have to disclose that I won the lottery? It should be my choice who I tell. And working in a factory doesn't make me a second-class citizen. You and PJ are no better than me and Linda. You may think you are, but believe me, you're not!"

"No? But we didn't win our money in a lottery."

"No, you're right, Angela. You didn't win your money. You stole it with all those corrupt business deals that you told me about. What the hell was I thinking of coming here with you? I must be mad! You're not in the same league as my wife, and do you know what? You never will be!" Brian storms out of the room without looking back.

"Don't forget your fancy clothes!" Angela shouts after him.

"Give them to one of your other boyfriends," he bellows back along the corridor.

*****

Once outside the hotel, Brian flags down a taxi.

"Can you take me to Long Island, please?"

"Sure, buddy," replies the driver, who then provides a commentary on the sights for Brian along the way.

This monologue allows Brian to contemplate how he could have been so foolish. He wonders why he hadn't seen Angela for who she really was and why he had felt so flattered by her.

Chapter Thirty-Three

It's almost six o'clock, and Linda still can't get in touch with Brian.

"What are the kids doing, Dan?" Linda hands him a bottle of beer and joins him in the back lounge with her glass of wine. She's forgotten how many she's had today, but it calms her nerves.

"They were watching Mrs Doubtfire with Karen, but she took them down to the beach park."

"The kids love having you and Karen around, Dan."

"And we love them, Linda. Everything will be fine, you'll see. It will all get sorted. Why don't you just pay Tom's debt? Get it out of the way and move on with your lives. You and Brian should be having fun with the children, not fretting about all this stuff."

"Dan, we can't let people threaten us like this. I don't owe them a cent, and the mood I'm in right now, well, they're picking on the wrong person." Linda wonders if she should slow down on the wine. She's beginning to feel irritated with Dan's views. Brian's radio silence is also working on her nerves.

"These are not your normal everyday people, though, Linda, and I'm really worried about you and the kids."

"You don't need to be. The police are involved now, and you heard what they said. They're patrolling the area. If you'd like to go to Spuds tonight, we'll be fine, Dan. You don't need to stay."

"I'm not leaving until Brian gets back."

"Yes, well, we don't know when that will be, do we? Brian's really let me down."

"It's so unlike Brian."

"Well, a psychologist would probably explain it better than me. But I honestly believe he's struggling with all the change. Having so much money is a huge transformation in your life. It changes everything. Look at how we quit our jobs and came out here. But going off like this with another woman, and one who I know is particularly interested in him! Well, it's just too much."

She puts her glass down on the side table and puts her head in her hands. "Our lives are changing in too many ways."

"I know, sis." Dan moves over to sit by Linda. He puts an arm around her shoulders.

It's been so long since she's had any time with Dan alone that, for a moment, Linda enjoys the old familiarity of their childhood and gives him a hug.

"Have you ever dreamt of winning the lottery?"

"Of course. Hasn't everyone?" Dan laughs.

"And what would you do if you won?"

"Hmm, that's a good question. When I was younger, I fancied opening an animal rescue farm."

"Gosh! I never knew that. Well, why don't you, Dan? I can buy you the land and the premises. You'd be brilliant at that. You love animals. And I think something like that kind of gives you a purpose in life."

"It would certainly keep me out of Spud's every day." Dan laughs.

"I know he hated the place, and it was very hard physical work, but I'm beginning to think that leaving the factory has thrown a spanner in the works in Brian's life. Do you understand what I mean?"

"Yes, I do. He was proud that he could provide for you and the kids. He had a goal in life."

"Now he's got all this money, but he doesn't have a clue what to do with it or where to start."

"Yeah, where do you start?"

"He keeps saying that some people aren't meant to have money. I didn't know what he meant by that. But now I'm beginning to think that—although he doesn't realise it—he's one of the people who wasn't meant to have money."

"He probably just needs time, Linda. I mean, you only won a couple of weeks ago."

"Yeah, but it still doesn't justify him disappearing with another woman and not replying to me all day!"

Linda's phone rings. They both jump up, startled.

"It's Debbie. It's a friend from back home. Excuse me, Dan."

Linda walks out to the pool, thinking how it seems such a long time ago since she spoke to Debbie. She wonders what's going on with Deano.

"Hi, Debbie, how are you?"

"Linda, am I disturbing you?"

"No, not at all. In fact, it's a pleasure to hear from you. I'm not having such a good day."

"Oh, I'm so sorry. Well, maybe this will cheer you and Brian up… I take back what I said about all men being pigs."

"Oh?" Linda laughs. She thinks back to their last conversation. "Why, what's changed?"

"Deano is here… He's with me at mine. I thought he'd run off with the house money, but he'd checked into rehab to straighten himself out."

"You're kidding?"

"No."

"So, you're okay? You don't need any money?"

"No, Linda. Deano's already bought our house."

"Oh, Debbie, I'm absolutely delighted for you. That's fantastic news."

"Well, I'll never prejudge anyone ever again in my whole life. There was me thinking that my man was up to no good."

Linda stays silent, mulling this over. This is exactly what she's doing to Brian—prejudging him.

"Next time, I'll give him the chance to explain before I jump in with two feet, Linda. Aren't we lucky to have Deano and Brian, Linda?"

"Debbie, I'm really glad you're both okay. And that you've bought the house. That's great news."

"I'll let you go, but thank you so much, Linda. If you can, thank Brian as well. We both want you to come over for dinner when you're back. How long are you staying out there for?"

"Oh gosh. We don't know yet. But I'll thank Brian for you when I see him. I'm really delighted for you both. Look, I'll have to go now, Debbie."

"Oh, okay. Well, enjoy yourselves, and we'll look forward to seeing you when you're back. We're so happy, Linda. Thanks again."

"You're welcome. Bye for now, Debbie."

"Bye."

*****

Linda doesn't feel lucky. She checks her phone again, but Brian still hasn't replied. She turns round to walk back into the house just as a man wearing a mask emerges from behind the bushes. She screams and drops her phone in shock. Another man grabs her from behind.

"So, where are the police now, Linda?" one of them growls into her ear.

Hearing Linda's screams, Dan rushes outside, shouting Linda's name. He punches one of the men to the ground, but the other pulls out a long knife and stabs Dan in the chest. Dan staggers and falls backwards into the house.

The man on the ground gets up and punches Linda to the ground. He kicks her in the stomach, and then he and his companion drag her back into the house, where she sees Dan bleeding out onto the carpet.

"Please! He's bleeding. You have to call an ambulance! Please, phone an ambulance! I can pay you if it's money you want. Please hurry! Phone for an ambulance." Linda hears her voice screaming at the men. She can't understand why they aren't doing anything.

"You should have paid earlier when you had the chance!" one of the men shouts at her.

Suddenly, there are two gunshots. The noise is deafening, and the two assailants drop to the floor. Linda turns round to see her neighbour, Rick, calmly walk through the living room with a gun in his hand. He stands over each of the men in turn to check whether they are alive.

"Are you okay, Linda?" he asks.

"I'm okay, but my brother, Dan... He's been stabbed." Linda hears the tremor in her own voice. She looks at the two dead men in her living room. She feels queasy but needs to focus. Dan needs help.

"Please call an ambulance, Rick! Please hurry!" Her voice is sobbing now. She sits on the floor with Dan's head in her hands. She needs something to stop the bleeding. She grabs a cushion from the sofa and pushes it hard against the wound in Dan's chest.

"Can you send an ambulance to 7 Sundrive? A man has been stabbed in the chest. He's bleeding pretty badly. It doesn't look good."

Linda looks over in horror at Rick as he speaks. It's fine. Dan will be fine. She just needs to keep the cushion pressed over the wound to stop the bleeding. She looks at the carpet around her, where blood has crept into a huge pool. "Stay with me, Dan," she begs. "Help is on its way. Dan! Dan! Say something!" As she screams at Dan, the doorbell rings.

"Answer the door!" she shouts at Rick. He moves quickly to the front door, sidestepping the bodies on the floor, and returns with two policemen.

"Someone's been stabbed in the chest," he says to the police. "I think it's her brother."

"Okay, the ambulance is on its way."

"It'll be too late!" Linda screams. "He's not responding!"

One of the officers joins Linda on the floor and starts CPR.

The other officer checks the two bodies and retrieves his radio to call it in.

"We have two males with gunshot wounds to the head, both deceased. We also have an injured male with stab wounds to the chest, unconscious and in critical condition. If the ambulance could speed it up, please."

Linda looks in horror at her brother. "No, no," she screams.

"Keep pressing hard!" the officer instructs her. "Don't let him bleed out."

Linda looks down at her hands, covered in blood, and gasps. She presses hard again and watches in a trance as the officer continues counting, pumping Dan's chest and breathing into his mouth.

"Dan, stay with us!" she shouts again. "Dan!"

Rick returns to the front door when he hears the ambulance sirens. Two paramedics come in with a stretcher and take over the CPR. One of them carefully removes the cushion from Linda's hands and looks at the wound. He then works rapidly to stem the flow with a huge dressing that reminds Linda of the sort of Fablon their mom used to cover the kitchen table with. The paramedics are asking questions, but she can't seem to answer. Rick and the police officers answer for her. "Less than ten minutes…" "No, we've not seen him conscious…" "Seemed to be a break-in…" All she can focus on is Dan's pale face and all the blood on the cushion and the carpet.

Dan is wheeled on the trolley stretcher out through the front door and lifted into the ambulance. Linda follows in a daze and sees Karen walking up the drive with the children.

"Oh my god!" Karen screams. "What's happened?" The kids are quiet, gawping at the ambulance.

"He's been stabbed, Karen. He's been stabbed."

"Who?" Karen asks blankly.

"Dan! They stabbed him. He's been bleeding. I couldn't stop it, Karen. I couldn't stop it. I tried, but I couldn't stop it," Linda is sobbing now.

"Oh no! Oh no!" Karen runs to the back of the ambulance, where the paramedics are still tending to Dan.

"Dan!" she shouts. One of the paramedics jumps out of the ambulance and starts to close the doors.

"We need to get him to the hospital urgently, madam. You're welcome to follow separately, but we really have to go now."

Karen nods without speaking.

Linda finds her courage. She turns to Ruby and Liam.

"Kids, something terrible has happened, but it's all under control. Uncle Dan needs to go to hospital, and I'll go with him. You can stay here with Auntie Karen, and I'll keep you posted on how he is."

"Excuse me, madam… I'm afraid the children can't go into the house just yet." The police officer who so calmly tried to save Dan's life has now switched to his police role. Linda remembers the two dead bodies in the living room and gasps again. She doesn't know what to do.

"Linda, they can come to mine," Rick says.

Linda considers this for a moment. If anyone else tried to attack her family, at least they would be safe with Rick. She doesn't know what would have happened without his help, but she pictures the shots he delivered to the assailants' heads. He killed two men and seems so calm. She decides she can't let her children go with him.

"Linda, he's my brother. I need to come with you."

"Okay, we'll all go. Get in the car, kids. God, where is Brian when you need him?"

The ambulance is already pulling out, and Linda follows. As they drive away, two more police cars and two ambulances arrive. In her mirror, Linda sees more paramedics enter the house. Too late for some, she thinks.

*****

The children are quiet for a while in the car. Linda has no idea where the hospital is. Liam, sitting forward in the back seat, points out which way the ambulance is turning to help her. The journey seems endless to Linda, and no one speaks. Linda is used to the children asking nonstop questions when they don't know everything about a situation, but it's as though they realise that they just need to keep quiet for her now.

Once at the hospital, they are all taken into a small family room and left alone for a few minutes. Ruby starts to cry.

"I'm sorry, Mummy, but I need to go to the toilet."

"It's okay, love. Liam, can you go find the toilets and stay with her? Don't let her out of your sight."

Linda gives Ruby a hug.

Liam looks worried but takes Ruby by the hand.

"Will you stay here, Mum?" he asks nervously.

"Of course," Linda replies. "Come straight back."

"Come on, Rubes," he says lovingly.

When they've gone, Linda turns to Karen.

"This is the bad news waiting room, where they come and tell you how sorry they are, but they tried their best. Why didn't I pay the money when they asked?" Linda sobs. "None of this would have happened if I'd have paid the money."

"No, it's my fault," Karen sobs too. "Getting you involved with Tom and his debts. It's all my fault."

The door opens again, but it isn't Liam and Ruby; it's Brian. He rushes over and holds Linda tight against him. "I'm so sorry, I'm so sorry!" he whispers. "Rick told me what happened. Are you okay? Where are the children?"

Linda pulls back from Brian and looks him in the eye. "They're fine. Liam has just taken Ruby to the toilet. They'll be back in a minute. But Dan's in a bad way. They're still working on him."

"Linda. I'm so sorry. I've been such an idiot."

"Don't go there, Brian, not now," Linda says quietly.

Liam returns, pulling Ruby into the room behind him.

"Dad, you're here," Liam says. The children run to hug their dad.

"I'll take you back home if you like," Brian suggests.

"I'm not leaving," Liam says. "Mum and Auntie Karen need us here."

Linda smiles at her son. He suddenly seems so grown-up.

"I want to stay near Uncle Dan," Ruby adds.

Linda looks at her children proudly but also thinks it might be better for them to go home with their dad. She wonders what's happening at the house.

"Brian, there's something I need to tell you about the house."

"Don't," says Brian. "Not with Liam and Ruby here. Rick explained everything."

Linda thinks of all the blood on the carpet.

"Mum, can't we all stay here, please?" Liam pleads.

"Sweetheart, we might be here all night. It's best you go back with Dad. Brian, maybe it would be best to ask the police if we can collect our personal things from the house and then you and the children could check into a hotel? I really think that would be best."

"If that's what you want," Brian says.

"Well, I think you'll find the police won't let us return at the moment. But Brian, stay with the children all the time! Do you understand? We can't be sure it's over yet."

"We'll phone you if anything changes," Karen says, pulling Liam and Ruby to her.

Brian and the children leave, and Karen goes to fetch some coffee to help keep them awake. Linda is left alone. She sits, and her whole body starts to shake. The images of the afternoon dart across her mind. Everything has changed.

*****

After several hours, a doctor and nurse join them in the waiting room. Karen and Linda jump up. Dr Tyler introduces himself and Nurse Wilson.

"Okay, your brother is out of surgery, but his situation is extremely critical. The stabbing missed his heart but perforated one of his lungs. He's also lost a lot of blood. We'll know how stable he is within the next hour or so. He's not awake, but you can go in and see him."

"What does that mean, one of his lungs is perforated?" Linda asks.

"It's not fatal. You can survive with only one functioning lung, but he'll need to learn how to deal with that. It's not uncommon, so don't worry."

They follow Dr Tyler into a small room in intensive care where another nurse is sitting on one side of Dan's bed. Linda's eyes well up when she sees her brother, the monitors, and the drip. Karen walks over and places her hand on Dan's. Linda follows her, trying hard to swallow.

"I'll be in the office at the end of the corridor if you need me." The doctor retreats.

"If you're worried about anything, just press this button here," Nurse Wilson explains, pointing to a button near Dan's hand on the bed. "We'll come straight away."

"Thank you," Karen says.

Linda leans over Dan. "Dan, you can do this. We're going to buy an animal rescue centre as soon as you come out. I love you so much, bro."

"Love you, Dan," Karen adds.

The two sisters pull up chairs on either side of the bed and sit reminiscing for a while. Linda thinks that if they talk enough about their childhood, Dan will eventually wake up and join in.

"Do you remember that tree Dan climbed and how I got the blame when he fell out? We could only have been around eight and ten at the time. Mom thought I should have stopped him climbing it."

"I don't remember that, but I do remember Dan stealing my favourite Barbie and hiding it in the loft. I can't remember why he did it, but he was mad at me about something."

"You'd broken his Scalextric. Do you remember? You'd put your foot through the track."

"Oh, god! Yes, that was it. Hey, Dan, sorry I broke your Scalextric. Wow, fancy you remembering that!"

Linda and Karen laugh, and each squeezes a hand on either side of Dan.

"Then, one day, he jumped in the pond after you. You must remember that!" Linda continues. "I still got the blame for you both falling in. But there was no way Dan was going to let you drown in that pond."

"Yes, I do remember that. He's always been a good brother."

They looked at each other sadly and then at Dan, who was breathing but still asleep.

Eventually, Karen quizzed Linda about what had happened at the house, and Linda whispered the story, stopping sometimes to take a deep breath. She still couldn't believe two men were dead. Her voice trembled when she recounted how she couldn't stop Dan's bleeding.

"Well, he's okay now, Linda. And the children are okay. Everyone's okay. Even Brian's back now."

"Yeah, pity he didn't turn up earlier, though. He's really let me down. He's broken my trust."

Suddenly, an alarm sounds. Linda and Karen jump up from their chairs as Dr Tyler and two nurses run in.

"His heart has stopped again," shouts Dr Tyler. A crash trolley arrives almost as he says this, and he places a defibrillator on Dan's chest.

"Stand back!" Dr Tyler commands.

One of the nurses ushers Linda and Karen to the back of the room, where they watch helplessly, Linda with her hand over her mouth.

"Stand back!" Dr Tyler repeats.

A constant beep resonates from the machines. Linda knows what this means. She and Karen both start sobbing, unable to control their emotions.

Eventually, all efforts draw to a close.

"I'm so sorry," Dr Tyler says, looking carefully at Linda and Karen in turn.

Karen takes hold of Linda's hand; they are both shaking from head to toe.

Chapter Thirty-Four

With Sundrive now a crime scene with a huge police presence, Brian needs to check himself and the children into a hotel. An officer at the front door of Sundrive allows him to fetch one or two things for the children.

"Stay there, kids. I'll only be a moment," Brian instructs the children, who sit wide-eyed, gawping at the uniformed officers who are combing the front lawn.

The officer escorts him into the house while the children wait in the car. Brian rushes up the stairs two at a time and heads for the children's room. He grabs their pyjamas and toothbrushes and Ruby's puppy teddy. He notices their swimming things on the floor, so he grabs them, too. He fetches his rucksack from his and Linda's room and adds his overnight things and his swimming trunks, too. The officer follows him around, repeatedly warning him not to touch anything he doesn't need to. Brian decides not to bother with clean clothes. They'll just have to wear the same things tomorrow. He can't think straight at the moment. He thanks the officer, returns to the car, and heads for the seafront. They may as well stay somewhere nice.

Brian has a choice of an extravagant-looking hotel next to the beach bar or the Silver Springs motel next to a Wendy's, which he'd never noticed before. He can see that the motel has a pool, so he chooses that one. At least the children can swim if they want to. Anyway, he's fed up with the rich life. The house manager barely registers their entering reception, and Brian has to cough to get his attention.

"Can we have a room, please? A family room would be great."

The man is unshaven and poorly dressed. Brian tries to hide his shock at the dishevelled appearance of the man.

"How long for? One night, two nights?"

"Oh, maybe a week, I don't know. Yes, say a week, for now, please."

"Okay, that's $75 a night for the family room deluxe. That's the only family room available for a whole week. Otherwise, you'll have to move out after a couple of days."

"Yes, we'll take the deluxe room, thanks."

"Well, there'll be a $100 deposit, too, and we like payment upfront, so that will be $625, please. You paying on a credit card or cash?"

Brian thinks he can smell whisky on the manager's breath. He wonders what state the 'deluxe' room will be in.

"Card, please."

"Okay, there's an extra 2% charge for using a card. There you go." The manager hands a machine over for Brian to insert his card. Once he's paid, the manager gives him the room key and directions to the room. The motel is laid out in a U shape with parking spaces on the inside. Brian decides to move the car outside their door. He grabs his rucksack and tells the children to follow him. The room isn't as bad as he expected. Everything looks clean, although there's a strange musty smell. Three beds, a double and two singles, line one wall and the opposite wall has a dressing table, minibar, and television.

The children are too tired to react to the room. Normally, Liam would be jumping on the bed in a hotel room, trying the television out, and exploring whether the mini bar included chocolate. Now, they both sit expectantly on the edge of the double bed, waiting for Brian to tell them what to do. They are quiet, and Brian knows they're frightened. He helps them out of their clothes and into their pyjamas. There's a basket of crisp packets on top of the minibar, and he throws a packet to each of them.

"Here, eat these and I'll get some pizza delivered. You guys must be starving."

Ruby opens her packet slowly and asks,

"Did Rifleman Rick kill someone, Dad? I heard Mum whispering to Auntie Karen about bodies. I'm scared, Daddy."

Brian smiles at hearing the nickname Rifleman Rick.

"We mustn't call him that, Ruby. It's just our name for him between us, but yes, he did shoot two men, Ruby. He was protecting your mum. It was a good job that he was there."

"Where were you, Dad?" Liam asks.

Brian looks at his son and feels a sense of shame. He wonders how to explain.

"I made a wrong call today, son. I'm so sorry I wasn't there."

"I'm glad you weren't here, Dad. You could have been hurt, like Uncle Dan." Ruby starts crying.

"Well, I'm here now." Brian pushes between his children on the bed and puts an arm around each of them.

"Okay, guys. What kind of pizza do you want?" Brian tries to make light of the situation but has a heavy heart. He can't turn the clock back, and he feels ashamed of his behaviour. He doesn't understand what's happened to him that he could behave in such a spoilt and selfish way. When their pizzas arrive, none of them eat very much. He lets them sleep in the double bed so they are together, and he goes to lie on one of the singles.

It's been a long day, and the kids soon fall asleep.

Brian can't sleep, though. He prays that his phone doesn't ring with bad news about Dan. He figures if it doesn't ring, Dan is still alive. After what seems like a very long night awake on his back, the phone finally rings. The sun is just rising, but the dirty net curtains aren't letting much light in. He can hear Karen crying on the phone, and his heart sinks.

"Dan didn't make it," she sobs.

"Oh, Karen, oh no. I'm so sorry."

"There was nothing they could do. He was too badly injured."

"Can I speak to Linda?"

"She's with Dan. I've just come out to let you know. The hospital is crawling with police. Linda has to give a statement, but she's exhausted. I asked them if they could leave anything else until later."

"Karen, I know this may not be the right time, but I saw your text message. I know you saw me getting into Angela's car. I wasn't thinking straight. But I swear to God, on the kids' lives, I didn't do anything."

"God, Brian! This is not the right time! I don't care what you did, but Linda needed you today, and you weren't here."

"I know, and I'm going to regret that for the rest of my life, Karen."

"We'll come and fetch the kids. We need to see Mom and Dad." Karen starts crying again. "God, they're going to be so shocked."

"Yes, of course. What can I do, Karen?"

"Where are you, Brian?"

"We're in the Silver Springs motel."

"The one by Wendy's on the seafront?"

"Yeah, that's the one."

"God, that's a dive, isn't it? Look, I've got to go. I need to get back to Linda. I can't leave her on her own. You need to tell the kids. They're going to be shocked. They loved Dan."

"They certainly did… I loved Dan, too, Karen. I'm so sorry."

There's a silence for a moment, and Brian hears Karen sigh.

"I know you did, Brian. And Dan loved you, too."

Brian chokes. The full force of the news hits him with Karen's words. "Thank you, Karen. It's kind of you to say that. You were a great sister to him. He loved you to bits."

"I know, Brian, but thank you."

"Please, Karen, tell Linda, I'll never let her down again."

"I've got to go. We'll be with you soon — we need to get off to Brooklyn as soon as we can."

*****

Liam is awake and wide-eyed, watching Brian. Brian leans over Ruby and gently wakes her.

"It's Uncle Dan, isn't it," Liam sobs before Brian can explain.

"Yes, Liam. His injuries were too severe. He couldn't be saved. So now we have to be very brave and remember all the happy times we had with him."

Ruby starts crying. Brian watches her tiny little shoulders heaving up and down. Finally broken himself, he hugs the children to him to hide his own tears. He rocks them for a few minutes until Ruby's cries finally die down. He helps them get dressed and explains that their mum and Karen are picking them up and taking them to their grandparents. Once dressed, the three of them sit in silence, waiting for Linda to arrive. Eventually they hear a car pull up outside and go out to meet her.

"I'm so sorry about Dan," Brian says.

"We're going to have to go," Linda says to Brian without giving him eye contact.

"Please, Linda, we need to talk."

"Not now, Brian."

"Let me come with you. I can look after the children while you talk to your parents."

"No, Brian. I need some space. Now's not the time."

"Linda, I…"

"No, Brian. Please." Linda waves her hands about in the air. The children watch on, forlorn.

"Get in the car, kids!" Linda bellows at them.

The children climb into the back, and Liam opens the car window. He shouts, "Why aren't you coming, Dad?"

Ruby is sobbing again now.

"I love you, Liam. Love you, Ruby. Look after your mum and Auntie Karen." Brian shouts back desperately as Linda reverses out of the parking lot.

Chapter Thirty-Five

Brian walks back to his motel room, trying to figure out what the hell has happened in his life the last few weeks. He wonders whether to join the motel manager for a few whiskies and drink himself to oblivion. But Linda might need him, and he doesn't want to let her down again. He must stay sober and be ready in case she called. He returns the hire car to the Hertz offices opposite the motel. He walks back to the room via the pool. He wonders how different this morning would have been if Dan had survived. Brian would have been splashing in the pool with Liam and Ruby. At least they had spent some fun time with Dan at Sundrive. The kids loved playing in the pool with him. Those would be their last memories of Dan. More than anything, Brian suddenly feels like he needs a shower and some fresh clothes. He wonders what's going on at Sundrive and whether he can get access again.

A lady he hasn't seen before is now sitting at reception in the motel. Too tired to walk back to the house, he asks her to call a taxi for him, and it soon arrives.

"Sundrive, please," says Brian to the driver.

"Are you with the Press, buddy? Sundrive is all over the news. Two people have been shot trying to break into somebody's house," says the driver.

"It's my house, actually," says Brian. "Well, I'm renting it at the moment. The two assailants were killed after stabbing my brother-in-law."

"Oh, I'm so sorry to hear that. Is he okay?"

"No. He died this morning." Brian takes a deep breath, remembering how the children took this news.

"Oh my god, that's terrible. I'm so sorry!"

As the taxi enters Sundrive, Brian sees that the place is still swarming with police.

He stands by the driver and retrieves his wallet from his back pocket.

"No, please, that's not necessary. I'm so sorry, buddy," the driver says.

"Thank you," Brian replies. The man's kindness brings tears to Brian's eyes, and he starts to shake. With Dan's death, not having slept, and Linda leaving without him and taking the children, he suddenly feels humbled by this small, kind gesture of a fellow human being.

He approaches the front door and catches sight of Rick talking to two police officers as they are standing at the entrance to the living room.

"Am I okay to pick up some belongings? This is my house," Brian asks one of the officers, feeling all the more dissociated from events by the fact that Rick knows far more about everything than he does.

"You can't at the moment, I'm afraid. Forensics are still collecting evidence," replies the police officer.

"I understand. That's okay," says Brian, wishing he'd asked the taxi driver to stay. He doesn't know what to do with himself. He decides to walk back to the motel. As he turns away from the house, Rick calls after him.

"How is Linda's brother?" Rick asks.

Brian looks Rick in the eye.

"I'm sorry. You haven't heard, of course. He didn't make it, Rick. Linda and Karen are on their way to Brooklyn to tell their parents."

"Oh my god! I'm so sorry, Brian. So, where are you staying? Your house is now a crime scene, a no-go area."

"I've booked into the Silver Springs motel until they allow us back in the house."

"That's an awful place! You can stay at mine, Brian."

"Thanks, Rick, but I've already booked in."

"Well, come and have a coffee at least."

Brian looks at the man whom he and Linda had frowned upon for using guns. He wonders what would have happened had Rick not arrived when he did the day before. He owes this man for protecting Linda.

"Sounds good, Rick. That's very kind."

They walk over to Rick's house. Brian is surprised at how similar the two houses are.

"I'd offer you a beer, Brian, but I haven't had a drink in years."

"That's okay, Rick. I've got to keep my wits about me in case Linda needs me."

"Coffee it is, then."

"So how did you get on with the police? I've no idea what happens now. Are you in trouble?"

"I've made a statement. But I'm an ex-cop, and most of those guys, well, the older ones, all know me. If I hadn't intervened, they would have killed Linda.

Some of what happened is even recorded on a camera that overlooks the pool, so I don't have to worry. My story is rock solid. What they can't see in the video, they can hear in the background. It's not very pretty, I'm afraid. I hope you never have to see it."

Brian shivers, wondering what Linda must be feeling like today.

"I'd like to ask some questions, though, if you don't mind, Brian. It would help piece the puzzle together."

"Sure. Fire away," says Brian, wondering whether Rick's picked up on their marital tiff, their lottery win or something else.

"What's with your brother-in-law and his gambling?" asks Rick.

"Karen's husband, Tom, is a compulsive gambler. He owes money to, well, almost everybody, including some gangsters, who are the assailants you shot, I guess. He'll feel pretty bad now, though, when he hears about Dan. They were close."

"Yeah, I've been down the drink and gambling road," Rick replies.

"I don't know what we'd have done without you, Rick. Linda could easily have been killed. How did you know what was happening?"

"I heard Linda screaming. I've heard those screams once before in my life, but this time, I knew exactly what to do. I just reached for the nearest weapon, which was my 19 mm handgun. It comes with fifteen rounds."

"I haven't a clue about all that technical gun jargon, and to be quite honest, Rick, until last night, I've always been opposed to guns."

"So was I until we were attacked."

"You were attacked? When?"

"Ten years ago. Our house was burgled late at night. I'd been drinking all day and was in no fit state to resist. I made the fateful mistake of challenging them without a weapon. They shot me in the shoulder, and they killed Betty with a shot to the back of her head. I haven't touched a drop of alcohol since that night."

"Oh my god, I didn't know. I'm so sorry. No wonder you're security conscious."

"So… do you not have any guns in the house, Brian?"

"No, none."

"Wow, none whatsoever?" Rick sits there shaking his head.

"No. I have two young children here, Rick."

"All the more reason to have something, Brian. You just never know. I mean, these assailants don't make appointments with you. You don't get any warning."

"No, I suppose not. So how many guns do you have, Rick?"

"I have different weapons for different needs."

"And you've obviously got a gun near your bed?"

"Either side, Brian. You just never know which direction an attack may come from. I swore that nobody would ever catch me in a vulnerable position ever again."

"No, I suppose… with what you went through, that's more than understandable. I really don't blame you."

"What do you think of Sundrive then, Brian?"

"I think Long Island is a beautiful place. My wife used to come to the beach here when she was little. We were looking to buy her parents a place here. I doubt they'll want to move here now, though."

"Yeah, but what do you think of Sundrive?"

"If I'm being totally honest with you, Rick, I'm not too sure about some of the neighbours."

"You mean Angela and PJ?"

"Ah… what made you say that?"

"I'm an ex-cop, Brian. I notice everything that goes on around here. I had to leave work after having a nervous breakdown. I was left some insurance money, but financially, I'm not in the same league as Angela and PJ. I've lived here for twelve years, and they haven't spoken to me since my wife was killed."

"I'm like you, Rick. I come from the poorer side of the fence. They're too good for the likes of us with their stocks and shares."

"Stocks and shares, Brian?"

"Yes, that's their line of business, isn't it?"

"Well, they may have invested some of their massive wealth, but I suppose you're not to know."

"Know what?"

"They're very bad people, Brian. In fact, they're evil people."

"I don't understand?"

"She's a high-class hooker, and he's got to be one of the oldest pimps around."

"You what?"

"She's a high-class hooker, Brian. And they blackmail people, including powerful politicians and judges. That's where they get all their money from."

"Oh my god!"

"Why, what's the matter?"

"I told Angela that we were buying a house for Karen's parents."

"So, they figured out you had money. You were probably going to be their next victim, Brian. They obviously assumed you had money."

"Oh my god! How could I have been so stupid?"

"I know a top judge who had to give them a huge amount of money."

"Linda didn't like Angela from the minute she met her. I feel so stupid."

"There was another couple. They actually lived at the top of Sundrive. Angela got intimately close to the wife. This was another blackmail case that my ex-colleagues investigated. After paying Angela and PJ, the couple ended up having to leave Long Island."

"How do you know all this?"

"I told you. I'm an ex-cop. Look, I still have friends in the force, but they've never been able to pin anything on them."

"I feel sick. That could have been me. I went to Manhattan with her. She kept kissing me in a bar."

"I bet she picked the bar."

"Yes, she did."

"You can guarantee that somebody would have been photographing you together. She was slowly gathering her evidence."

"Oh my god. She told me she loved having fun."

"She does, but at other people's expense."

"And she took me to a hotel in Manhattan."

"I'll also bet she picked the hotel room as well."

"Too right!"

"I'm sorry, but the room will have been rigged from top to bottom with cameras."

"Well, fortunately, nothing happened. I walked out after she got angry. She discovered that Linda had insulted PJ in front of clients. Linda had revealed that I wasn't a successful businessman and that I won my money in the lottery. Angela got really mad and said that I'd lied to her. I didn't want everybody to know my personal business, so I just let her assume I was a successful businessman. I hadn't actually told any lies."

"She's a psychopath. She must have felt that you were conning her instead of her conning you. What a shock for her!"

"She was very angry. I couldn't believe how quickly her mood changed."

"Thank god it did, or it would have cost you a lot and possibly even your marriage, Brian."

"I think I've already screwed that up myself, Rick."

Chapter Thirty-Six

Early afternoon, Rick drops Brian back off at the Silver Springs motel.

"Thanks for the lift, Rick. And thanks for the coffee. It's been really good to talk to someone. I'm grateful for your time."

"You're welcome. It's not a good time, I know, but hang on in there. Why don't you take my number, in case you're stuck for a lift or anything? Just call me if you think I can help."

"Yeah, thanks, Rick. What's your number?"

Brian types Rick's contact details into his phone and then sends a text so that Rick has his number, too.

"Look after yourself and pass on my condolences to Linda."

"I will. Thank you."

Back in his 'deluxe' bedroom, nobody has touched the beds or removed the half-eaten pizzas. Brian flops on the bed, exhausted. He rings Linda. There's no answer, but within a couple of minutes, Karen calls him.

"Hi Brian. Linda can't speak right now. Mom and Dad are in shock. They're trying their best not to break down in front of the kids."

"God knows what you're all going through. Just tell Linda to phone me when she's up to it."

"I will, Brian."

"And Karen…"

"Yes?"

"Thanks for phoning me back."

"You're welcome, Brian. Bye for now."

"Bye."

Brian closes his eyes. He can't work out how his life can have nosedived in this way since his massive win. This isn't how he was expecting things to be. Here he is in Long Island with seventeen million in the bank and without a clue what to do next. The whole situation is driving him mad. He decides there's only one thing to do. He walks to the nearest liquor store and buys a bottle of whiskey. Back in the room, he switches on the TV and pours himself a large drink.

Just then, his phone starts ringing. He jumps up, hoping it's Linda, but sees that it's Deano. He feels like he's time-warped into a previous life.

"Hi Deano, we've been worried about you. Where are you, mate?"

"At Debbie's, of course."

"At Debbie's?"

"Yeah, didn't Linda tell you?"

"No… Erm, I haven't seen much of Linda just lately. So, where have you been?"

"Debbie rang Linda to let you guys know I was in rehab getting my act together. Best thing I've done in years."

"That's good, Deano. That's brilliant news. Well done, mate! So, are you still getting the house?"

"God, Linda hasn't told you anything, has she? I've already bought the house. We're just waiting to move in. Is everything okay? You don't sound too good. What's the deal with Linda? How come she didn't tell you? Is she okay?"

"To be honest, Deano, no, everything's not okay. Linda's brother has been murdered. Linda and the children are with her parents in Brooklyn right now. She and her sister… well, they are all in shock. I'm sitting in a motel in Long Island waiting to hear from her."

"Oh my god. What the hell happened? Is Linda okay? Are the children okay?"

"It's a long story. Karen's husband, Tom, owes money to some gangsters. Poor Dan ended up in the middle of it all and got stabbed. Yes, Linda is okay, just, and the children weren't there, thank god, when it happened, but they're pretty shaken up now, of course."

"God, there was me thinking you were surfing on the beach somewhere."

"I wish I was. The whole trip hasn't been quite what I expected."

"I'm sorry." Brian can hear that Deano is still on the line, but he doesn't say anything. After a short pause, Deano resumes the conversation.

"Brian, I was phoning to tell you about another death, actually, but you won't be too bothered about this one. Juicy died."

"What happened to him?"

"A drug overdose. He won't be missed."

"I wouldn't say that," Brian says generously. "He's still a human being."

"I thought you'd be glad! He threatened your family!"

"Deano, the poor bloke, never stood a chance in life. He obviously made a few bad choices, but he never got the same breaks as you and I."

"Brian, have you joined one of those American religious groups or something?" Deano laughs.

"Well, imagine how different your life would have been if you couldn't have had rehab or if you had never met Debbie. Everything that's been happening the last few weeks has made me think about life, Deano."

"Yeah, I suppose so. Listen, I've got to go, Brian. Debbie wants to go and choose the carpets. I'm trying to get everything ready before we move in. Give Linda our love. Tell her I'm so sorry about her brother. Say hello to the kids, and I'll speak to you soon, buddy."

"Okay, take care, Deano."

Brian flicks through the channels and thinks about how Juicy's luck eventually ran out. He can't help wondering if his own luck has also come to an end.

His phone rings again. He sits bolt upright, hoping it's Linda, but he's surprised to see Angela's name on his phone screen. He isn't sure whether to answer, especially after what Rick told him, but his curiosity gets the better of him.

"Hello!"

"Hello, Brian. I had to call. The police have taken over Sundrive. I'm so sorry to hear about your wife's brother. I'm also sorry for the way I behaved the other night."

Brian isn't sure whether to hang up but is still quite intrigued. Angela has probably realised by now that he has millions in the bank and wants to get her hands on some of it.

"Her name's Linda, Angela."

"Sorry, Brian. I don't know why I find it so hard to remember her name. What was her brother's name?"

"Dan," Brian says quietly.

"Well, I'm really sorry about Dan, and I hope you have happy memories of him to help you through."

Brian's exhaustion overwhelms him. Angela's words all sound kind, but now Rick has told him about her and PJ's con artist activities, Brian wonders at the tenacity of the woman. He considers leading her along a little. He's curious to see what she will do.

"I'm sorry too, Angela. I shouldn't have spoken to you as I did at the hotel. You just seemed so angry, and it was all so sudden. It rather took me by surprise."

"I know. I really am sorry, Brian. I've thought about what you said. I wouldn't want everybody knowing I'd won the lottery either. I get that. By the way, I can see the police going in and out of your house. How long will they be there for?"

"I'm not sure."

"So, where are you now?"

"I've had to check into a hotel."

"Is Linda with you?"

"No, she's had to go with her sister to break the news to her parents."

"Oh, how awful… Which hotel are you in?"

"Oh, hold on, Angela, I've got to go. Her sister Karen is phoning."

"Sure, speak soon, Brian."

Brian is relieved his small deception deflected Angela's questions. He needs time to think. He phones Rick.

"Hi, Rick, sorry to bother you. You'll never guess who just phoned me."

"Angela?"

"Correct. She conveyed her condolences and apologised for her behaviour the other day."

"You know what this means, Brian? She's still after your money, pal."

"I told her Linda was at her parents, and she asked me where I was staying."

"Did you tell her?"

"No chance. She won't be hearing from me again. And you're right. It looks like she just came back, hoping to get her hands on the money. I got her off the line, told her I had another call."

"Brian, you don't have to do this, and it's completely your decision, but there may just be a chance here to stop this evil pair for once and for all."

"How do you mean?"

"Well, you could pretend to go along with whatever she's planning, and we could expose them both."

"I'm sorry, Rick, but I don't want anything to do with her. I'm in enough trouble with Linda because of Angela. If she knew I'd just spoken to her, well, that would definitely be it!"

"And there lies the problem, Brian."

"How do you mean?"

"Angela and PJ can get away with whatever they like because their victims fear the risk to their relationships. Apart from the shame and embarrassment, victims don't want their partners to find out. It's the perfect crime."

"You can't blame people for that, though, Rick."

"No, you can't." Rick sighs.

Brian can tell that Rick is disappointed and doesn't know what to say.

"Brian, can I level with you?"

"Sure."

"When Betty, my wife, was killed, we found out that the henchmen who shot her had been delivering parcels to PJ and Angela for several weeks."

"I don't understand."

"We already knew that PJ was dangerous, but after Betty's death… Well, it's possible Angela had named us as easy targets to burgle. I was a heavy drinker at the time. We were easy prey."

"Did the police question them about it?"

"Sure, but PJ and Angela laughed it off, claiming I had my wires crossed, with being an alcoholic and all that. I had to leave the police force around that time because of my drinking, and my complaint was never investigated properly. Nobody was ever charged for Betty's murder."

"I'm sorry, Rick. That must be hard. And you're sure the men who broke in were associates of PJ and Angela's?"

"Brian, I swear on Betty's grave, I've seen them numerous times with PJ and Angela."

"How can you carry on living here, Rick? You're torturing yourself. You need to get away and start afresh, mate."

"This is my home. It's where Betty and I lived. Anyway, I haven't given up on catching them out yet."

"Good luck with that! What I don't understand is that if they have so much money, why does Angela continue to con and blackmail people?"

"They're hooked. The more they earn, the more they spend—yachts in the south of France, villas in Italy, they even had their own helicopter for a while and hired a pad by the beach. And she's a psychopath, Brian. She enjoys risk."

"Well, even if I were to go along with your suggestion, how would it help? I'm not prepared to do anything they could blackmail me for, and surely they can't be arrested for putting a few cameras in a hotel room?"

"I don't care whether they're arrested, but so long as their activities are exposed, the publicity would finish them. Their fake stocks and shares charade would also be exposed for what it is, a complete and utter sham."

"But that's hardly justice for Betty, is it? Would this really help you, Rick?"

"Yes, Brian. I let Betty down."

"You didn't let her down, Rick. You were both attacked by evil people."

Rick remains silent.

"You were there for my family the other night, Rick, and I owe you for that. So yes, I'm in; what do I need to do?"

"Thanks, Brian. You're a star! Phone her back and go along with whatever she wants. She'll probably suggest a hotel. I'll do the rest."

"Okay, Rick. I just hope I'm doing the right thing."
"Believe me, Brian, they don't come nastier than these two. I've been waiting for this moment for years. I'll speak to you soon."

Brian is now fired up for action. He feels sure that Angela plans both to rob him and to destroy his marriage. What kind of a woman does that? Rick had also seemed pretty sure they were involved in Betty's murder.

He phones Angela.

"Sorry about that, Angela. It was Linda's sister."

"How are they all?"

"Not good."

"What about you, Brian? Don't tell me you're on your own again?"

"I'm afraid so."

"Right, where are you? I can't leave you on your own, Brian. Not at a time like this."

"I'm at the Silver Springs motel."

"Silver Springs? Why the Silver Springs, Brian? You can afford better than that!"

"I had to get somewhere quick. I had the kids with me. It was just a panic thing. We couldn't get access to the house. It was late. I was tired."

"Right, I'm just going to get changed. I'll be about half an hour, and I'll be round there to pick you up."

"Okay, Angela. That's kind. I could do with a distraction."

Brian gives Rick a quick call to update him, and within half an hour, he sees Angela parking up by reception. He texts Rick quickly to keep him informed: She's arrived. Don't call me. I'll phone you.

Rick responds immediately: Good luck!

Feeling a sense of déjà vu, Brian climbs into Angela's blue convertible. She's wearing a tight mini-skirt and a figure-revealing boob tube. She looks older than he remembered, and the shape of her nose gives her a harsh profile from where he's sat in the passenger seat.

"Wow, Angela. You look great," he says with a smile.

Chapter Thirty-Seven

"Brian, we never got to have that Italian meal. Would you still like to go?"

"Why not? I'm only sitting in a motel waiting for Linda and the kids."

"Why are you staying in a motel? I thought a man of your wealth would be staying in a five-star hotel, not a dump like that?"

"I only picked it because it had a pool for the kids."

"Always thinking of others, Brian." Angela takes her hand off the steering wheel and places it over his.

"I still feel bad about the way I spoke to you. I don't know what came over me."

"I was rude to you, too, Angela. I guess we were tired."

"Let's put it behind us now, but I'm going to make it up to you, Brian." Angela smiles at him seductively, holding eye contact just a moment longer than needed.

"Watch the road, Angela," Brian asks nervously as she swerves past a braked car in front of them.

"Manhattan, here we come!" Angela laughs as she puts her foot down on the accelerator.

"So, are we going back to the Highgrove then?"

"Yes, you never got to see the restaurant, and believe me, you've never experienced anything like it."

They continue in silence. Brian wonders how Linda and the children are doing. He's never felt so distant from her in their marriage, and it worries him. He also needs to speak to Rick and let him know what's happening. He considers how to ask Angela to stop so he can make a call.

"Angela, when you get a chance, can we stop by a garage? I could do with a coffee. I haven't been sleeping too good."

"Sure, there's a gas station coming up shortly. We can stop there."

When they reach the gas station, Angela parks up.

"I won't be long. Do you need me to get you anything?"

"No, I'm okay, thanks."

As Brian enters the store, he looks back and can see Angela on her phone. He assumes she's making plans to rig the room at the hotel.

He pops into the toilet to make his call, just in case Angela decides to join him in the store.

"Hi, Rick. I have to be quick. We're going to the Highgrove Hotel again. As soon as I know the room number, I'll let you know. Is somebody going to be there? I'm beginning to feel a bit nervous. I don't want this wrecking my marriage… I've no intention of doing anything with Angela." Brian can hear his voice rising in volume as his nerves get the better of him.

"It's fine, Brian. Calm down, and oh, yes. There'll be a welcome committee for her."

"Okay, Rick. I have to go now, but I'll call you when I can."

"Text me if it's easier. Just make sure she doesn't catch you."

Brian finds the coffee station and pays for a latte. As he returns to the car, he sees Angela drop her phone back into her handbag.

"Stocks and Shares. Do you know much about the financial market, Brian?"

"Not a thing."

"It's terribly boring, but it pays the bills."

Brian knows exactly how Angela and PJ pay the bills: by ruining other people's lives. And today, they are planning to ruin his. Suddenly, he doesn't feel nervous at all. Knowing what kind of people Angela and PJ are makes him determined to stop them. He has to remain cool, though.

"So, you must have been delighted winning the lottery, Brian?"

"Well, yes, but it was also a bit of a shock, really, you know, not something we were prepared for."

"I bet it was. Do you mind my asking… how much did you win?"

"£17 million. Well, a bit over."

"How much?" Angela brakes sharply to avoid the car in front. "Oh my god, £17 million! You're made for life, Brian!"

She smiles winningly at him. "What fun you can have with that, Brian. You guys don't seem very together, though. Is Linda unhappy? Why aren't you with her now, especially at a time like this?"

"To be honest, she's very annoyed with me. Her sister, Karen, saw you and me together. She thinks I should have been there when Dan was attacked. Instead, I was with you." He tries to hide his feelings from Angela and makes his voice sound neutral. "She's distraught, of course. Dan was her baby brother. So, she's overreacting about us, of course."

"I see. And how would she react if she found out we were together now?"

"Oh my god," Brian laughs loudly. "If she knew, she'd probably divorce me!"

Angela smiles and raises her eyebrows. She seems to take the bait. "You're afraid of her, then?" she asks.

"Oh god, you have no idea. My life would not be worth living. But it'll be fine. There's no way she or Karen will ever find out." Brian smiles at Angela.

"Well, we're both mature adults, Brian, and you're right. She won't find out. We can have some fun. Are you happy to be with me?"

"Yeah, sure I am."

"Good! We only live once. How long is she staying in Brooklyn?"

"I'm not sure. She's going to have to look after her parents, and I don't think she's in any hurry to rush back to me."

Angela looks up and raises her eyebrows.

"It must be very difficult for you too, Brian."

"I must admit, it is quite hard, Angela. I was very fond of Dan, too."

Angela takes his hand in hers. "I can think of a way to distract you."

*****

Once they arrive at the Highgrove, Angela abandons the car to the valet, and they make their way to reception.

"Would you be a darling and get me a glass of champagne in the Piano Bar? I'll book the restaurant at reception."

"Yeah, sure." Brian heads for the bar and takes the opportunity to phone Rick again.

"Rick, she's at reception now. Is there somebody here ready?"

"They're on their way. Don't worry, Brian, everything's organised."

"I've got to go, Rick. She's coming."

Angela walks back into the bar like she's walking on a catwalk.

"Was there room available in the restaurant?"

"I had to use some influence, but we've managed to get a table."

"That's great."

"That wasn't Linda on the phone, was it?"

"No, it was a friend from Liverpool. He's moving into a new house. He's pretty excited and wanted to update me."

"Do you fancy a drink in the tourist bar we went to?"

"Yeah, I quite liked that bar."

They both raise their glasses to drink their champagne, and Angela's phone starts to ring.

"Excuse me, darling. Let me just answer this. It's business." She walks away, presumably so he can't hear.

"No problem," Brian says amiably and wonders if she's coordinating the preparation of the hotel room for her sting. He watches her speaking animatedly to someone on her phone over by a window. When she's finished, she returns to him, once again emphasizing the swing of her hips.

"Right then! Shall we go?"

The bar is near Central Park, and it doesn't take them long to walk there. Once inside, Brian orders a bottle of champagne, and Angela is soon laughing and dancing; she's the life and soul of the party, grabbing him at every opportunity. She moves close to kiss him and places his arms around her waist.

Brian knows this is all part of her plan. He looks around for a photographer, but nearly everyone is taking photos on their phones, so nobody in particular stands out. Everyone seems a little wild, and the conversations they are having sound shallow. He wonders why he thought this was fun when he first came with Angela, and he starts to feel a little queasy from the champagne. He wishes Linda was with him. Angela orders another bottle of champagne and chatters on.

"I just love New York City, Brian. Isn't it great fun?"

"Yeah, it sure is." Brian tries to inject some enthusiasm into his voice.

"Brian, you sound tired. Shall we go back to the hotel and prepare for our meal?"

"Yeah, sounds good."

"I've booked us a room to freshen up."

Of course, you have, Brian thinks. Out loud, he says, "That's great. Is it one of the skyscraper rooms overlooking Manhattan?"

"Yeah, it's the Duke of Windsor suite. It's on the second to last floor and has a delightful balcony. It's my treat for being mean to you the other night."

"No need, Angela, but sounds great."

They walk back to the hotel.

"Would you get me some more bubbly, please, while I check at reception that the room is ready?"

"Okay." Brian orders another bottle of champagne and quickly gets his phone out. He texts Rick the name of the room: Duke of Windsor Suite on the second to last floor.

Rick responds immediately: The team will be waiting to pounce.

Everything is going to plan. Brian can't wait to get up there and see Angela's face when she realizes the tables have been turned.

"Our suite is not going to be ready for another hour, but they've said we can go up to another room while we're waiting and sit on the balcony there. Let's bring up our drinks," Angela says on her return.

The room they have been given to wait in is very small, and Brian sees that there's no balcony.

"It's only for an hour while we're waiting for the suite to be cleaned," Angela apologizes.

She switches on the TV, tunes to a music channel, and turns the volume up.

Suddenly, there's a knock at the door.

"Oh gosh, maybe the room is ready already," Angela suggests.

Brian opens the door and is knocked to the floor with a punch from a giant of a man. Two more follow the giant into the room and begin kicking Brian on the floor.

"Do you think I'm stupid, Brian?" says Angela. "You're not dealing with your factory friends in the north of England now. You're in a different league, you moron!"

Brian feels a throbbing in his head and takes another kick to the stomach. The three men stand around him like great tree trunks. He wonders if this is it, and an image of Linda and the children flashes in front of him.

He tries to raise his head and tastes blood in his mouth. He hears a groaning and realises that he's making the noise himself. The three giants are still surrounding him. Though his vision is blurred, he can see them smirking at him. He hopes they aren't going to kick him anymore. There's also a ringing in his ears, which he thinks might be his phone. It must be because Angela grabs it from his pocket and puts it to his mouth.

"Brian, what's going on? Why are you making that groaning noise?" Linda asks.

Brian tries to say something, but only a grunt escapes.

"Hello, who is this?" Angela asks.

"Linda, Brian's wife. And who the bloody hell is this?"

"It's Angela. Can I help you?"

"Yeah, you can tell him to fuck off back to England. I don't know how he could do this to me. Tell him he'll never see me and the kids again."

Chapter Thirty-Eight

Brian slowly moves his head. He can't hear anyone else in the room and tries to get up off the floor. As he gradually arches himself up into a sitting position, the pain sears through his head.

He's unsure what has happened, and as he looks around the room, he feels dizzy. Then he remembers. Brian's a big bloke, but there wasn't much he could do when he was attacked by three men, all larger than himself.

He somehow manages to get to his knees, then to his feet, and staggers into the bathroom. He's not a pretty sight when he looks in the mirror. He's bleeding from his mouth and nose, and his left eye is swollen. He runs the cold water tap and grabs a glass from above the sink. He fills it and washes his mouth out. He reaches for a pristine white towel from a pile at the end of the bath and soaks it under the tap. He wipes it around his face and dabs carefully at his eyes. The towel is now blotted with blood, and he throws it into the bath.

He staggers slowly back into the bedroom and lowers himself into a chair by the bed. He catches sight of his phone on the floor and remembers Linda phoning. He replays in his mind Angela taking his phone and speaking to Linda. He'll never be able to explain this to Linda.

He crouches down to pick up the phone and dials Rick.

His voice sounds hoarse and laboured, as though it's someone else speaking, and his words come out slower than usual.

"Is everything okay?" Rick asks.

"You weren't kidding when you said she was evil!"

"Who? What's going on?"

"Angela. I think we underestimated her."

"Why? What's happened?"

"Well, apart from getting her heavies to beat me up, she's also wrecked my marriage."

"Brian, are you okay?"

"I'll survive. But Angela knew… She knew about our plan. She pretended our suite wasn't ready and said reception had offered us another room whilst we were waiting. Then three guys… big guys… came into the room and gave me a good thrashing. How could she have known, Rick?"

"I'm sorry, Brian. I should never have let you do this. Maybe she has people in the police on her payroll."

"These cuts and bruises will heal, but I don't think my marriage will."

"Why? Tell me what happened!"

"Linda called when I'd been punched to the floor. I was in a pretty bad state, Rick, moaning and groaning in agony. Angela made sure Linda could hear me and that she would get the wrong end of the stick. It worked, and all I could hear was Linda screaming that she was my wife, that I could fuck off, and she'd never let me see the kids again."

"You mean Angela made it seem like you were together?"

"Yes, definitely."

"I'm so sorry. I don't know what to say. I shouldn't have got you involved in this. Do you need an ambulance, or shall I take you to a hospital?"

"No, I'll be okay. But you could pick me up if you don't mind. I don't want to get into a taxi looking like I've just finished fifteen rounds at Maddison Square Garden."

"Give me an hour. I'll phone you when I'm outside."

"Okay, see you soon."

Brian phones Linda but isn't surprised when she doesn't answer.

He sends her a WhatsApp message:

This is hard to put in a text message, but you've got this all wrong. Would you please answer your phone and give me the chance to explain?

He checks his phone a few minutes later, but Linda hasn't looked at it.

It seems to Brian that since he won the lottery, he's had nothing but bad luck.

He drifts off to sleep and is startled when his phone rings.
"I'm outside," Rick says. "Can you hurry so I don't need to park up? I'm not supposed to park here."

"I must have fallen asleep. Okay, Rick, I'll be right down."

Brian tries avoiding eye contact with people in the lift. Once at the ground floor, he quickly makes his way out of the hotel and jumps into Rick's car.

"Oh my god. Your face…it's… I'm really sorry, Brian."

"It's not your fault."

Rick takes off his sunglasses and passes them to Brian, who puts them on to hide his swollen eyes.

"Linda's not responding to my calls or WhatsApp messages."

"I'm sure she'll come round. The police have left Sundrive now, Brian. Do you want to go back there?"

"No. I won't be going back there. If I saw Angela, I'd probably do something worthy of a life sentence. And after what happened to Dan, I've definitely had enough of the place."

"Yes, I'm sure. In fact, Brian, I'm beginning to feel that way myself. I contacted a real estate agency last week, even before all this happened—I was thinking of leaving myself. I could move back to New Jersey. I've still got nephews living there."

"That would be a wise move."

"So, is it back to your motel for you, Brian?"

"Yes, please. God, you couldn't make this shit up. How do I explain what I was doing with Angela? What must Linda's family think of me right now, especially with Dan lying in a morgue? Oh Christ." Brian takes a deep breath. "My marriage is over. There's no way back from this."

When they eventually arrive back at the motel, Brian struggles to get out of the car.

"Thanks, Rick. I'll speak to you later. I need to rest right now."

"Phone me if you need anything."

Brian surveys the motel room. The beds are still rumpled from how the children left them. It seems such a long time ago since they were there. He pours himself a large glass of whisky. This is followed by a few more, which seem to ease the pain. It isn't long before he falls asleep, and again, he doesn't wake until his phone rings, by which time several hours have passed.

When he wakes and remembers everything that has happened, he does something he hasn't done in years; he starts crying. More than anything, he wants the call to be from Linda, his beautiful lady Linda, but it's Rick.

"Hi, Rick," he says, trying to hide his disappointment. He wipes the tears from his face, glad that Rick can't see him.

"You've been drinking, haven't you?" Rick challenges.

"Yes, but don't lecture me, Rick. I need it to ease the pain right now."

"Physical or mental pain, Brian?"

"Both." Brian tries not to break down.

"Look! I understand. I really do. I used to do exactly the same. So, no lectures, I promise, but just make sure that you're eating too."

"I will. Can I call you back when I'm feeling a bit better, Rick?"

"Sure. Just don't forget to eat!"

Brian is awoken again from a deep, alcohol-induced sleep by Rick's next call.

"Rick, what day is it?" Brian asks.

"Tuesday. You've slept for about sixteen hours."

"I feel exhausted."

"That's the alcohol. Have you eaten?"

"I'll take a shower and then get some sandwiches."

"Okay, call me back when you've had something to eat."

Brian checks his phone again, but there's still nothing from Linda. He decides to phone Karen, and fortunately, she answers.

"Karen, I take it Linda isn't speaking to me?"

"Well, what do you think?" Karen replies in an angry tone.

"I guess I understand."

"Oh, you do, do you? Dan's just died, and you jump into bed with a neighbour! God almighty, Brian. What were you thinking?"

"It didn't happen, Karen."

"Linda heard you both, Brian, and that brazen hussy had the audacity to come to the phone. I understand entirely why Linda doesn't want anything more to do with you. Now, if you don't mind, I've got my brother's funeral tomorrow, and I've still a lot to do."

"Dan's funeral is tomorrow?" Brian exclaims. Everything feels unreal to him.

"Oh, you didn't know? Well, if you'd been with your family as you should have been, you would have known."

"Will it be at St Michaels? What time?"

"Linda doesn't want you there."

Brian closes his eyes. How much has changed? Dan is dead. Linda doesn't want him with her.
"Karen, can you let me explain?"

"What's there to explain, Brian?" Brian can tell that Karen has lost all patience with him. She, too, is mourning, and Brian doesn't feel the energy he needs to defend himself.

"Karen…"

"Let me save you the trouble, Brian. We don't need any more lies. When Linda and I went to collect our things from Sundrive yesterday, we found an envelope at the door with photographs of you and your new woman kissing in a bar. There was another note from the woman, Angela, saying what a great time she'd had with you at some hotel."

Brian frowns.

"She said she was sorry PJ sent his men to beat you up, but he'd found out about your affair. So there's no point denying it, Brian."

"Affair? Karen, that's not true. It's a lie."

"So you weren't beaten up then?"

"You don't understand, Karen. She…"

"Did you get beaten up, Brian?"

"Yes, I got beaten up, but not for having an affair with Angela."

"So why did you get beaten up, and what were you doing in a hotel room with her, Brian?"

"It's not what you think. I went to a hotel with her to…"

"You went to a hotel with another woman when we'd just lost Dan! What's the matter with you, Brian? You're finished with our family. I've heard enough."

"Karen, I went to… Hello? Karen?"

Karen has hung up.

Brian sits on the end of his bed with his head in his hands. He raises his head and looks into the mirror opposite him. Jesus, how quickly life could change. Only Rick understood everything that had happened. How quickly Brian had also changed his view of this neighbour who saved his wife's life. He dials Rick's number and updates him about Angela's letter. Brian feels completely lost now.

"It's Dan's funeral tomorrow, and I'm not welcome." Brian finally gives way to his emotions. "I'm broken, Rick." He tries to swallow but can't, and there isn't anything else to say anyway. After a pause, he adds, "Sorry, mate. Not your problem. Don't know why I called you."

"What if I go and speak to Linda? Where's the funeral?"

"Karen didn't say, but it's probably at St Michaels in Brooklyn. That's their parish. But how can you explain Angela kissing me in that bar? You're wasting your time, Rick. Anyway, a funeral isn't the time or place to explain something like that. It's all over, my friend. I'm going back to Liverpool. I've had enough. There's a flight to Manchester in a few hours, and there's still a seat available at the moment. I'm going to book this before it's gone."

Brian promises to phone Rick later when he's booked his flight. He manages to get the last seat to Manchester, and Deano agrees to pick him up at the other end. He makes one last call to Rick to thank him. Rick offers to take him to the airport, but Brian declines. He invites Rick to stay if he's ever in Liverpool and thanks him for everything he's done.

Once at the airport, Brian has a couple of drinks at the bar. He's soon invited to the gate. On the flight, he stares out of the window, numb from everything that has happened.

Chapter Thirty-Nine

Brian is restless on the flight and finally lands in Manchester. With only a small hold-all bag, he's soon through passport control and customs.

Deano, as arranged, is waiting for him in the short-stay car park outside the terminal. Brian phones him to locate where he's parked and spots him almost immediately as he dials.

"On your own? Where is everybody?"

"Don't ask. They're not with me. Let's just get out of here, Deano."

"What? Is that a black eye you've got there, Brian?"

"The trip has been an absolute nightmare."

"I did wonder when you phoned me. You didn't sound your usual self."

Brian is exhausted. Although he doesn't want to talk to Deano or anyone else about everything that has happened, he feels that he owes Deano an explanation. He starts to explain everything, starting from Tom's gambling, moving on to Dan being murdered, and how Rifleman Rick had saved Linda, to his failed attempt to trap Angela and PJ.

Deano focuses steadily on the road ahead, taking them back to Liverpool, and occasionally whistles under his breath.

"So, what's the situation with Linda, Brian? Surely this is only temporary? Linda knows you wouldn't do anything with another woman, and you guys have always been rock solid. You're the strongest couple I've ever met."

"We're finished, Deano. It's all over."

"I can't believe that, Brian."

"I wish we'd never gone to the States. I prayed last night for the first time in years. If God gives me one last chance, I'll give the money back. If we hadn't won the lottery and gone to the States, Dan would still be alive. It's absolutely true what they say, Deano: you can't buy happiness."

"You can still sort things out with Linda, though. She's a decent woman. She'll understand when you get the chance to explain to her."
"She won't Deano. She'll never forgive me for not being there when Dan was killed. She thinks I've had an affair, and worst still, she thinks I was doing it when her brother had just been killed. She and her whole family are disgusted with me."

"Well, I believe you, Brian, and I think that when you get the chance to explain, Linda will too. You just need to get her to listen to you."

"She saw photographs of me and this neighbour of ours in Long Island. The woman was kissing me in a bar. It's too late; it's game set and match, Deano."

"Yeah, but from what you've told me, this Angela was setting you up. Surely you explained that to Linda at Dan's funeral?"

"Dan's funeral is today, and it was made quite clear that I wasn't welcome. I'm absolutely gutted not to be there. Dan was like my own brother."

"Yeah, I know, mate."

"By the way, when is Juicy's funeral?"

"I haven't the faintest idea. There won't be many people there, I'm sure."

"Don't you think that's sad?"

"Well, he didn't do himself any favours, Brian, with the kind of life he chose."

"I wonder if he did choose that life, or did the life choose him?"

"That sounds rather philosophical. What do you mean?"

"Well, what's happened to me in the last few weeks has shown me just how quickly your life can change. I went from rags to riches. I also went from being one of the happiest people in the world… to this. Perhaps if Juicy had had the chance to change, he would have done?"

"And how could he have changed?"

"Well, what if his dreams had come true?"

"His only dream was about where his next fix was coming from."

"I thought I had it all with those six lucky numbers, Deano. How wrong I was. I already had it all. I just couldn't see it. And I'd give the money back tomorrow if I could get my family back."

The trauma, his break-up with Linda, and his complete exhaustion have finally reduced Brian to sobs. His shoulders shake as he lets his anguish out. He puts his hands over his face. He's embarrassed to break down there in the car in front of his best mate.

"Brian, you'll still be able to see the kids. You've got to pull yourself up, mate. It's going to be okay. Trust me!"

Deano puts his left hand on Brian's shoulder but remains silent for a while. His friend continues sobbing until finally, he starts taking deep breaths and rests his head back against the headrest.

"I'm sorry, Deano. I'm losing it. Sorry, mate. You shouldn't have to see this."

"Forget it. What are friends for? You've been there for me, God knows!"
"What am I going to do, Deano? Where did this all start?"

"It sounds like telling people about the win let the genie out of the bottle. Your fate was no longer in your hands."

"You're right. I wish I'd never told anybody."

Brian shivers as Deano pulls up alongside his family home. He feels like a different person to the one who left for the airport with his wife and children. He remains sitting in the car with Deano for a moment and then looks up at him.

"Just as well, I kept the house," he says as he climbs out of the car. He rummages in his pocket for his wallet. "Let me give you some petrol money."

"I don't need it, Brian. Honestly, get yourself a good sleep, and I'll call you in the morning."

"Thanks, Deano. I'll speak to you tomorrow."

Brian enters the empty house and switches on the TV to try to fill it with some noise. He sits on the sofa and stares at the screen without taking anything in. Sometime later, he wakes lying full out on the sofa. He's still dressed, and it's 9.30 a.m.

He phones his mum.

"Hi, Mam. How are you and Billy?"

"Good morning, love. How are you? How are Linda and the kids?"

"We're all fine. I've just come home. I've got a funeral to go to. Linda's still over in the States with the kids."
"Oh, sorry to hear that. Anybody we know?"

"No, you didn't know him, Mam. He was one of the lads from the pub. I'm just showing my face at the service to pay my respects."

"How sad. How long are you home for, love?"

"I'm not sure yet. I've got a few things to sort out while I'm here. Mam, I'm just going to jump into the shower, and I'll come round to see you. I'll be about half an hour."

"Okay, love."

Brian feels a warmth talking to his mum. She's okay, and that's something. He ponders on how he hadn't appreciated his life before all this happened. Going forward, he would appreciate everything. Yes, he was glad his mum was okay. He felt guilty for not having contacted her much while he was in the States. He thought about Deano, too. Deano had been through a lot recently and pulled himself up. He'd gone to rehab and sorted his life out. He should thank Deano for being there for him today. He was a really good friend. After his shower, he dresses and sets off to see his mum. On his way, he phones Deano.

"Hiya Brian, did you have a good sleep?"

"Yeah thanks. Slept fully clothed on the sofa as soon as you dropped me off! I just wanted to thank you for picking me up and, you know… being there when I reached rock bottom."

"You're all good, mate. It's good to hear you with a bit more energy in your voice."

"By the way, Deano, can you do me a favour? Can you find out when and where Juicy's funeral is?"

"Brian, I know you feel pretty bad about beating him up in the shop that time, but it's not your fault he died."

"I know that! I just want to pay my respects. I feel like I need to do this."

"Fair enough. I'll make some enquiries. It shouldn't be that hard to find out. Can I phone you back? Debbie's ringing me."

"Yeah, speak to you later."

He arrives at his mum's and knocks on the door. She answers and gives him a big hug. He walks into the front room, and Billy is sitting there.

"Hiya Billy. How are you feeling, mate?"

"I'm fine, thanks, Brian. How's things with you?"
"Would you like a tea or coffee, Brian?" his mum asks.

"I'll have a quick tea, please, Mam. I'm sick of all that American coffee."

"So, how do Liam and Ruby like America? I bet they love it."

"Mam, I didn't want to tell you over the phone, but Linda's family are going through a bad time… her brother was killed last week."

Sandra sits down abruptly on the sofa next to Billy. They look at each other for a moment in shock.

"Oh my god, you mean Dan? What happened?"

"It's a long story, but he was stabbed. I don't really want to go into it now if that's okay. I'll tell you all about it another time. Mam, do you and Billy need anything while I'm home?"

"God, I can't believe it… No, we're okay, love. We get almost everything delivered now, thanks, love."

The three sit in silence, and Brian finishes his cup of tea.

"Okay, I'm off, Mam. I'm very tired and just need a little space for a few hours. Phone me if you need anything."

"God, you're always in a hurry, love," says his mum. She watches him as he walks away from the house.

Brian heads back home and calls a taxi. He goes to the local leisure centre, where he swims over thirty lengths. He's never been a swimmer and hardly went in the pool at Sundrive, but he feels something is locked inside of him that he needs to let out. In the water, nobody can talk to him. He can just process everything that's happened. When he's on his thirty-fourth length, he starts to get cramps in his left leg and decides to get out. He goes to sit in the sauna. It's dry and hot, so he takes a ladle from the wooden bucket and pours some water on the coals. The water sizzles and spits, and he sits back against the bench to relax. He's soon too hot and goes to shower off and swims another ten lengths. He continues for a couple of hours, switching between the pool and the jacuzzi, steam room, or sauna. He watches others come and go and wonders what he'll do with the rest of his life. Eventually, he starts to feel hungry and decides to head home, where he calls for a Chinese takeaway. As soon as he rings off, Deano calls him.

"Right, my friend. Juicy's funeral is eleven o'clock tomorrow morning, at Eastville crematorium."

"Thanks, Deano."

"By the way, I've only just discovered that Juicy's name was Sean Barker."

"See what I mean, Deano, that's how sad it all is. I bet hardly anybody knew his name. Oh well, thanks for that."

"No problem. What are you up to? Do you fancy a few drinks somewhere? Or do you want to come over and eat with us?"

"No thanks. I'm not the best company to be around at the moment, and anyway, I've just ordered a Chinese. Maybe in a few days. I'm going to watch a movie or something. But I appreciate the invitation, Deano. Thanks, mate."

"Okay. I'll speak to you tomorrow. Take it easy, Brian."

Brian's meal arrives, and he sits down to eat it with a cold beer.

Chapter Forty

Brian is up early after a restless night. He throws the remains of last night's takeaway in the bin and makes a cup of tea. He switches the TV on to hear the news.

After a few minutes, he goes upstairs to get ready for Juicy's funeral. He wears a dark suit and white shirt but can't find a tie.

He phones a taxi, which only takes a few minutes to arrive.

"Hello mate. Eastville Crematorium, please," he asks as he gets into the car.

"Sad day, my friend?" asks the driver.

"Yeah, but to be honest, I didn't really know the guy that well. I'm just paying my respects."

"Yeah, you need to sometimes, don't you? I've been to many a funeral where I've just gone to show my face. Not sure why, but it seemed the right thing to do."

"So, how's business?" asks Brian, wanting to change the subject.

"Oh, you know, up and down. It's a lot quieter during the day, but I don't mind. I can't be doing with the nights anymore. Too many people now are off their heads on drugs."

"Yeah."

"Here we are, Eastville crematorium. You must be early. There's nobody here yet."

But Brian knows that they're not early.

"I don't think many people are expected, to be honest."

"That'll be £6.50, please."

Brian gives him a £10 note and tells him to keep the change.

"Thanks, mate," says the driver through the window as he moves his vehicle slowly away from the crematorium.

As Brian expected, there's hardly anybody there.

There's a row of about ten benches on either side of the service hall. They are all empty, apart from the front row. Sitting on one side are three young men, who Brian assumes must be friends of Juicy's.

Standing alone on the other front row is a petite middle-aged woman. Brian assumes this must be Juicy's mum.

Brian sits at the back.

A couple of minutes later, a woman in a dark suit emerges from a side door.

"Good morning. My name is Helen, and I'm the celebrant for today's service. Thank you for coming here to pay your respects on Sean's final journey. Sean wasn't a religious person, so I won't be going through a religious service. I've been asked to read out a small tribute to Sean's life."

The celebrant smiles at the woman in the front row.

"Sean was born in Marquis Street in 1972. He was an only child and attended Regent Street infant and junior school. He later went to Derwent High School. Although he didn't really enjoy the academic side of school, he had many friends and enjoyed sports, especially football. On leaving school, Sean had many short-term jobs, mostly in factories and working as a labourer."

Brian recognises some parallels between his own and Juicy's lives.

"Sean struggled to keep his jobs due to mental health problems but enjoyed fishing and would often spend his time on the banks of many different local ponds and lakes. Sean would also be the first to admit that he had made some wrong choices in life, and he tried many times to rectify this. However, despite many attempts by others to provide help and support, Sean's personal problems, unfortunately, proved to be one battle too many."

There is a murmur amongst the young men on one side of the crematorium. The celebrant ignores it and continues.

"Sadly, we say goodbye to Sean today and hope that his final journey is a peaceful one."

The curtain behind the celebrant slowly closes.

The celebrant walks over to the lady in the front row and shakes her hand, and they speak for a couple of minutes. The woman then leaves her seat and slowly walks out, followed by Juicy's three friends. Brian waits for them all to leave before following them out.

Once outside, Brian acknowledges the three men with a slight nod. They quickly walk away, leaving him standing next to the woman. She's slight and looks weathered from life.

Under her eyes are dark rings, her cheeks appear hollow, and her skin a pale grey. A gust of wind catches a wisp of her hair, which she tucks under her black skull cap, from which a black lace veil partially hides her eyes. She looks up at him expectantly, and Brian feels compelled to say something.

"I'm so sorry for your loss. I had to come today. Are you Juicy's... so sorry... I mean... are you Sean's mum?"

"No, I'm not. I work in one of the hostels that Sean used to stay in. It's a shelter for people who don't have anywhere else to go, you know, if they're struggling in life with drugs or other issues. You must be a friend of Sean's, or did you know him as Juicy?"

"I only knew him as Juicy. I wasn't a friend of his. I only met him a few weeks ago."

"So, how did you know Sean then? Are you a police officer?"

"No, no, sorry, no, I'm not. I just had to come and pay my respects, though I'm not so sure that I'm doing the right thing now. I was hoping to meet with one of his family."

"I'm sorry, I can't help you there, but I did know Sean for many years, which is why I'm here. I used to fill out his welfare forms and look after his medication, among other things."

"I really need to speak to someone who was close to him. You seem to be the closest person to Juicy — I mean, Sean — as he doesn't even have family here." Brian feels an enormous need to talk to anyone who knows Juicy, anyone with whom he could share his own history with Juicy.

"Yes, perhaps I was his closest acquaintance, sadly."

"The thing is, we got into a fight."

"Yeah, that sounds like Sean."

They begin to walk slowly away from the building.

"So, I take it then, you didn't get on well with Sean."

"I stopped him stealing from a corner shop. We ended up having a fight. A few days later, he turned up outside my house and threatened me and my family."

"I'm sorry to hear that. He was in a very bad place, I'm afraid. We'd better move further away. I think people are gathering here for the next service."

They start to walk over to the remembrance garden, where a single wreath of white lilies lies on the lawn in memory of Juicy. Further along is a huge array of wreaths and a gathering of mourners chatting together, trying to console one another over their loss. Brian feels Juicy's loneliness in comparison, with only him and the woman standing by his single wreath.

"I know now that he was in a bad place." Brian starts the conversation again.

He bends down to read the card on the wreath. It reads, God Bless, and Rest in Peace, Sean. You will be remembered.

"I guess these are from you?"

"Yes... Let's walk on. There's a path around the garden here. Tell me, why did you feel you had to come today if you knew Juicy so little?"

"Well, if I was to tell you something. This is really starting to affect my mental health. You see, during the fight in the shop, Juicy dropped some lottery tickets in the fracas. He left without them."

"I don't understand."

"Well, after he'd gone, I just kind of picked them up and never thought any more about it. I didn't even realise they were still in my hand when I left the shop."

"Go on."

"Well, like I say. I never gave it another thought until the following Saturday when I was checking the tickets."

"Was there a winning ticket?"

"Yes."

"A big win?"

"Massive. A jackpot win."

"And you kept the tickets?"

"I don't know what I was thinking. That's why I had to come today. Juicy could have had a different life if I hadn't taken his tickets."

"Do you have the money now?"

"Well, I gave some to a friend to help him buy a house and some to help my sister-in-law. But to be perfectly honest, I don't want the rest of the money. I don't want any of it anymore."

The diminutive woman seems to have grown in size in front of him. Her confidence is clear, and her gaze holds him. He notices that her eyes behind the veil are a deep brown. He imagines that she does her job caring for people in the hostel very well. She was probably a great support to Juicy.

"Well, well, well! You're something else!" she says slowly, nodding her head.

"I know. I'm so sorry. I feel ashamed. At the time, I thought Juicy would only spend it on drugs. I had a close friend who seemed to be getting totally wasted all the time and who was following the wrong track. Perhaps that made me prejudiced. I disrespected Juicy. I looked down on him. I also selfishly saw a chance to improve my own life. Once I'd made that decision, I couldn't seem to backtrack, however much I thought about it and however guilty I felt. Then, things happened so quickly. I'd never had money before in my life. I was able to leave the job that I hated. My wife did the same. We went to see my wife's family in the States. She hadn't seen them for years. The temptation was all too much. I knew deep down that it wasn't my money, and I had no rights to it, but I couldn't turn back."

The woman stops walking.

"Can I ask you something?"

"Yes."

"Why have you really come here today? Why do I get the feeling that something else has happened in your life to make you want to confess all this to someone?"

"Is it that obvious?"

"Yes."

"Since I got this money, I've had nothing but bad luck. My wife's brother was stabbed and died. My wife and I have separated. She thinks I had an affair, which I didn't. I feel like I've lost my family, and I don't want to carry on." Brian unashamedly lets tears run down his cheeks now. There's no one to see him except this one lady whose name he doesn't even know.

"All this bad luck… you feel it's related to your actions, don't you?"

"I don't know what's happening, but I haven't been able to live with myself knowing what I've done. I'd give every penny back tomorrow and go back to working twelve-hour shifts in the factory just to come home to my beautiful wife and kids once again. Before the curse of this money, I had everything. I just couldn't see it." Brian wipes the tears from his face with the back of his hand.

"What's your name?" she asks.

"Brian. Brian Jackson."

"Brian, I'm Barbara, Barbara Cooper. There's probably only a handful of people in this whole world who would have come here today and confessed what you have. But listen to me. You haven't done anything wrong."

"But they were his tickets. He could have…"

"He could have what? He was a drug addict who just couldn't help himself. I sent him to rehab numerous times, but he always returned to the drugs. Unfortunately, this latest dip killed him. He'd have overdosed anyway with any amount of money. We had to keep money away from him in the hostel to keep him safe. If anything, you might have prolonged his life by depriving him of money for the supply he couldn't resist. And anyway, I bet you anything they weren't his lottery tickets."

"Well, he definitely left them on the floor."

"You obviously didn't know Sean. He was incapable of buying anything in a shop. He had no concept of value. He couldn't even buy a bottle of beer. But stealing wasn't a problem for him. We had to buy his food and drinks for him because he gave his every last penny to dealers.

He could have stolen those tickets from anywhere. He most likely stole them from somebody's house. He even stole from me once. You can rest assured that you didn't take his tickets."

Brian is still crying. His tears are falling silently, but he doesn't seem to be able to stop the flow.

"Have you told anyone else your story, Brian?"

"No. You're the only person I've been able to speak to."

"I can see you're a good man. Your coming here today proves that. But it's over now, Brian."

"What's over?"

"Your guilt. Don't tell anyone else what you've told me. You need to bury this once and for all. And as far as I'm concerned, no one is going to hear it from me. Promise me that you'll bury this now, Brian?"

"Yeah, yeah, I promise," Brian whispers, frowning.

"Keep the money, and don't give up with your family. In my job, I've seen too many people do that. Your courage coming to speak with me today tells me that you can certainly sort things out with your wife."

"I would, but she's in the States."

"Well, if the mountain won't come to Muhammad..."

"What, you think I should go back to the States to see her?"

"Of course! Straight away! Without a doubt."

Brian looks down at his feet. He feels like a great burden has been lifted from his shoulders.

"What hostel do you work in?" he asks.

"I'm the care manager at the Quadrant Hostel on Queens Road."

"I know where it is. I'd like to make a donation."

"That would be very much appreciated, and if you ever want to visit, you're welcome to come and see the work we do."

"I'd like that very much."

The two stand awkwardly, strangers bonded through their mutual acquaintance with Juicy. Barbara steps forward with her arms open, as if tentatively enquiring whether he would like a hug.

Brian wraps his arms around her, dips his head to rest on her shoulder for a moment, then raises it and looks down at her.

"Thank you. You're probably the only person in the world who could help me right now."

"So, you're going to the States to sort things out with your wife?" she asks.

"I'll get a flight today."

"Today?"

"I have some other unfinished business that needs sorting."

"You do?"

"Yes. They're called Angela and PJ."

Printed in Great Britain
by Amazon